SUIT OF HARTE'S

THE COMPLETE COLLECTION

JACQUELINE GREY

CONTENTS

www.jacquelinegrey.com

TRICKS AND BIDS

ONE

"Hey. Wanna play?"

Dillon glanced up to find a young man leaning against the hood of his car. At Dillon's pointed look, he took a step back, so he no longer touched the automobile.

"What gave you the impression I want company?"

"You obviously didn't find what you were looking for in there" came the reply with a nod back at Harte, the BDSM club Dillon had just exited. "If you had, you wouldn't be leaving this early."

"And you think you're what I want?"

The boy shrugged.

Dillon peered at him. He appeared to be in his midtwenties, fit and tight in the way Dillon remembered being before he'd hit thirty-three. He was shorter than Dillon with dark-brown hair long enough to grip: two things Dillon liked in a submissive. There was something familiar about him as well. If Dillon wasn't mistaken, he'd seen him heading into a nearby motel a few times and never with the same "date."

"Are you a prostitute?" Dillon asked.

The blunt question evoked an expression of surprise, but it rapidly morphed into a smooth smile. "'Prostitute' sounds like a job. It's more of a hobby."

"One you get paid for."

"It's a good hobby."

Dillon cracked a smile. "How much do you charge?"

"Depends on what you want to do."

That was reasonable enough, and if he'd been waiting outside Harte, he must know to expect kink and charge for it accordingly. "Are you clean?"

"Yes, and condoms are necessary and at your expense."

"Expense? That sounds like a job term to me," Dillon teased.

He considered his options. The boy was right. He hadn't found what he was searching for in the club, and he held no illusions he ever would. Even after six years, he couldn't help comparing every submissive he came across to the lover he'd lost. Harte called him a stubborn old goat, but the thought of building a relationship from scratch exhausted him. It was so hard to find someone whose rhythms and tastes fit with his own. Granted, the club was designed for negotiation and mutually desired play, but that was for the scenes that took place there. What about the rest of the time?

Dillon didn't want a casual play partner. That did nothing more for him than scratch an itch that would return in no time. He wanted someone he could build a life with. He wasn't going to find that with a prostitute, but something about the stranger brought forth yearnings Dillon hadn't felt in years. He could take the boy home with him, indulge in what he wanted in his own territory and under his own rules. It would be a purchased illusion, but it beat going home alone and sleeping in an empty bed.

"Come on," he said, pulling his car door open and unlocking the other side. "We'll talk details when we get to my place."

"Your place? Don't you mean a hotel?"

"My place," repeated Dillon. "I don't do quick fucks."

Mike hesitated. He never went to a trick's home. That was one of the rules he'd established for himself when he'd decided to continue having sex for money. Never make the first move, never go to a client's house, never let the client choose where they would go or take him someplace crowded to fuck, and always, always take half the money up front.

He'd already broken one of his rules by approaching first. When he'd seen the Dominant exit the club, muscular arms bulging from a leather vest, he'd thought, *Now there's someone who could manhandle me in all the right ways.* It was a risk to proposition someone who clearly had the strength to do just that, yet something in his eyes had also spoken of loneliness. Mike could make a few hundred off an expression like that but approaching was one thing. Going home with a john was another.

"You're welcome to call someone to let them know where you're going if it will make you feel safer."

That was nice of him, but Mike couldn't think of anyone to call. His school friends were acquaintances at best, and none of them knew about Mike's "hobby." The offer went a little way to easing Mike's nerves as did the patience with which the Dominant waited for his decision. Mike assessed the man, and what he saw in his eyes melted the rest of his uncertainty. It was hope. None of the arrogance, hunger, or lust he'd seen in other clients. Hope. Mike didn't know what the Dominant was hoping for, but he wanted to give him what he'd need to fulfill his wish.

"Okay," he said, "but if I want to leave at any time, I want money for a taxi."

"That's fine."

Mike opened the door and slid into the passenger seat. "Where are we going, anyway?"

"About twenty minutes north of here."

That was a relief of sorts. He'd still be in familiar territory.

They didn't talk as the man drove, and soon they were parked in front of a house with a neatly manicured lawn and columns stretching up to the second floor. Now that he had to get out of the car, Mike's initial doubts returned with a vengeance. "Are you sure you want to let me into your place?" he asked. "I could be a thief, you know."

"I could be a serial killer."

The thought had crossed Mike's mind. "You're not, are you?"

"Would you believe me if I said no?"

Good point. Mike scrutinized the man again, searching for any signs of "crazy psycho killer" on his face. He didn't see any, but from what he'd seen on *Criminal Minds*, people like that could blend in.

The Dominant reached into his pocket and pulled out a wallet. He handed Mike a twenty.

"What's this for?"

"Your taxi. If you want to go, I won't stop you."

There it was again, hope. Mike had a feeling the man didn't want him to leave, but he'd let him go without question. He pocketed the money. "I'm okay. Let's head inside."

The man opened the car door and led the way toward the house. Mike followed him inside, down a short hallway, and into a living room. The place was ordinary enough. Nothing to indicate Mike would soon be locked in the basement or chopped up in the freezer. That was reassuring. Sort of.

"Would you like something to drink?"

"Water, please."

Alone for the moment, Mike surveyed his surroundings. The room appeared to be the result of an argument between someone's grandfather and an interior decorator magazine. A studded, brown-leather wingback chair sat in pride of place facing a semimodern fireplace, which, from the looks of the soot still in the grate, had been used recently. Soft, cream-colored carpet muffled his steps as he moved around. The rest of the furniture was plush, but less well used. Overall, the room felt comfortable, and he appreciated that—he'd never understood the concept of living rooms that weren't lived in

—but something about the place made him feel uneasy. Like the Dominant, there was more to the room than met the eye, but Mike couldn't figure out what it was. He was still pondering when his host returned.

"Here," he said, handing Mike a bottle. "It's still sealed, so you don't have to worry."

Mike gave the bottle a squeeze to make sure there weren't any needle holes in it. He'd been dumb enough about this whole situation so far; he didn't need to be drugged too. When no liquid escaped, he cracked the container open and took a few deep swigs. "You said we'd discuss details when we got here."

"Yes," the man said as he took a seat in the well-worn chair. The fabric creaked, but Mike couldn't tell if the sound came from the furniture or the guy's tight leather pants. "Have you ever experimented with BDSM?"

"I've had some guys who were into being all Dom on me." Mike shrugged. "Maybe a bit sadistic too."

"Do you like pain?"

"I can take some flogging or a paddle, stuff like that. I don't do heavy though."

"What about spanking?"

Mike smirked. He could imagine the man enjoying the sight of him naked over his knees. Something about that image appealed to Mike as well. "Sure. I could go for that."

"I'm not doing any of that tonight. For things like that, we need a deeper level of trust than can be acquired after knowing each other for only half an hour. If tonight goes well, and we decide to meet again, we can discuss that then. As for tonight, if you agree, I'll have you naked with your wrists cuffed to the hook in the ceiling above you."

Mike glanced up. There was indeed a hook in the ceiling above his head. He noticed other little details about the room he'd missed before like the small trash can hidden in the corner, and the way the carpet in front of the fireplace wasn't perfectly smooth. The nagging feeling he'd had made sense.

He wondered what the Dominant used the uneven section of floor for.

"I will cage your cock and balls," his client continued, recapturing Mike's attention, "so you will be unable to come. And while you're in that state, I am going to fuck you senseless—with a condom, of course." He smiled. "After which, we will retire to my bedroom where you will be cuffed to the bed by your ankle. The chain is long enough for you to easily reach the bathroom, and you are welcome to close the door for privacy, but you will return to the bed as quickly as possible and be available for my pleasure at any time during the night if the mood strikes me. In the morning, I will release you and bring you to orgasm before you leave. You will not be gagged or blindfolded at any time tonight.

"If anything occurs that you feel was not covered by our contract for the evening, I expect you to bring it up, and we will negotiate. If at any time you feel it necessary to leave, all you need to do is say the word 'stone,' at which time everything will stop, and I will release you and send you home with half of our agreed-upon price. Does that suit you?"

Mike stared at him for a whole minute before he realized he was gaping. He closed his mouth with a snap of his teeth. Most men went for a fuck, and if they wanted anything more, they just assumed they were free to do as they pleased and went for it without warning. He didn't know what to do with a whole plan set out in advance.

And yet, the plan made him feel a lot better about the scene. Between the money for a taxi, the suggestion Mike call someone to let them know where he was going, and now this, it was clear the guy was treating him like any sub he'd find at Harte. Although Mike wasn't sure he liked the idea of being chained to a bed for the whole night, he was reasonably confident he'd be released if he invoked the safeword.

What client had ever given him a safeword before?

It was risky. It was stupid, but so was picking up a

stranger inside a club. You never knew who you were meeting.

When it came down to it, he knew it was the idea of being manhandled by strong arms that made the decision for him. Mike wanted to indulge himself, and a strong Dominant—no, this Dominant—having his way with him would scratch that itch in just the right way.

"That's acceptable," he said.

"Now that you know the details, how much are you planning to charge?"

Mike considered. This was kinkier than anything he'd done before for money, not to mention it was for the whole night. Who knew how many times the guy could get it up? His price couldn't be cheap. It had to match the risk and the work, but he didn't want to scare him off. More than the money, Mike really wanted this man to fuck him.

"One thousand dollars for the night," he said. He pretended he'd be okay if the answer was no. He could always find another client. He just didn't want to.

"Done. Do you need anything before we get started?"

"A bathroom?" Mike asked, feeling the need for a moment alone.

His host pointed. Mike followed the direction and found a bathroom just down the hall. He closed the door behind him and leaned against it, wondering what he had gotten into.

The first time he'd taken money for sex, he hadn't known what was going on until the trick had handed him fifty dollars and told him he'd take care of the hotel bill. Although Mike had thought they were randomly hooking up, the other man had thought Mike was the prostitute he'd been expecting.

On a whim, Mike had tried it again, this time on purpose, and he set his own price for the fuck. It had seemed so easy at first. A simple and fun way to supplement his income while he went to school part-time. He was paying his own way for college, and a hundred dollars a fuck put money in his pocket a lot faster than working at Starbucks. He liked being his own boss too. He worked only when he wanted to, fucked only who he wanted to, and set his own prices for everything.

It hadn't been all fun and games, of course. There were times when he'd considered never doing it again, maybe even moving to another town so no one would know his face, but the benefits outweighed the cons, and soon he found he'd set his studying to the wayside, taking fewer and fewer classes.

Now was not the time to be thinking about that. He should be focusing on the hot guy in the living room who was about to fuck the shit out of him, and the thousand dollars he'd get for it. Mike couldn't help grinning. Yeah, this was a lot better than school.

He made use of the facilities, washed his hands, and returned to the living room. He opened his mouth to say he always took half up front but stopped when he spotted a pile of bills on the couch.

"Count them."

Mike picked up the money. He appreciated this client understood the business aspect of the evening. "There's one more thing I need from you before we begin," he said as he finished counting the bills and put them in the inside pocket of his jacket.

"Yes?"

"Your name."

The man smirked. "Dillon."

Mike nodded. "I'm Mike Nol—er, Michael. Where do you want me to put my clothes?"

TWO

The chain above Mike's head was just long enough for him to keep his feet flat on the floor and the pressure off his shoulders. Leather cuffs kept his arms immobile above his head. Dillon sat in what Mike assumed was his favorite chair, his gaze roaming over every inch of Mike's body like a physical touch. Dillon had said he'd fuck Mike senseless, but he might not need to touch him to do it.

"Next time, I'll light the fire," Dillon said. "The flames would look beautiful reflected on your skin."

Mike was already exposed, but the compliment made him feel more so. "Thank you, Sir," he managed, fighting to keep still. He didn't think fidgeting was possible with the way his body was stretched, but he wasn't used to being still for so long.

Dillon shifted in his seat, and Mike's skin tingled in anticipation. Were Dillon's warm massive hands going to touch him again? He wanted nothing more, even as his arms began to ache from their position.

When Dillon first put him into the cuffs, he had done so by issuing simple orders or guiding Mike into place. His touch hadn't been exactly gentle, nor had it been harsh. When other men had tried to dominate him, they'd moved forcefully, thinking a shove was a display of power. Dillon kept things simple, his tone matter-of-fact as if Mike disobeying was inconceivable. Mike found it easier to obey when he spoke like that. He found he *wanted* to follow Dillon's orders.

Dillon rose and stepped forward. He placed a hand on Mike's stomach as he walked behind him. For a moment, Mike forgot how to breathe. His cock tried to harden further, but the metal rings encasing it pressed against him. He hissed when it began to hurt.

"Painful?" Dillon asked.

"Frustrating, Sir," Mike answered.

There was no reply, but the hand on his stomach disappeared, and he heard a pop. He knew Dillon hadn't moved. The heat of Dillon's body remained behind him, a presence he found impossible to ignore. Dillon's hand returned to steady him and was immediately followed by slicked fingers at his ass. Dillon wasted no time teasing. He slid his fingers between Mike's cheeks and pressed. The movements were slow and controlled, easing inside him gently.

"I'm not a virgin, Sir," Mike offered. "I'm used to rough treatment."

Dillon did not reply, and the entry of his finger did not change its pace. It moved back and forth within him in that same slow rhythm as if Mike hadn't said a word. Dillon's finger was thick and filling, but Mike soon found himself wanting more. He arched his back in offering, but there was nowhere to go as he hung from the ceiling.

Dillon inserted a second finger, and a moan escaped him. He hoped Dillon didn't mind a noisy sub. Between the feel of Dillon's fingers and the cage preventing his cock from expanding fully, there was no way he'd be able to keep silent.

He made a frustrated sound, and as if in reply, Dillon crooked his fingers to hit his prostate. Mike gasped, then groaned. His straining dick began to weep. The heat of Dillon's body intensified as he moved closer. He peered around Mike's shoulder as he teased the sensitive spot again.

Mike responded reflexively, his body fighting both to prolong and to escape sensations he had no choice but to accept.

"Sir… Dillon…" The words escaped him as Dillon continued. He seemed fully content to torture Mike the entire night.

"You can call me Master."

Mike had had clients demand that from him before, but the title had never been so easy to say. "Master," he begged. "Please."

Dillon didn't reply, and after a few more moments of teasing, he leaned back and slid a third finger inside Mike. The thickness of the digits stretched him, and Mike's hands clenched and flexed, seeking anything to grasp hold of, but there was nothing within reach. Suddenly, he was empty. A disappointed mewl escaped him, but he was reassured by the sound of a condom wrapper tearing. It was soon followed by the blunt head of Dillon's erection pressing against him. He pushed in steadily, and Mike groaned. Dillon was a big man, and from the feel of it, his cock was proportional to the rest of him.

A slow burn crept through Mike's body as Dillon eased himself in to the hilt. He rested there for a few moments, letting Mike remember how to breathe and relax his muscles. Then, he took hold of Mike's hips and began to move. Long, deep thrusts from head to hilt drilled in and out of Mike's body. Dillon's cock felt bigger than anything Mike had experienced before, and he moved with precision, holding nothing back.

Dillon hadn't been kidding when he'd said he'd fuck Mike senseless. Mike's eyes rolled up into his head, and the rhythm of his moans matched each and every thrust. He tried to form words, but they were lost as sensations built within him. His cock grew harder in its bonds, the pain from the cage contrasting sharply with the pleasure spearing him from behind. He shook his head, unable to contain it all, yet with no way to find release.

"I… I…" he panted. *I want to come*, but he couldn't say the words, no matter how true the statement was. He knew when he would be allowed to come, and he was sure no amount of begging would change Dillon's mind. Instead, he abandoned the use of words and let the moans tumble from his lips as they may.

———

Dillon approved of Michael's responses. He didn't beg for release, only expressed the sensations building inside him, and Dillon would fuck him through them all. It had been a long time since he'd had someone fully at his mercy in his house. There was a difference between playing with a sub at Harte and claiming one in his home. He had missed this.

He drove on, pounding into Michael's body again and again until the boy's pulsating moans became a constant symphony, built on the pain of restriction and the pleasure of penetration. Dillon, a smile curving his lips, made sure to hit Michael's prostate every time, knowing exactly how it would drive him crazy.

No matter how wonderful the submissive felt wrapped around his prick or how well he moaned for Dillon, the moment couldn't last forever. With one final thrust, he came, buried balls-deep in Michael's body. He stayed for a moment, riding the wave of pleasure and in no hurry to leave it.

Eventually he pulled out, firmly holding the condom over his softening erection before tying it off and disposing of it in the trash can in the corner.

Returning to Michael, he lifted the boy's chin and peered into his face. Michael's eyelids were heavy, his expression far away. He was obviously worn out and unable to stand. Any of the hesitation he'd shown earlier was gone. The knowledge that Dillon had gained such trust from his submissive never failed to take his breath away. It made him want to take care of him, spoil him. He wanted to tuck Michael into bed, wrap his arms around him, and never let him go. The feeling shocked Dillon. It was the same feeling he'd had after an intense scene with Clover. He'd never wanted to do that with anyone but Clover before.

He should not be thinking about Clover when he had a boy to take care of who needed water and sleep. "I'm going to release you," Dillon said. "Hold on to me when I do."

The smallest of nods was the only sign he'd been heard. Dillon stepped closer and put an arm around Michael's waist. Bracing the submissive's body against his own, he reached up to unhook the first cuff. Michael's wrist dropped, and Dillon moved it to hang over his shoulder. Michael groaned as his erection rubbed against Dillon's pants. Dillon could imagine how sensitive it must feel after the intensity of their scene and being unable to come. He was careful not to stimulate it too much as he freed Mike's other arm and looped it around his neck. He lifted the boy up as if he weighed nothing, then carried him upstairs to the bedroom, making sure to grab a bottle of water on the way.

―――――

"How are you feeling?"

Mike cracked open his eyes and jumped. For a moment, he'd forgotten where he was and glanced around frantically.

"Drink some of this," Dillon said, holding a bottle of water in front of his face.

"Did I pass out on you?" Mike asked, his voice rough.

Dillon shrugged. "It happens." He gestured with the water until Mike took it and drank. When Mike had downed half the bottle, he said, "The bathroom is right over there. Go get ready for bed."

Mike nodded and rose. He was a little unsteady at first, so he waited until he was sure he wouldn't topple over before making his way to the bathroom. There wasn't much to do since he had nothing to change into. When he emerged, a cuff lay on the bed with a chain attached to it. The chain connected to the foot of the bed on the right side. Dillon stood next to the bed beside the cuff.

"Come here."

Mike went.

"On the bed."

He crawled onto it and lay with his head against the pillows and his foot next to the cuff. Dillon didn't say anything more as he latched it around Mike's ankle.

"Make yourself comfortable while I get ready," Dillon said before he headed into the bathroom. Once he was gone, Mike leaned forward to examine the cuff. Like the ones used on his wrists, it had signs of long use, and he wondered who had worn it before him. Was this how the other person had gone to bed every night? He picked up the chain and noticed it was indeed long enough to reach into the bathroom, but he wouldn't make it too far outside the bedroom with it on.

Not wanting to be caught disobeying, Mike pulled the covers down and snaked the chain beneath them. He snuggled down under the blankets and was beginning to drift off when the bathroom door opened, and he forced himself awake. He turned toward Dillon and gaped. The man was stark naked and *gorgeous*, perfectly sculpted with smooth brown skin Mike wanted to lick all over. Dillon obviously spent at least part of his time at a gym, and Mike would happily trace every line of muscle on Dillon's body with his tongue. His mouth watered at the idea, and his eyes remained glued to Dillon as the older man walked around to his side of the bed and climbed in.

"I don't sleep with fish," Dillon said.

It took a minute for Mike to realize his mouth had been hanging open the whole time. He promptly shut it.

"Lie down and go to sleep."

Mike hesitated. "Are you sure you don't want anything more?"

"The night's not over yet," Dillon replied. "Sleep."

Mike lay down, and before he knew it, he was out.

It was pitch black in the room when the touch of a hand startled Mike awake. He was unaccustomed to sleeping with someone else and made to fight off the intruder.

"Relax," came Dillon's voice in the dark. "You're safe."

Something about the sound calmed him instantly, though Mike wasn't sure why. Though they'd fucked that evening, Dillon was still a stranger. Yet he didn't object when Dillon reached for him again, pulled him close, and turned him over. Mike followed the direction and lay on his stomach, waiting to see what he wanted. Dillon hastily acquired a condom, and in no time pressed his thick cock against him.

"On your knees," Dillon ordered.

Mike pushed up onto his hands and knees. The bed shifted as Dillon moved behind him. His broad body covered Mike's like a blanket, and his strong arm braced the bed beside Mike's. When Dillon's weighty hand took hold of the back of his neck, panic threatened to spike through him, but he forced himself to relax. No one was harming him. Dillon pressed his upper body down, gently but firmly, leaving nothing but his ass in the air.

Dillon's hand didn't move after Mike complied but remained as Dillon pushed into him. His ass was sore from earlier, but the pain soon mixed with pleasure. He lay exactly as his Master had positioned him, offering his body to be used as the other man saw fit, and Dillon did. He thrust deep into Mike's body, his fingers tightening in the hair at the base of Mike's head and holding him in place. Mike groaned from the force of the thrusts and the restriction of being held down. His cock wept from the joy and frustration of it. He couldn't remember being this hard in a long time, especially with a client.

Dillon rode him without breaking stride until he plunged all the way in and came. He remained in that position for a few minutes. Mike was swiftly learning Dillon liked to bask in the bliss of his orgasm before moving to deal with necessities. That was fine with him. His cock throbbed with need. The ache was painful, but he remained patient until Dillon released him. Once Dillon had dealt with the condom and lain back against the pillows, Mike gathered he was allowed to move and turned onto his back. Their activities had bunched the sheets around their ankles, but neither man moved to reposition them.

As moonlight filtered through the bedroom curtains, Mike's eyes had adjusted enough that he could see Dillon staring at his straining erection. Dillon brushed a finger over the head, making him cry out from the sensation. He didn't do it again, but Mike still felt him watching.

"Are you a sadist?" Mike asked.

"You could say that."

"Meaning?"

"I love to torture a sub. Seeing you like this, enduring the pain of not being able to get an erection, let alone relieve it, turns me on. I love making a sub beg for release, and yes, I do like giving a sub pain."

"You also like having someone at your beck and call, don't you?" Mike asked. "I would guess not all Doms chain their subs to the bed every night?"

"Some do."

"So I'm noticing."

Mike had done some kinky things with a few guys at college. He'd done it with clients too, but he wouldn't classify any of those guys as a Dom. He'd never trusted a trick not to take advantage, so the list of what he'd been willing to do with them was small. And yet, he'd allowed Dillon to do much more than that. There was something about him that made Mike believe he wouldn't exploit his trust.

Dillon was a real Dominant. He'd shown Mike respect and patience, taken his well-being into consideration, and hadn't pushed beyond what Mike had allowed. He supposed Dillon was what they called a lifestyle Dominant. Mike knew the mechanics of the concept, but he'd never met anyone he could fathom doing something like that with.

"What else do you do with a sub who's yours?"

Dillon raised an eyebrow as if to question the motivation of the inquiry, but he answered anyway. "Clothing is not an option in this house," he said. "My sub cooks for me, cleans, and is available for my pleasure at any time. Occasionally, I put him on display much like you were in front of the fireplace. I do like something pretty to look at when I unwind. He kneels patiently beside me when I am home, and he is proud to be called mine when I take him to a club."

"Doesn't sound too bad."

"And if it did?"

Mike shrugged. "Not my problem beyond tonight."

"No…" Dillon said.

Mike wondered at the hesitation he thought he'd heard. "You had a sub?"

"Yes."

Dillon's tone left no room for further questions. It wasn't Mike's business to pry anyway, so he just said, "Okay."

There was a moment of silence before Dillon said, "Go to sleep."

"Yeah. Never know when you're going to wake me up again," Mike teased.

"I'm not into brats."

"Sorry, Sir," Mike said, but the hint of amusement in Dillon's voice made him smile.

———

Dillon took advantage of his evening's acquisition one more time during the night. The next time Mike woke, it was morning. Dillon was still asleep, and Mike admired him in the light streaming in from the window. With his short brown hair, there was nothing to obstruct Mike's view of the man's chiseled face. He could have been an artist's sculpture. The line of his jaw had just the faintest touch of a shadow to it, and the stern gaze that had watched him so intently the night before was relaxed in sleep. A straight Greek nose led down to slightly parted lips Mike was tempted to kiss, but he was struck with a better idea. Wondering how the Dominant felt about a sub taking initiative, Mike burrowed under the covers and wriggled carefully closer. Normally, he wouldn't offer a client services for free, but his mouth had been watering for this ever since Dillon emerged naked from the bathroom. Besides, he'd charged a flat fee for the night, so technically, the service was included.

The massive cock that had rammed him throughout the night was half-hard and already an intimidating size. Mike was not deterred. He reached for it and licked a long line up its length. Dillon didn't move, but his dick stirred in approval. Mike did it again, then swirled his tongue around the crown. He kept playing with it as it grew larger and larger before him. Finally, he encased the head with his lips and began to suck. He didn't stop when the sheet above his head was lifted and removed. He rolled his eyes up to focus on Dillon watching him.

"Couldn't wait for breakfast?"

Mike laughed around the cock in his mouth, creating vibrations that had Dillon groaning softly as his eyes fell closed. Loving the sight of the man's reaction, he did it again before working his mouth up and down on the shaft as far as he could go. Plunging down, he deepthroated as best he could and still had an inch to go to the base. He used a hand to pump the shaft, keeping time with the rhythm of his mouth. Dillon rested his hand on his head. He expected Dillon to guide him with it, but he only ran his fingers softly through Mike's hair. Mike welcomed the touch.

He did his best to please, using every trick he knew and making note of which ones Dillon liked the most. Dillon's pleasure was visible in the way his lips parted and the rhythm of his breath. Finally, the hand in his hair tightened, and he knew Dillon was close. He let Dillon take control, holding still as his Master came in his mouth. He swallowed —another thing he didn't do with clients—and stayed in position even after Dillon was spent. Only when Dillon released his hair did Mike slide the softening cock from his lips.

"Morning," he said.

"Good morning," Dillon answered lazily.

"I hope you didn't mind…"

"Not at all. I consider morning blowjobs a gift when I wake in the middle of them."

Mike grinned. "You're welcome then."

Dillon smiled. He took a deep breath and regarded the sun shining in the window. "It's time."

Mike's merriment clouded with disappointment. He didn't want to leave yet.

"What about breakfast?" he asked.

"You just had yours," Dillon pointed out.

"I eat more than that in the morning, you know?"

"I didn't fill you up enough already?"

Mike was too surprised by the tease to respond.

"Come here."

Mike slid up to lie beside him. Dillon pushed him to lie on his back.

"Ready?" Dillon asked. "This is going to hurt."

Confused from that warning, Mike didn't realize what Dillon was doing before the cage was off and blood rushed to his prick. He was painfully erect, and the change was so overwhelming Mike cried out. When Dillon gently brushed his cock, it was too much, and Mike grabbed the man's wrist to stop him.

"I…"

Dillon smiled. He leaned forward to kiss Mike's temple. "I'm going to suck you off now," he said. "Scream all you like, but I'm not stopping until you come."

Mike groaned. He didn't think he could take more than that simple touch. When Dillon licked up the underside of his erection, fire ran through him, and he screamed. He clutched at the bedsheets as Dillon swirled his tongue in intricate patterns as if tracing the design of a complicated lollipop. Overwhelmed, Mike shook his head from side to side in a plea the Dominant simply ignored. The teasing continued, and Mike was unable to form words to beg, though what he would beg for he didn't know.

When Dillon encased him in his mouth and began to suck, he screamed again, and his vision blanked to white. His hand flew to Dillon's short hair and tried to hold on to the strands, but they weren't long enough to grasp. Dillon grabbed him and locked his massive hand like a shackle around Mike's wrist, pinning it to the bed. The restriction only made Mike moan harder. His body rocked, coaxing Dillon to continue, though his mind begged for an alternative. Eventually, one word escaped him, one plea that could make it past his lips in more than just vowels.

"Master…"

As if in answer, Dillon picked up the pace and worked him purposefully. Gradually, the fire was replaced by the need for release. It built and built, but even without a physical restriction, Mike found himself unable to come. It was as if his body had forgotten how.

"Please. Please," became a mantra as Mike begged his Master for help. Dillon couldn't give him a verbal order without releasing the cock from his mouth, but he squeezed Mike's wrist, and Mike came. The orgasm ripped through him with a vengeance, spilling from him in long spurts that filled Dillon's mouth. He swallowed everything and waited for Mike to be fully spent before releasing him. Dillon crawled back up the bed to lie beside him and brushed stray strands of hair off his face.

"Beautiful," Dillon said.

Mike didn't answer as he drifted back to sleep.

———

When he woke, he found himself alone in the bedroom. His ankle had been released. A sense of loss beat in his chest at the cuff's removal, but he reminded himself this had been a business transaction, and he was a professional. Just because it had been the best night he could remember did not mean he was allowed to get sentimental.

He made his way downstairs to the kitchen where Dillon was making coffee.

"Hi," Mike said.

"Hi. Do you want coffee?"

"Yes, please."

Dillon nodded and brought another cup down from the cabinet. "Do you need me to drive you somewhere?"

"Nah, I'll take a cab. You did give me money for one."

Dillon's lip quirked. "Call it one of my expenses. Are you sure? I'm headed out anyway."

Dillon's offer to drive him back to the club felt like the ending of a date. Mike wondered if he wasn't the only one who needed a reminder of the nature of the arrangement between them. Still, he found he couldn't flat-out refuse. "Next time."

The coffee was ready, and Dillon moved to pour. "Do you want there to be a next time?" he asked.

Mike hesitated. There was a fine line between a good trick and getting attached. He wanted to come back, but he didn't want to get caught up in something that wasn't there.

"You're the client," he said. "I think that's your call."

Dillon nodded, accepting the answer though he didn't indicate what his decision might be. "How do you take your coffee?"

"Black, two sugars."

Dillon doctored the coffee and handed Mike his cup. "I put the rest of the money on your clothes. Count it before you go."

Mike nodded. "Thanks." He took a careful sip of the coffee

and found it too hot to drink. "I'll get dressed while this cools."

Dillon nodded, and Mike wondered if he'd just asked for permission to get dressed or not. Either way, he put the cup on the kitchen table and headed for the front door. As Dillon had said, the money was in a neat pile on top of Mike's jeans. He counted it and put it in the pocket of his jacket with the original amount—which he also double-checked out of occupational paranoia. Once he was dressed, he returned to the kitchen. The coffee had cooled enough to drink.

Mike sipped it in awkward silence. He never lingered with a client. Hell, there'd never been a morning after with a trick before. He wasn't sure if he should make conversation or chug his coffee and get the hell out of there.

"Do I dare ask?" said Dillon.

"Ask what?"

"Why prostitution?"

For Mike, the moment immediately went from awkward to disappointing. He'd had clients try to "fix him" in the past, but their attempt to convince him to stop having sex for money usually stemmed from their own guilt of sleeping with a prostitute. He hadn't pegged Dillon for the type.

"It pays better than Starbucks," he said.

"So do a lot of other things."

"You going to tell me I should stop? That it's dangerous and not worth the risk?"

"Last I checked, controlling your life wasn't in our contract."

Mike blinked, realizing Dillon wasn't trying to convince him of anything. He was just making conversation. "It started as an accident, actually. Some guy mistook me for the prostitute he'd been waiting for. I'd wanted to hook up with him anyway. The extra fifty bucks was a bonus, so I tried it again, figuring it would help me pay my way through college."

"With the price of tuition, that's not a bad idea."

Mike was surprised Dillon agreed with him. It was nice

having someone listen to him who didn't tell him he was an idiot or wasting his life. He hated to continue his story, but a part of him believed he could share his situation with Dillon. "Yeah, it was, but I haven't been taking many classes lately."

"Many, or none at all?"

Mike dropped his gaze. "None." He hadn't gone to class for a full year now.

"Why not?"

Mike shrugged. "I don't know what I want to do. Felt like a waste paying for classes that may not mean anything in the long run."

"Makes sense. Though you must know your current career doesn't have a built-in retirement plan."

Mike laughed. "You make it sound like any other job."

"In a way it is, though I thought it was supposed to be a hobby."

"At this point, it's probably more than a hobby."

"Yes." Dillon took a long sip of his coffee. Mike wondered what he was going to say next if he was taking the time to consider his words. He braced himself for a lecture, hoping he wouldn't get one. He'd liked how Dillon had talked with him so far. He didn't want to feel like a child Dillon thought he had to take care of.

As if he could sense Mike's tension, Dillon said, "I'd say this to any of my clients. Don't forget about the things you want to do in life just because your current situation is comfortable or it's easier to stay there. I'm not telling you not to be a prostitute, but I will tell you to plan for the future. There is no 401K for you, and you're not going to want to be standing on street corners when you're sixty. You don't need to know what you want to do, but you do need to think about it occasionally."

That was better than he'd expected. Still sort of a lecture but not terrible. "What do you do?"

"I'm an accountant."

"I didn't know being an accountant paid so well."

"I have a few high-end clients."

"No prostitutes, I'm guessing?"

"Why? You looking to hire a CPA?"

"If I am, I'll let you know."

Dillon nodded. He swigged back the last of his coffee and rose to put the mug in the sink. Mike took that as his cue to leave. "I better get going," he said, hoping the reluctance didn't show too badly.

"Let me walk you out."

He followed Dillon to the front door, but Dillon didn't open it.

"What's—"

Dillon turned to look at him, and his expression silenced Mike in an instant. It was the face of the Dominant, the man who had tied him up and held him down all through last night.

"Next week," his Master said. "I'll pick you up in front of the club at ten. *Do not* be late. We will discuss details and pricing when we get here."

Mike's cock, so recently spent, tried to rise at Dillon's tone, and it wasn't the only part of him to respond. "Yes, Sir," he said.

Dillon quirked an eyebrow, and Mike corrected himself.

"Yes, Master."

THREE

"You *what?*"

Dillon had never seen his friend's eyes go that wide before. He and Jesse Harte had known each other since high school, so that was saying something.

"He could have been a thief. Or worse."

"And I could have been a serial killer," Dillon replied. "We had that conversation, actually."

Jesse sighed. "Dillon, it's been a long time since Clover, and you know I am the first person to say it's time you started meeting someone for more than a club scene, but to pay for it? How much did he charge you anyway? I assume a scene wouldn't come cheap."

"No," Dillon admitted, "but it was worth every penny." He'd been half-hard all day from remembering the feel of Michael's skin beneath his hands, the warmth of his body enveloping his prick, and the sounds the boy had made when begging for release.

"He must have been something to tempt you," Jesse said. "You have it out of your system now, though? Think you can go back to looking for a submissive who doesn't cost a small fortune?"

If you only knew. Jesse would kill him then. "I'm meeting him again next week."

A muscle in Jesse's jaw twitched, and Dillon knew his friend was trying hard not to snap at him or lecture. Finally, he asked, "Are you sure about this?"

"Do you think I'd spend the money if I wasn't? I think you'd like him. He has a sense of humor you'd appreciate."

"I'd appreciate him more if he didn't make my friend pay for sex."

Now it was Dillon's turn to hold his tongue before replying. "I'll see you later, Jesse."

"Be careful, Dillon."

Dillon nodded and left his friend's office. He made his way downstairs to the back entrance of the club. For the first time, he wondered what had drawn Michael to stand by that door and not the front entrance. Granted, prostitution wasn't something that could be easily advertised, but the BDSM theme of the club's upper floors was well-known even if it was members only. Members entered from the back if they didn't feel like pushing through the dance floor crowds. Michael had to have known what he would find when he chose Harte as his hunting ground last night.

Dillon stepped out into the brisk cold, his breath clouding the air in front of him. The parking lot was empty save for his car and Jesse's. No hot submissive waited for him to emerge.

What could Michael have been feeling out here in the cold? What had made him call out to Dillon? For all Dillon knew, he could have been anyone for Michael. There were plenty of Dominant members at Harte. Any one of them could have come out and caught Michael's eye.

A part of him railed at that thought, and he shoved the emotion aside. His time with Michael was a diversion, a fantasy. He had no right feeling any claim over him. Yet he couldn't help remembering how shy Michael had been when admitting he hadn't taken any college classes lately. He hadn't been embarrassed when defending his choice to be a prostitute, but clearly, he wanted to do more. The protective side of Dillon wanted to help Michael find the direction he needed to make him feel proud of all facets of his life. He couldn't though. He'd told Michael he wouldn't judge, and he had no right to try to change the boy's life. All he could do was look forward to seeing him again.

In the meantime, he turned his car in the direction of his own office. He had statements to reconcile, and his clients' quarterly reports wouldn't write themselves. If he let his work slide, he wouldn't be able to afford to see Michael at all.

FOUR

"Dillon!" a voice called, and Dillon turned to find Michael leaning against a wall in clear view of the back entrance to Harte.

"You're shivering," Dillon said.

"Didn't think I'd need a heavier coat when I left this morning. I was wrong."

"Get in the car," Dillon said as he walked toward the parking lot. Once they were inside the vehicle, he turned the heater on full blast.

"Can't fuck me if I'm an icicle?" Michael teased.

"I'll fuck you anyway, but you might enjoy it more if you aren't numb."

"Thanks." Michael held his hands to the vents to soak up more of the warmth. "Know what you want tonight?" he asked.

"We'll discuss that when we get to the house," Dillon replied.

"You don't chat much, do you?"

Dillon didn't answer, and the rest of the car ride was quiet.

———

Dillon hadn't realized just how much he'd wanted to see Michael again. The instant he'd spotted the boy leaning against the bricks, he'd had the sudden desire to shove him back against the rough surface, strip him bare—cold or no— and fuck him senseless. The whole ride home he'd fought to get his hormones in enough order to negotiate properly. He reminded himself Michael wasn't his. He was just renting him for a while. The only time he had any right to do as he pleased was within the allotted time and their agreed-upon terms; a contract that only began once Michael agreed to the details and placed his clothing on the table beside the front door.

"Have a seat on the couch. I'll make us some coffee."

"Are you sure you don't want to—"

The look in his eyes must have expressed enough because Michael shut up and moved to do as bidden.

Dillon berated himself for not controlling his expression better. *Calm down. He's not your submissive. There's only so far you can push until you have your contract for the night made.*

He went into the kitchen and put on the pot to boil. Lately, he'd only had the patience to wait for instant coffee. Clover had been the one to take the time to make a really good cup of coffee.

The thought of Clover made him pause. Jesse was right. Six years was a long time to mourn someone. He wouldn't dishonor Clover's memory if he found someone to share his life with, but to find a submissive and one who fit him as well as Clover had…that seemed impossible.

The pot began to boil, wrenching his attention back to the present. He poured the water into two mugs and carried them back into the living room where he was happy to see Michael sitting patiently on the couch as instructed. He handed him one of the cups. "Careful. It's hot."

"Thanks," Michael said. He appeared warmer already.

Dillon took a seat in his favorite chair and carefully sipped from his own mug. It tasted like instant, and he tried not to wince. All those years of drinking good coffee had spoiled him, and even after six years, he still suffered from the inferior taste.

"I would have thought you'd drink one of the better brands," Michael said, interrupting his thoughts.

"You want better coffee, you go make it," Dillon replied.

For a moment, it seemed as if Michael would get up and do so, but the boy hesitated. Dillon's inner Dom didn't like the hint of defiance, but he kept it in check.

"Think it's time we discussed tonight's details?" Michael asked.

"Yes." Dillon set his cup on the table beside him. "Tonight, I'd like to take you downstairs to the dungeon." He took stock of Michael's reaction as he continued. "I have plenty of equipment we could discuss for use in the future, but tonight, I thought we would use the sling and some hot wax candles. Would that be okay with you, or is that outside your limits?"

Michael appeared hesitant, and Dillon waited patiently for him to speak.

"I've never played with hot wax before," he said.

Dillon understood the concern. "The candles in my stock are custom made for this purpose. Their burning temperature is quite low, even lower than many candles I've found in stores that are specifically made for wax play. If you agree, we'll go down, and I'll show them to you. I'll also test one on your arm before setting you in the sling, and if you change your mind, we'll renegotiate our plans."

"Are all Doms so accommodating?" Michael asked.

"No," Dillon said, "but that depends on the Dominant. I'm not so accommodating either. If you were officially my sub, we wouldn't negotiate before each scene. We'd have sorted out limit details before our contract was even signed, so any decisions would be mine to make. This is a different situation, and you're inexperienced, despite what fools may have tried to do with you. I don't know you well enough to decide what you may be able to endure on your first try with something. That power is completely yours in this relationship."

Michael quietly considered the idea. "I'd like to try it."

Dillon gave a curt nod of acknowledgment. "As before, after our scene, you will accompany me to my room where you will be chained by the ankle to the bed, and you will not be allowed to come until morning when I bring you to orgasm."

Michael nodded again. "That's fine."

"Would you like to change our price from last time?"

"No," Michael replied. "I think we can leave it standing."

"Okay," Dillon said, satisfied with the negotiations. "Are there any concerns you'd like to address before we begin?"

"Condoms go without saying?" Michael asked.

"Absolutely."

"Then all is fine with me."

"Good. Now, if you are ready, please undress and set your clothes by the front door. When you return, you can take your coffee and kneel beside my chair here on the floor. You are welcome to use a pillow for your knees if you'd like."

Michael rose from the couch, set his coffee on the table, then exited to do as he was bid. When he returned, he was gloriously naked. Dillon's eyes were glued to the younger man's cream-colored skin as he picked up the mug and took his place beside Dillon's chair.

"I did offer you a pillow."

"Thank you, but the carpet is plush enough," Michael said. His lips parted in a soft gasp as he obviously remembered something he hadn't mentioned before.

"Yes?" Dillon prompted.

Michael's gaze lowered to the floor. "Do I call you Master?"

A shiver of pleasure ran through Dillon, and though he knew it was a bad idea to get too used to the submissive calling him that, he couldn't stop himself from answering, "Yes."

FIVE

"Give me your arm."

Mike did as ordered, and Dillon took hold of it in a firm grip. Mike wondered if the Dominant expected him to run at the first sight of flame. The candle had been burning long enough for a small pool of wax to gather around the wick. Dillon lifted the candle and held it a good distance above Mike's arm. It was higher than he had expected, but he didn't have time to ask before a drop of wax hit his skin, and he flinched with a gasp.

Dillon's grip remained steady as he asked, "Was that too much?"

Mike shook his head. The sting of the wax's initial touch seeped into his skin and warmed the small area it covered. "It was a surprise but not bad."

Dillon lowered the candle a few inches, and another drop of wax fell on Mike's arm. The sting was a little more intense, and the heat took a little longer to settle. Dillon lowered the candle once more and dripped again.

"This is as hot as the wax should get. I will not put the candle any closer to your skin, or it could become dangerous. Keep in mind, I will not be dripping it over your skin as slowly as this, and the more wax that covers you, the more intense the sensations will become. Do you still want to go through with the scene?"

Mike's curiosity was piqued, as was another part of his body. "Yes," he said.

Dillon scrutinized him, and self-consciousness made Mike want to cover his beginning erection, especially when Dillon frowned.

"I'm going to have to shave you," he said.

"Wh-what?"

"I don't want the wax getting caught in your hair. It's not supposed to be too problematic, but it would be much easier if you were clean shaven, and we didn't have to worry about it."

"We discussed nothing about razorblades near my junk when we were upstairs," Mike pointed out, ready to call the whole thing off if necessary.

"You're right," Dillon said. "It's your call."

This was way past the line he was already crossing. Letting some stranger come at him with a razor was insane, but as he thought about it, he realized it wasn't much different from letting a perfect stranger tie him up and cuff him to a bed or any of the other things he'd done with Dillon so far. "Do it."

Dillon studied Mike's face, making him feel uncomfortable.

"Are you sure?"

Mike was having trouble making eye contact. "Yes, just—"

"Look at me, Michael."

The order was irrefutable. Mike obeyed.

"Are you sure?" Dillon repeated.

"Yes," Mike answered. "I'm sure."

After a moment, Dillon nodded. He set the candle on the table. "Come with me."

He led the way to the corner of the room toward what Mike assumed was the sling. He had heard of them but had never seen one in person. Leather straps hung from a frame and he had a general idea where he'd be placed in the middle of it, but as for the rest, there were too many options to determine what Dillon had in mind.

"Stand here and face me." Mike moved into position, and before he knew it, Dillon had lifted him and placed him into the center of the sling. Leather straps supported his rear end, his back, and his head so he was in a comfortable lounging position.

"Give me your foot."

Mike lifted his left leg, and Dillon took hold, bringing another strap over to hook his ankle into a cuff. After doing the same with Mike's other leg, he made a few adjustments, bringing Mike's legs up high and into an accessible spread-eagle position.

"Hand."

Mike automatically moved his hand toward the voice, and in no time at all, his wrists were cuffed and arranged to Dillon's liking. There was little give in any of the restraints, leaving him fully to Dillon's mercy. It was a concept that was both arousing and worrisome, especially when Dillon moved to a small cabinet and returned with a can of shaving cream, a towel, a small bowl of water, and a razor.

"The razor is brand new," Dillon assured him as he knelt between Mike's spread legs.

"I wasn't worried about that."

Dillon eyed him. "Are you nervous?"

"I would be stupid not to be," Mike said.

"You're also turned on," Dillon pointed out, using a finger to pull down Mike's cock before letting it bounce back up. Mike wanted to squirm, but the sling wouldn't allow it.

"You know what to do if this becomes too much for you," Dillon said. "I won't stop otherwise."

The words were as much a reminder as a warning, but Mike felt reassured. He lifted his head to see the other man better, but it was useless at this angle.

"Are *you* turned on by this?" he asked instead.

Dillon smiled, and the twinkle in his eyes told Mike all he needed to know. Still, the Dom answered. "Oh, yes."

———

Dillon was treading a very thin line, and he knew it. Michael had placed an immense amount of trust into his hands, and it was his responsibility not to abuse that trust in any way.

He dipped his fingers into the warm water in the bowl and spread some of the shaving cream on his hands. He took the opportunity to massage Michael's skin as he lathered it up, teasing his cock and balls just because he could, and because it would help the sub relax. Michael may have been nervous, but he was hard as well. His cock stood proudly, pointing toward the ceiling and not at all concerned with how the rest of him may be feeling.

Dillon wiped his hands on the towel, then picked up the razor. He placed a firm grip on Michael's inner thigh to keep him steady as he began to shave him. His concentration narrowed to his task, making sure Michael would be shaved clean, and there would be no mishaps along the way. He had done this for Clover many times, but it had been a while.

As he cleared the hair between Michael's legs, he realized he'd been missing this. He had always enjoyed doing this for Clover. Clover used to tease him that it was one of his kinks, but it was more than that. It was about the care he had to put in, the trust he received, the knowledge that the freshly shaved skin would be that much more sensitive to his touch, and the feeling that the body before him was *his* to do with as he pleased. His attention was never as focused as when he had his sub helpless and at his command, even for something so basic as shaving.

Once the skin was clear and he had wiped any remnants of cream from Michael's skin, he snaked out his tongue and licked up the underside of Michael's cock. Michael cried out from surprise, and Dillon grinned.

"Sensitive, isn't it?"

"Are you going to drop wax on my dick?" Michael asked.

"Don't you think that's a question you should have asked before I tied you up?"

The submissive frowned. "Yes."

Dillon toyed absently with Michael as he answered, enjoying the sight of his captive trying to squirm and failing. "I'm not going to drip directly on it this time, but it remains a strong possibility for the future." He rose and gathered the shaving supplies to set them aside. He returned, rolling a snack tray with wheels over toward the sling. On the tray were candles of various colors and a lighter as well as a few washcloths and a clean bowl of water.

"Ready?" Dillon asked.

————

Ready? There wasn't a breeze in the basement, but every movement of the air danced on Mike's freshly shaved skin. He could only imagine what the wax would feel like on it.

As if in defiance of his worry, his cock began to drip at the prospect. He frowned, but Dillon took his body's reply as his answer rather than waiting for a verbal one. He lit the candles and lifted one above Mike's body.

"Usually, I would have you blindfolded for this," Dillon said. "So, feel free to close your eyes."

"You have got to be—"

Mike's words cut off with a gasp as the first drop of wax fell on his skin. Dillon had chosen a spot on his chest, and the bead of wax rolled a little before it cooled and hardened. Mike exhaled, but before he could think, another drop fell. He cried out as it hit one of his nipples. Other drops followed, fully covering the sensitive nub. He began to moan from the sting.

This time Dillon let the heat sink in before moving to another point on his body. Though Mike's eyes were open, and he watched the Dominant's movements, from his angle he couldn't see where exactly the drips would fall. Dillon chose Mike's thigh next, and he let a small river of wax dribble from the candle.

"Aah!" Mike panted as the wax rolled down from his knee toward the sensitive fold where his thigh met his groin. Dillon had said he wouldn't drip on Mike's cock directly, but he obviously had no problems creating heat on the sensitive skin around it. Mike groaned again as his other leg received the same treatment. The wax ran down his thigh, then shifted course to run down next to his balls. As if to complete a circuit, Dillon's next hit was Mike's other nipple. He saw stars as the wax gathered, heat building on his chest in the small area. His hips rocked, and his arms tugged at their restraints.

"That's it," coaxed Dillon. "Good boy. Enjoy it, Michael."

"I...I..."

More wax dripped, making lazy patterns over Mike's chest and stomach. Each new touch had Mike rocking more in the sling. Somewhere along the way, his head had dropped back, and his eyes had closed. He no longer tried to follow Dillon's movements and jumped when they surprised him.

"One day I'll cover your cock completely in wax," came Dillon's voice in his ear. "Then I'll suck you off right after I peel it clean."

Mike moaned and bucked his hips. Warmth had enveloped his body, and he was aching to come. He braced for the next drip, but none came. Cautiously, he opened his eyes and lifted his head to look at Dillon. The man watched him intently, and he smiled when their eyes met.

Dillon slid a warm hand over Mike's knee and up his body to a piece of wax on his chest. With a flick, the edge of the wax was lifted, and Dillon peeled it off Mike's skin.

"Oh my god," Mike groaned.

Dillon brushed a thumb over Mike's newly revealed skin. "All of your body is going to be sensitive like this," he said. "I'm going to peel you slowly and lick you all over. Think you'll be able to keep from coming?"

It wasn't a question that required an answer. Mike wasn't allowed to come, but he now had an idea of how hard he would have to work to follow that order.

Unfazed by the challenge he had set for his sub, Dillon peeled the wax from one of Mike's nipples. Mike moaned as the wax was lifted. Dillon followed it with his tongue, and Mike gasped. Sometime when he hadn't been paying attention, Dillon had put ice in his mouth. The contrast of the intense heat from before to the cold was too much for Mike to process, and he groaned again as his head fell back in surrender.

Dillon continued to work over Mike's body, peeling and licking in one small area after another. Mike could do nothing but lie back and take it, his voice escaping him despite his inability to think.

The last piece of wax was not followed up as expected. Instead of licking over Mike's hip, Dillon's mouth enveloped Mike's erection in a mix of hot and cold that made Mike scream. It took his entire concentration to keep from falling over the edge in that instant. Dillon's eyes sparkled as he teased Mike to the brink, then let him settle back, only to do it again.

Mike fell into a series of pleas that were ignored. It wasn't until he screamed the word "Master!" that Dillon finally stopped and released Mike's cock from its captivity.

Mike fell back into the sling, exhausted. He was unable to move, even as his Master released him from the restraints. After checking all the candles were out, Dillon lifted him into his arms and carried him upstairs to the bedroom. He laid him gently on the bed, locking his ankle in the cuff before covering him with a blanket. He set a bottle of water on the night table beside Mike, then undressed before sliding in next to him. He pulled Mike close before drifting off to sleep.

———

Sometime later in the night when exhaustion gave way to even sleep, his sub shifted, turning his back toward Dillon. The movement was familiar, and even Dillon's sleep-addled mind recognized his lover wanted to be cuddled. He reached out and pulled the boy closer, wrapping him even tighter in his embrace and throwing a leg over the young man's for good measure. As if to reassure his possessive instincts, the rattle of a chain tinkled with the movement. Dillon smiled, his hands caressing the body beneath him. He reached up for the boy's collar, needing to feel the strip of leather around his sub's neck, but his fingers found nothing.

He woke in an instant, pushing himself up and leaning over the submissive with a growl. With a start, his boy woke, staring up at him with wide eyes.

"Where's your collar?" Dillon demanded angrily.

There was a moment's pause before the boy answered, "You never gave me one."

Dillon gradually focused on the face beneath him. He remembered where he was and whom he was looking at. Ashamed and angry with himself, he sat up and turned away, swinging his legs over the side of the bed. He wouldn't leave the room, but he couldn't bring himself to face the man beside him.

The silence stretched until Michael asked, "How long has he been gone?"

Dillon was quiet for a while before he said, "Six years."

"Have you talked to anyone about it?"

Dillon hesitated again, but he didn't take as long this time. "Harte knows." Michael didn't know who Harte was, but Dillon wasn't up for explaining.

"Knowing isn't the same as listening," Michael said. Dillon said nothing. "How did you two meet?"

Dillon should have been annoyed with the questions. He didn't like to talk about Clover, especially to someone who hadn't known him, but instead of telling Michael to shut up, he found himself sighing and opening up to him. "Jesse and I met in high school. He was a stubborn twat even then. One day, he just came up to me and introduced himself…"

Dillon's voice drifted off as the memory came back to him.

"Hi. I'm Jesse Harte." The boy stood directly in Dillon's path with his hand outstretched, waiting patiently for Dillon to do something. What Dillon wanted to do was continue walking down the hall to a corridor where he could find a place to smoke, but that didn't appear to be an option anymore.

"Dillon Spade," he grunted, ignoring the outstretched hand.

Jesse grinned and let his hand drop. "I know. It's like we're half of a deck of cards."

"What?" Dillon asked, despite himself.

"Hearts and spades," Jesse said. "Two suits in a deck of cards."

"Yeah, well, when you find the other two, let me know." Dillon turned to walk away.

"Can I hold you to that?"

Dillon's brows furrowed. What was with this kid?

"If I find the other two suits," Jesse continued, unfazed, "you'll have to be friends with us."

Dillon turned to glare at the boy. "And if you don't?"

"I think that would be your terms to set," Jesse replied.

"If you don't," Dillon said, "you leave me alone. And you also leave me alone until you find them."

Jesse considered and then nodded. "Okay. Any other terms you want to set?"

No use letting this stupid thing drag on forever. "You have until the end of the year."

"What about the names?" Jesse asked. "Ours are last names. Do the other two have to be as well?"

Dillon shrugged, already fed up with the conversation. "Whatever you want, as long as it fits."

Jesse smiled and stuck out his hand again. "It's a deal."

This time, Dillon had no choice but to grudgingly take it.

• • •

Turning his attention back to the present, Dillon continued. "A week later, he thrust this scrawny kid in my face and told me how he'd saved him from some bullies. The kid's name was Evan Gloverfeld, but we were going to call him Clover. The kid wasn't thrilled with the idea, and I tried to point out that clovers were not a suit in a deck of cards, but Jesse had already made up his mind. Once that man has set his mind on something, there's little you can do to get him to change it."

———

Mike didn't say anything. As he'd talked, Dillon's body had gradually relaxed, and Mike didn't want to do anything to make him tense up again.

"Even though I had told Jesse to leave me alone, once Clover was with us, I found them both around me all the time. I kept telling Harte to fuck off, but I couldn't bring myself to say it to Clover, and I think he knew. The kid was so uncertain, it was no wonder people bullied him, but the more time he spent with us, the more confident he became. He grew from staring at the floor, hesitant to attempt conversation, to voicing his own opinions and even standing up for himself against his own bullies. He became—" Dillon's voice softened, and it spoke more than the word "beautiful" that left his lips. Things clicked into place for Mike as he listened.

"About three weeks before the end of the school year, Danny Stone was pulled into our group and that was it. Jesse had won, and we've been best friends ever since."

Mike couldn't let that be the end of the story. "And Clover?" he prompted gently.

Dillon's shoulders softened again, and he turned his head, staring off into the distance. "Clover..." He swallowed. "Clover was something else, something completely unexpected. He changed during high school and college, but I never knew how much until one night he threw himself at me at a party. Literally. I thought the kid was raving drunk, but he kissed me and looked up at me with clear sober eyes and said, 'You're mine.'

"He was right," Dillon said, pushing himself into a better position on the bed. Mike made sure not to touch him, in case it would spoil the moment. "One moment we were in a room crowded with people, and the next I had him alone, my hand grabbing hold of his hair and forcing him to his knees. I had no idea if he would be into anything rough, but I already knew I was, and I couldn't help myself or stop to ask." His voice became deeper as he spoke, and Mike shivered at the note of irrefutable possession it contained. The chain on his ankle felt flimsy by comparison. "Clover was mine," Dillon said, "and that night, I staked my claim on him."

There was silence for a moment as Dillon was lost to memories. Mike could only wait for him to return to the here and now while pretending a stab of jealousy was not ripping through him. It was ridiculous to be jealous of a client's past lover and completely unprofessional.

"We learned together, Clover and I." Dillon's voice came softer now. "We stepped into the world of BDSM together, created our routines together, and fitted our lives to match perfectly." A slow smile curved the Dominant's lips. "He loved to wake me with a blowjob," he said, "and boy, would I return the favor. Clover would be trembling and begging before I was done with him, and even then, I could never let him go. It was a daily challenge for him to convince me to let him out of bed, so he could make breakfast for the two of us, and I could get to work on time. Jesse used to tease me that without the chains we'd be a blissfully married vanilla couple, and Clover would scold him for making fun." Dillon laughed. "I loved when he'd put Jesse in his place. My Clover was brave and beautiful," he said. "He was proud and perfect, and one day, a drunk in an SUV took him away from me."

The resounding silence was heavy, and Mike had no way to fill it. He didn't know how to lend comfort to a man who had lost someone he had loved so deeply. He couldn't even reach out to touch Dillon, afraid any offer he gave would be rejected. To call this man Master now would be an insult, and it hurt him to feel so helpless.

In the end, he resorted to his job. His presence in this bed wasn't the only thing being paid for, and if that was the motivation that could make him mobile, so be it. He reached for Dillon, taking hold of the man's arm and using it to pull him closer. Dillon turned with Mike's guidance as if in a daze. Mike slid his arms around the bigger man, his legs opening in invitation. Dillon registered the cue and took the lead, pressing them both down against the mattress and coaxing Mike's hips higher with his knees. Mike took care of the condom, relieving Dillon of the responsibility, and when he was ready, he pushed his hips forward in a silent plea. Dillon slid inside him carefully, wrapping his arms around Mike's body and pressing their chests together.

It was different than any other time he'd been taken by this man, and he couldn't help clinging to him in return. Dillon set a rhythm, and Mike held still, offering his body to be used as needed.

The faster Dillon rocked his hips, the tighter his embrace became, and Mike held him tighter in return. Faster and faster, the slap of Dillon's body against his filled the room, accompanied only by their panting breath. Finally, in a jerking shudder, Dillon came. He collapsed onto Mike and rested there.

Mike waited patiently, breathing shallowly beneath the weight. Eventually, Dillon moved to dump the condom, but he made no move to let go of Mike, pulling him close as he drifted off to sleep. He did not let go for the rest of the night.

SIX

Mike woke to the feeling of warm, wet lips around his cock. It was a truly pleasant sensation, and it took him a moment to realize who was attached to the delicious mouth. Once he knew, his eyes flew open with a gasp.

Dillon, his eyes locked on Mike's face, chuckled. The vibrations were a dancing tease that made Mike squirm. Leisurely, Dillon slid his mouth away.

"And here I thought you were going to sleep and miss the promised orgasm of the morning," he said.

"Wouldn't that be breaking the rules somehow? I'm sure I'm supposed to be awake for the orgasm in our agreement."

"There is nothing in our agreement about you being conscious for it," Dillon pointed out.

"Well, I'd like to add that for next time," Mike said.

Dillon smiled. "Noted."

"Um…Dillon? Are you just going to leave it like that?"

Dillon chuckled again. "You're still mine until that ankle cuff comes off. I can leave it as long as I'd like."

Mike wanted to squirm, but Dillon's body had trapped his legs. He was sure the man had chosen the position on purpose.

"Please?" Mike asked, wondering if begging would work while Dillon was in a teasing mood.

"Please what?"

"Please suck my cock, Dillon?"

Dillon frowned, and Mike's heart skipped a beat. "You should know better than to say that," Dillon said.

Mike scrambled to figure out where he'd fucked up. He would have kicked himself once he realized if only his legs had been free. Tentatively, he asked, "Please suck my cock...Master?"

The smile returned, easing some of Mike's anxiety. "That's better." Dillon shifted to straddle Mike's body, and Mike gasped in surprise.

"You're not going—"

Dillon's raised eyebrows cut off the protest, but the thought of the Dominant riding him was too much for Mike to take. He swallowed.

"I'm sorry, Master. Please do as you'd like."

Whether Dillon was curious or cared about his outburst, he made no sign. Mike wondered if his apology had been enough, but he soon found out.

"For forgetting your place," Dillon began as he lazily stroked Mike's cock. He must have been toying with it for a while. Mike hadn't realized how hard he was. His prick was dripping, and a slow throbbing began as Dillon teased him. "And for forgetting to call me Master, you are going to be punished this morning." Dillon's hand tightened, intensifying his stroking, and he flicked over the head, making Mike want to squirm again. Dillon didn't say anything more but continued to work him. Mike soon found himself tightening his muscles to keep from coming without permission. It became harder and harder to hold back, and he trembled from the effort.

"That's it," Dillon said. "Almost there..." He kept working until a small sound escaped Mike. "Perfect." Dillon smiled. He shifted forward, leaning his body over Mike. "No coming until I give you permission. Remember that." He waited until Mike gave a nod. Sweat had broken out on Mike's brow, and he was afraid to speak. "Good," Dillon said. "Now, open your mouth so I can fuck it."

Mike let out a moan and had to concentrate even harder to keep from coming. He opened his mouth gingerly, afraid any movement on his part would send him over the edge.

"Wider."

He opened his mouth wider as instructed.

"And don't forget to cover your teeth. I'll slap your face if you scrape me."

A whimper escaped Mike at the thought of what that would feel like. He wrapped his lips around his teeth and opened his mouth as wide as he could. Dillon angled his cock with one hand then thrust down. Bracing himself against the wall, he did nothing less than what he'd promised. He fucked Mike's mouth, taking hold of Mike's hair to angle him better. When Dillon's dick slid deep and entered his throat, Mike's concentration shifted from not coming to not choking. Dillon worked it a few times before pulling back enough to let Mike breathe. Mike felt tears running down his face, but he couldn't let them distract him. His focus was only on pleasing Dillon and following orders. He would take his punishment well.

With a final deep thrust, Dillon came, his seed sliding down Mike's throat, and Mike hurried to swallow as best he could. The massage of his mouth working milked every drop from his Master. Spent, Dillon pulled back enough for Mike to breathe again, but he kept his cock in Mike's face. Mike took the cue to lick the Dominant clean, worshiping the taste and opportunity. Dillon's gaze was full of approval when he pulled back fully, and Mike smiled.

"You didn't come, now, did you?"

Mike's heart jumped into his throat, and he panicked. He couldn't see beyond Dillon's body, and at some point, he had totally forgotten to concentrate on keeping himself from orgasm. Dillon was not kind enough to let him see. Instead, he reached around and took hold of Mike's erection. Mike cried out, and Dillon smiled broadly.

"Good boy. Looks like you're still begging for me." He slid back and lay on his stomach, trapping Mike's legs once again beneath his body.

"Take hold of the headboard. If your hands come off it just once, I won't finish you off."

Mike gripped the rungs until his knuckles turned white. Dillon resumed playing with him as if he were a lollipop. One long lick from the base to the tip of his cock had Mike whimpering. The pain of need overwhelmed the pleasure, and tears streamed down his face once more. When Dillon swirled his tongue around the head, Mike stopped breathing for a moment, but then there was nothing.

"Open your eyes, Michael. Look at me."

Slowly, Mike forced his eyes open. Dillon's attention was locked on his face.

"Good. Keep looking at me. I want to see all of it."

Dillon lowered his lips once again. Mike had to fight to keep his eyes from rolling back into his head, but with Dillon's eyes on him, it was easier. Dillon's mouth plunged down on him and sucked hard, making Mike scream. The corners of the older man's eyes crinkled in a smile at his pain.

The sucking softened, and the Dom moved his mouth up and down. The sensitivity made Mike want to squirm, but he was trapped. Instead, he cried and stared back at Dillon until, eventually, pleasure took hold. He saw in his lover's eyes when the man wanted him to come, so he came. Dillon drank everything, his eyes dancing with approval.

He sat back and freed Mike's ankle, bringing an abrupt end to their evening. Mike didn't have a moment to enjoy the afterglow before disappointment hit him. This was only the second time he'd left this bed, but it felt harder than the first. If this kept up, he wondered how long he'd be able to keep Dillon as a client.

"I'll be downstairs making coffee," Dillon said as he slid out of bed.

"Should I be doing that?" Mike asked, then froze, realizing what he'd just said.

The question seemed to startle Dillon as well. He was slow to answer. "That's not in our contract," he said, finally.

"Of course," Mike hurried to correct himself. "I'm just going to use the bathroom, and I'll meet you downstairs."

He practically threw himself into the bathroom to avoid facing Dillon. He took his time using the facilities before heading downstairs to find the man already pouring two cups of coffee. What threw Mike off more was Dillon was fully dressed.

"Get dressed while this cools," Dillon said.

Yes, that was a very good idea. Mike felt too vulnerable and exposed to remain naked. He hurried to the front door where he once again found a pile of bills waiting for him. He counted everything before getting dressed and slipping the money into his jacket.

"Thank you," he said when he returned to the kitchen and accepted the cup of coffee. Dillon didn't reply immediately, and Mike's brow furrowed. He took a seat across from him. "Is everything okay?"

He wondered if the events of the evening, the story Dillon had told him, had been too much. He wondered if Dillon would say they wouldn't be seeing each other again. He found himself holding his breath as he waited for any sign from Dillon, not wanting that to be the case.

"You have my apologies," Dillon said, "for this morning."

"What?" Mike asked, confused. "What are you talking about?"

"The punishment this morning," Dillon replied. "It wasn't my right to do that to you, and my actions weren't within the bounds of our contract. If you'd like some sort of compensation, you just have to ask. If you'd rather we not meet again, I can understand that as well."

Dillon stared at Mike as he spoke, and that somehow made things worse. Even clothed, Mike felt exposed, and he didn't know how to answer. He dropped his gaze to the table, giving himself some space to think. Dillon was right. They hadn't negotiated the punishment, and Dillon's actions had bordered on breath play, which had never been discussed in the terms of their agreement. It was up to Mike to decide how this would play out.

"I could have stopped you," Mike said. He looked back up at Dillon. "But you're right if you're thinking I wasn't in the right mind to do so. I haven't done D/s like this before, but from what I know, it is your responsibility as my Master to keep aware of things like that, and in that respect, you made a mistake." He took a breath, feeling as if he were on a ledge, knowing he was on the verge of an offer he should not be making to a client. "But we also did not agree that you were my Master during this time period. Not officially. I had no collar, and you had no claim; therefore, the responsibility for my well-being also rested on my shoulders. It was a shared oversight. As no one was hurt, I think we can accept it as a mistake with shared blame and move on, but I also think we need to adapt our contract to prevent similar mistakes in the future." He took a sip of his coffee to steel his nerves. "For future scenes, we will still negotiate as we have been. All negotiations and payments will be agreed upon before the scene. As for sleeping together after the scene and the ankle chain, I think we can take that as a given for the contract, as well as no orgasms on my part until the one promised to me in the morning. Any alteration of those details can be brought up if necessary; otherwise, they are assumed. Any objections so far?"

Dillon shook his head.

Mike had already crossed the line. His next words would only take him further beyond it. He braced himself, wondering how much of a mistake he was making and how badly Dillon would take it.

"The terms of our contract are in place from the moment my clothes are placed on the table by the door until the time I've retrieved them for morning coffee. During this time period, you will be my Master with all the responsibilities that includes. My well-being will be in your hands, and I expect you to take care of me as you would any sub put into your care." Mike tried to ignore Dillon's widened eyes and rushed on. "The responsibility extends both ways. During the time period we are together, I will take the responsibilities of your sub and all that entails. If I do not behave accordingly, punishments will be your responsibility to dole out as long as they are within the boundaries of the evening's contract. I still hold the right to call a halt to any scene as well as the right to call a negotiation of anything that does not fall clearly within the terms of the evening's contract." He forced himself to keep eye contact as he asked, "Do you agree to these terms?"

The other man appeared to be frozen in shock. Mike resisted biting his lip in worry, taking a sip of his coffee instead. He didn't taste it as he waited, but at least it was something to do.

"Are you sure about this?" Dillon asked.

Mike found himself backtracking. "It's not a live-in permanent contract," he said. "This is only for the times you employ me as a client. As your tastes are specialized, I felt it would be right to alter our agreement accordingly." The fact that he wouldn't even consider offering something like this to anyone else made his stomach churn with worry. What was he doing?

Dillon took his time drinking his coffee as he considered Mike's proposal. The thought the Dominant put into the offer made Mike feel a little better. He wasn't committing suicide by letting a client have this much control. It was Dillon, and Dillon was different.

And Mike was an idiot, obviously.

"That didn't answer my question. Are you sure about

this? You don't have to do it. I don't mind keeping things the way they are."

"Well, I…" Mike stopped talking and thought about it. He could find many reasons for and against the idea, but that wouldn't answer Dillon's question or the real one he should be asking: Did he want to do this? When he set aside his job and his anxiety over what he should or shouldn't be doing, the answer was easy. "Yes."

"I accept your offer," Dillon said.

Mike was startled into glancing up. "You do? Uh, good. Do you want to arrange another meeting then?" he asked, attempting to employ his professionalism, even though he seemed to have misplaced it somewhere.

Dillon smirked. "Finish your coffee, and I'll check my schedule."

SEVEN

"You met with that boy again."

It wasn't a question, so Dillon didn't answer. Instead, he made himself a cup of coffee and took a seat on the couch in Jesse's office.

"I'm worried, Dillon," Jesse pushed. "I don't like the thought of that kid taking advantage of you."

"What makes you think he's taking advantage of me?"

"It's obvious you like him. I haven't seen you like this since…" Jesse sighed. "Since Clover was alive," he finished.

Dillon took a thoughtful sip of his coffee. Had he been acting different lately? He hadn't noticed. But he felt different. He felt happier than he had in a long time.

"So, what's the problem?"

Jesse moved to get his own coffee and leaned against the wall while he stirred sugar into his cup. "I'm worried he doesn't feel the same way. He obviously treats you well, or you wouldn't give him the time of day, but when it comes down to it, you're still a client, and he's still working a job."

Dillon kept his eyes on the dark liquid in his cup. He didn't want to admit it, but he'd been thinking the same thing. Having Michael scene with him in his house was a boundary he had never crossed with any of the one-nighters he'd picked up at the club. Not to mention the edges of their scenes reached into areas far outside what he'd consider casual, let alone professional. The negotiations following their wax play scene had proven that. They'd met a couple of times since then, and although they'd handled the evenings the same way as before, it was only a matter of time before they crossed the line fully.

"I know," Dillon said finally. "My bank account will start protesting soon."

"Do I even want to know how much he's charging you?"

"No."

Jesse sighed again. "Just be careful, okay? I don't want to see you get hurt."

"Yeah, yeah," Dillon said as he pushed up from the couch. "Sure thing, Ma."

Jesse rolled his eyes. "Fuck off."

"I will after I finish this." Dillon gestured with his cup.

"Actually, would you be willing to scene on the stage tonight? We've got a slot to fill, and the members would love to see you. It's been too long since you've been up there."

"What has it been? A month?"

"Try three."

"You've got to be kidding."

"Nope. Time flies when you get old."

Now it was Dillon's turn to roll his eyes. "I can't. I'm meeting Michael tonight."

"Do you think he'd be interested in going up there with you?" Jesse asked.

Dillon paused, sipping his coffee. He liked the thought of putting Michael on the stage. Stripping him down and making a claim in front of an audience. Dillon grew hard at the idea, but he pushed the thought away. That wasn't just outside their negotiations; it was on another planet altogether. He swigged the last of his coffee and stood.

"We've never talked about it," he said. "If he would, it wouldn't be tonight."

Jesse shrugged. "Next time then."

With a nod, Dillon set his empty cup on Jesse's desk, waved, and headed off. A smile curved his lips as he headed downstairs and outside. He was looking forward to seeing Michael again.

———

The back door to Harte pushed open. Mike glanced up from his crouch against the wall and smiled when he saw Dillon in the doorway.

"Dillon!" he called, standing and waving.

Dillon found him instantly, and a shiver that had nothing to do with the cold ran down Mike's body. He'd expected Dillon to stalk over to him and rush them off to the house, but he didn't move. Backlit as he was in the doorway, Mike couldn't determine his expression, but something felt off.

"You okay?" he asked, then wanted to kick himself. If Dillon was having doubts after their last time together, it wouldn't do to encourage them.

"Would you be willing to do a scene on stage with me?" Dillon asked.

"What?"

"Harte asked me to scene on stage tonight, and it got me thinking. I haven't done a scene here in a while, and it would be nice to take the stage again."

Mike froze. Alarm bells that had never rung around Dillon were suddenly clanging loudly. "Are you kidding?"

"No."

"That's not in our contract," Mike said, his mind scrambling to make sense of the unexpected change of plans and his new anxiety.

"I know. We would have to make a new one," Dillon said. "Obviously, the basics would remain the same, and I'd still expect you to come home with me afterward, but we'd negotiate the details. Price as well, of course."

Mike took an involuntary step back but forced himself to stop there, resisting the impulse to break into a run. "I…" It was too much. Mike searched for something to say or a question to ask, but nothing came to him.

"You can say no," Dillon said, and the simplicity of his tone cut through Mike's fear and anxiety.

"No," he said. "I don't want to do it."

Dillon was quiet for a moment, and Mike flinched inwardly, wondering if he'd ruined everything.

"I shouldn't have brought this up here. Are you all right? Do you still want to come back to my place as originally planned?"

"Um…" Mike swallowed. His heart raced, and he couldn't slow it down. The feeling of comfort and safety he usually felt in Dillon's presence had vanished. "I'm not sure how good I'll be for you right now."

"We can take our time. We don't have to go to the house until you're ready."

"I'm…" Mike hesitated.

"Would you rather call it a night and reschedule?"

The alarm bells had quieted after Mike had said no, but now he felt as if they would return. He didn't want to leave Dillon. He was afraid if he walked away now he would never be called to the Dominant's side again, but the part of him that craved the man's company had nothing to do with his job. Maybe he did need some space to get his thoughts straightened out and his feelings in order. This was a business relationship, nothing more. He had to remember that. If he couldn't, he couldn't be in this relationship anymore.

"Yeah," he finally said. "I think it might be best to call it a night."

Dillon nodded. "Do you need a ride anywhere?"

Mike shook his head. "I got it."

"Okay. Have a good night, Michael."

"Good night, Dillon."

EIGHT

Once Michael left, Dillon returned to Harte's office and pulled a bottle of scotch from the cabinet.

"What are you doing back here?" Jesse asked.

"Change of plans."

"What happened?"

"I might have just fucked things up royally."

Jesse leaned against his desk and stared at Dillon expectantly.

Dillon drank some of the scotch. "I asked him if he'd want to take the stage with me," he said. "It completely shook him up. I didn't think it would be that big of a deal, but I really know nothing about this kid. He was so rattled, we called everything off for tonight."

"Are you going to see him again?"

"We said we'd reschedule."

"Then what's the problem?"

Dillon sighed and sat on the couch. "I let him go home upset. I don't feel right leaving him alone with his thoughts like that, but I have no right to insist he stay with me."

Jesse took a seat next to his friend. "Maybe being alone with his thoughts will help him figure out what he might want from you."

"What do you mean?"

"You're not planning on paying for sex forever, are you?"

"No."

"So, at some point you'll have to ask him if he'll be willing to transition from a professional relationship to a real one. You need to let the kid make up his own mind when you ask him. If you coddle him now, how can you expect him to make a rational decision?"

"You really think I should collar the boy?"

Jesse laughed. "Come on, Dillon. You already know what you want. You did the same thing the first time you saw Clover."

"I did *not* want to collar Clover the first time I saw him."

"No, but your protective streak flared up royally. Why do you think he always gravitated toward you? You looked at him, and he was yours. This kid is the same. In your head, he's already collared."

Dillon swirled the scotch in his glass. "That's what's making things so difficult," he said. "It's hard to keep the line when you feel like you're past it."

"The next time you two meet, you need to put all your cards on the table. It's your responsibility to make sure those lines are clear, and if you can't keep them that way, you shouldn't be playing at all."

"I know," Dillon said. "I know."

NINE

Mike hadn't called to reschedule, but neither had Dillon. They'd exchanged numbers after their second night together when their negotiations had clearly been moving toward a regular thing. He was glad he had a way to contact Dillon that didn't require standing outside Harte in the cold, hoping the man was around, but picking up the phone felt harder than that.

A week had gone by since they'd last seen each other, and Mike still wasn't sure what he should do. He knew he could trust Dillon. If he hadn't, he never would have broken so many of his rules with him. But maybe he'd given Dillon too much leeway for Dillon to request to scene in public with him. There was nothing wrong with asking, but Mike had had bad experiences with clients in public, enough that even the thought of doing so with Dillon made him freeze up in fear.

He hadn't expected to react so strongly. Maybe that was a sign he should end their arrangement. It had to happen sometime. The money was great, but how long could he expect Dillon to keep paying a thousand dollars every time they saw each other? Not to mention, his relationship with Dillon had been affecting the rest of his business. He didn't exactly have a revolving door of clientele, but repeat customers were few, and he saw other tricks in between them. He hadn't seen anyone else in the few weeks he'd known Dillon, but the real problem was he hadn't been motivated to. Sex with Dillon blew his mind, and he was hard-pressed to imagine another client who would be able to stack up against him. He'd become spoiled, and he knew he was getting too attached.

On top of his issues with Dillon, he'd also received notification class registration was approaching again. The email reminded him of Dillon's words about thinking of the future even if he wasn't taking action yet. He knew he'd been out of school for a year, but he hadn't realized how long it had been since he'd even considered going back. He'd opened the link to the class catalog and scrolled through it. As usual, nothing stood out to him. He'd closed the browser, feeling stagnant and hopeless, but instead of falling into the same old pattern, he'd wondered if he was searching in the wrong place. College wasn't the only way to find a career. There were trade schools, apprenticeships.

It was time to stop waiting for inspiration to hit him and go out and find it. He needed to make some changes in the way he did things, and not just with school. Reluctantly, he admitted one of the first things he needed to change was his relationship with Dillon. He reached for the phone, but Dillon was already calling him.

TEN

Mike was nervous. When Dillon had called saying he wanted to talk, it had shaken his resolve to end things with him over the phone. He didn't think it would be any easier in person, but he could hear Dillon out before they parted ways. After the last time they'd seen each other, he wasn't sure how things stood between them. It would be best to clear the air before he let go of Dillon as a client.

He felt awkward as he arrived at Dillon's house. Dillon did nothing to ease the tension when he opened the door. Without a word, he stepped aside to let Mike enter. Mike headed into the living room and stood in front of the fireplace, unsure what to do with himself.

"Have a seat," Dillon said.

Mike sat.

"I want to talk to you about the other night and about our boundaries in general."

Mike nodded. That was fine. Mike wanted to talk about the other night as well. As for boundaries…that wouldn't be a problem soon.

Dillon appeared to hesitate before continuing. "If you'd like, we can go somewhere else to discuss this. I don't want you to feel influenced by your surroundings."

"I'm fine," Mike said.

Again, that hesitation. What would make a man like Dillon hesitate?

"Can you tell me what bothered you the other night about scening on stage?"

Mike forced himself to remain relaxed. "I'm not sure."

"Have you done anything like that before?"

"No."

"Does it bother you to be seen by others?"

This time it was Mike's turn to hesitate. Dillon nodded as if that were answer enough. "Do you trust me, Michael?" he asked.

"Of course," Mike immediately replied. He'd never trusted anyone more, and that was the problem. He did trust Dillon. He liked Dillon. He liked the time they spent together, the way Dillon made him feel, especially how safe he made him feel. Mike let his guard down around Dillon, and he couldn't do that and still consider himself "safe" when it came to his job.

"Why?"

"You've never given me a reason not to." That wasn't the whole truth. Yes, Dillon had never betrayed his trust, but that wasn't enough of a reason. There was something else that drove his instinct to place himself in Dillon's hands, but he couldn't put the feeling into words.

"I hope I never give you a reason to distrust me," Dillon said, "but there was something about the other night that you didn't feel comfortable with. I'd like to know what that was."

"I…" Mike didn't want to talk about this, but that's what he'd come for, he supposed. He took a breath and tried again. "I don't like being in crowded places with a client," he said. "It doesn't always work out well. Sometimes…things don't go according to plan. People take advantage. That's why I have them take me to a hotel or just fuck me in the bathroom."

"Others have tried to share you?"

Mike nodded. "Or just pass me along as if they own me. As if it's not my choice who I fuck."

Dillon was quiet for a long time. Mike feared the man was disgusted with him and had to fight to finally look up at his face. What he saw in Dillon's expression rocked him to his core. Dillon was *furious*. His jaw was set tight, and it was obvious he was trying to calm down before speaking again. When he saw Mike eyeing him, he bit out three words: "I don't share."

Mike wasn't sure how long he'd stopped breathing, but he didn't start again until Dillon broke eye contact by turning toward the kitchen.

"I'll make us some coffee," he said before heading off.

———

Dillon was losing it. When he'd heard how Michael had been treated, he'd wanted to find those men and rip their balls off. More than the thought of defending Michael, the idea of anyone else touching him had set fire to his veins.

Jesse was right. If he couldn't get hold of himself and draw clear lines with Michael, he couldn't see him anymore. It was unfair to them both, not to mention dangerous. He couldn't wait any longer. It was time to stop feeling the submissive out and lay his cards on the table. He set about making two mugs of coffee, and with one last deep breath to brace himself, he headed back into the living room.

"Careful, it's hot," he cautioned as he handed a cup to Michael. Once free of the duty of host, he took a seat in his big leather chair. The comfort and familiarity of its embrace helped him to put some of his worries aside and focus on the moment at hand. "I'd like to negotiate a new contract with you," he said.

Michael had been in mid-sip when he spoke. He carefully lowered the cup to his knee and regarded Dillon. "What did you have in mind?"

Dillon fought to keep from blurting everything out at once. Michael would know better than to interrupt, but it was still difficult not to rush things. He made himself take a careful sip of his coffee before speaking.

"Our sleeping arrangements shall remain the same," he began. It was easier to start with the simple things. "I still expect you to be available to me at any time during the night, same as before.

"I would like to lay out specific boundaries of what you are comfortable with and where your limits are, so I can use that information to determine what we do in future scenes without having to make suggestions you've never considered. If there is something you'd like to try, please tell me. I want to know what you're interested in. My goal is that as we scene together and we learn more about each other, you will eventually be able to trust me to know your limits, so I won't have to explain the full specifics of a scene before we do it."

Michael's brow had furrowed. He seemed a little wary, but he hadn't objected so far. After another sip of coffee, Dillon continued.

"If either you or I suggest something we have not previously considered, we would discuss the idea, but overall decisions within the boundaries we have set would be mine to make. I would like to discover your limits and interests. This may mean pushing you to try new things, but it may also mean delaying something you want because I don't think you are ready for it. I'll expect you to trust my judgment, but I'll also expect you to be honest about what you're feeling and thinking, so I can make the correct decisions. If you find yourself fully against something, it's mandatory you bring it up. I will not have an unwilling submissive, nor do I want to do anything detrimental to your health or well-being. You will still have your safeword to stop any scene or situation you deem necessary. This will not break the contract, and I will fully expect to discuss why you used your safeword once we have resolved the situation."

The crease between Michael's brows had deepened, but he continued to be silent, so Dillon pushed on.

"This contract will also extend to regular duties around the house. I will expect you to make breakfast, lunch, and dinner when we are both home. If you are not going to be home, I expect you to have something prepared for me. If I decide to surprise you and cook or let you off the hook for an evening, you will be notified beforehand. You remember I told you I may tie you up in front of the fireplace just to look at you?"

Dillon paused, and it took a moment for Michael to realize he expected a response. Finally, he nodded.

"I like to read in front of the fire, and I may do so for hours on end some evenings. I like to have something to admire during that time, and you will be it.

"There will also be rules and punishments in our routine. I expect you to follow the rules, and if you do not, you will be appropriately punished. I will not punish you unreasonably."

Now he was getting to the more obvious details. Dillon found it harder to face Michael as he spoke, not wanting to see an answer in the boy's eyes before he had finished speaking.

"If you agree to this contract, I will take responsibility for your care and safety. I will provide for us both with a roof over our heads, food for the kitchen, and clothing for when you venture outside. Indoors, clothing will not be necessary. There are other details to discuss, and I fully expect us to learn and adapt as we work out the specifics, but final decisions will be mine." Dillon gathered his courage and fixed his gaze on Michael. "Above all of the details I have mentioned, there are two items that cannot be negotiated." He hoped the roiling fear in his belly did not show as he forced the Dom to the surface and hid the rest behind a screen of steel. "This will be a live-in, exclusive contract," he said, his voice brooking no argument, "and it will not be a professional one."

Mike found himself frozen once again. Dillon's last words rang in his ears like deep bells, yet he still wondered if he'd heard them correctly. "You want me…as your sub? Like a real sub, not a once-a-week thing?"

"The only sub I have ever had lived with me," Dillon said. "I don't want it any other way."

"You could have anyone though, couldn't you? I'm sure there are tons of subs at Harte who would kill to be yours."

"I want you."

Mike didn't know what to say. He'd come here to end things with Dillon because he had been getting too attached. Now Dillon was asking him to commit to a full-time contract. It was too much all at once.

"You can say no." Mike could see how much it hurt Dillon to utter those words.

Despite his hesitation, Mike wasn't sure he wanted to say no. He liked Dillon. That had been the problem. Question was, did he like him enough to try having a relationship with him? Especially one that required a contract?

"I'm not him," he said. "It isn't going to be the same."

"I know. I want to create something that works for the two of us. And I know it'll take time, trial, and error. What I'm asking for today is your willingness to try this with me."

Dillon filled a need in him he couldn't get from other clients. He couldn't trust them enough to really let go. He didn't think he'd ever trusted anyone the way he did Dillon. The Dominant made him feel safe, and with this contract Mike could feel that way all the time. All he would have to do is give up his job. It wasn't like he'd been taking other clients anyway, and he did have money saved for college.

"What about school?" he asked.

"Are you interested in going?"

"Yes." Not that he'd figured out what he wanted to study, but when he did, he wanted to be free to pursue it.

"You're welcome to go to school whenever you want, and if you need help, I will be happy to assist you."

Mike shook his head. "I want to pay my own way through school. And I want to be able to take a job after I graduate. I may be your submissive, but I do not want to be completely dependent upon you."

Dillon smiled. "Does that mean you accept my terms?"

Mike took a deep breath. He could think about it all he wanted, but he already knew his answer. Setting his coffee mug aside, he rose and undressed. Once he was completely naked, he crossed the room and knelt in front of Dillon's chair.

"Yes, Master," he said, his head bowed.

There was no response, and Mike chanced a look up. The bright smile on Dillon's face made him grin.

"You owe me a collar."

"Brats don't get to demand collars," Dillon replied. "I decide when you get one."

Mike shook his head. "It's only a decoration. I'm already yours."

Dillon's gaze softened. He pulled Mike up into his lap and kissed him deeply. "Yeah. You were mine the moment I saw you."

EPILOGUE

Seven months later…

"Happy birthday, Clover." Dillon set the flowers down in front of the gravestone and knelt to say a few silent words. Mike stayed back to give him some space. After a few minutes, Dillon rose and gestured for Mike to stand beside him. "I'd like you to meet someone. This is Michael. He's—" The words caught in Dillon's throat, and Mike put his arm around him. Dillon leaned into him. "I hope you are happy for me."

"I'm sure he is," Mike whispered.

Dillon held him tight as they stood there.

"We never spoke about what would happen if one of us was gone. We never thought that far ahead."

Mike didn't know what to say, so he kept quiet. In his head, he said his own silent words for the man he'd never met. *I'm sorry you had to leave him. I hope you don't think I've taken him from you. You will always be in his heart, but there is room for me too. I love him, and I'll be good to him. I'll take care of him, I promise. Please watch over us and give us your blessing.*

"Do you want a few minutes alone with him?"

Dillon shook his head. "I'm almost done."

"No rush."

Later, when they were making their way back to the car, Dillon said, "How do you feel about going on a date?"

"A date?"

"Yes. Dinner, a movie. We can go to Harte later tonight too."

They had been to the club a few times since their relationship had changed from professional to something more. Dillon hadn't asked to do a scene with him onstage again, but Mike knew he was warming up to it. Mike didn't mind. Knowing he was Dillon's alone made him feel like he'd be able to give it a try this time. He eagerly awaited the day Dillon asked, so he could say yes.

"I'd love to go on a date with you, but would you mind helping me with something first?"

"What did you have in mind?"

"I think it's time I went back to school, but I don't want to do the whole bachelor's degree thing. There are certificate programs for stuff, and I was hoping you'd help me figure out what I might like to go for."

"I'd love to."

"I should have enough money to get started, but I also think I should get myself a job."

"What kind of job?" Mike knew he tried, but Dillon couldn't fully hide the concern in his voice.

Mike grinned. "Starbucks."

Dillon laughed. "I think you'll be good at it. You already make great coffee."

Yes, he did. At the first opportunity, Mike had dumped the instant at Dillon's house and refused to let him buy it again.

"Let's go home. We'll get comfortable in front of the fire, and we can talk about it."

That was Dillon's way of saying Mike had been clothed for too long, and he wanted his submissive naked. Mike leaned in to give Dillon a kiss. "Yes, Master."

Dillon squeezed his ass before giving it a pat. "Into the car with you."

Halfway home the words he'd thought to Clover came back to him. Though they'd had a few snags along the way, he'd easily settled into life with Dillon. He couldn't imagine being anywhere else. He'd always felt safe with his Master, but he hadn't noticed his feelings had grown so much. It wasn't fair that only the dead knew about them.

"Dillon?"

"Yes, Michael?"

He was sure it was unfair to say this to a person who was driving, but now he'd realized it, he didn't want to wait any longer. "I love you."

Dillon's mouth spread into a wide smile. Though his eyes remained on the road, he reached for Michael's hand and gave it a squeeze. "I love you too."

Joy filled Michael's chest like a balloon, and he found it difficult to stop grinning. It may have been a stupid decision to go home with a stranger that first night, but it was the best decision he'd ever made.

SHOOT THE MOON

ONE

"We're going to Harte."

Ash said this as if Adam would know what the hell he was talking about.

"Where?"

Ash waved the question away with a flick of his wrist and an expression that clearly said it didn't matter. "You'll know when we get there. Now, come on." He linked their arms and half dragged Adam out the door.

On the taxi ride to wherever they were going, Adam tried to get more details, but all Ash would tell him was that Harte was a local nightclub.

"You didn't let me get dressed."

"Why do you think I lent you that shirt to begin with? You look fantastic. Trust me."

The crowd outside the club wrapped around the side of the building and back again. Thankfully, it wasn't too cold out, or they would have frozen solid before getting inside.

"Is this place always so crowded?" Adam asked as they took their place at the end of the line.

"Packed like sardines," Ash confirmed. "Best place in the city for good drinks and dancing."

A man in skintight leather pants and what Adam guessed was a harness walked by. "Varied crowd," he said.

Ash spotted the man and did that wrist-flick thing again. "He's headed around back for the upper floors."

"The upper floors?"

"Yeah, the nightclub is only on the first floor. It's got three dance floors, each with their own bar, and a backroom, which was most likely meant to be a bathroom but is usually otherwise occupied. Upstairs is the kinky stuff. From what I hear, Harte has the best dungeon in the city, and he's known to be top-notch on safety. It's pretty well-known despite being members only up there. The entrance to the second floor is in the back, though, because there's a difference between exhibitionism and indecent exposure."

"Huh." Adam had never been to a kink club. Granted, they didn't have plans to head upstairs, but this was the closest he'd ever been to one.

Eventually, they made it inside. With the beat of the music and the press of sweaty bodies grinding around him, it was easy for Adam to be distracted from thoughts of the upper floors. It wasn't long before he'd lost Ash to the throng as well. His friend tended to sidle toward the nearest hot guy before passing him up for the next one on the dance floor. It gave him more exercise than the dancing itself. When he wanted a break, he'd pop up next to Adam as if finding someone in a crowd was the simplest thing to do.

Tonight, Ash's method fit Adam's mood. He scanned the floor for someone to dance with. It didn't take him long to find what he was searching for.

The man was dancing alone and, apparently, without a care in the world. He seemed lost to the music, his body moving with enviable grace and confidence. He was lean with boyish good looks and the kind of face that would still look thirty when he was fifty-five. His light-brown hair was just long enough to be spiky, and though his clothes were casual, he dressed stylishly.

When the dancer turned his head, he caught Adam staring. A jolt ran through Adam, but he couldn't look away. Even from a distance, the man's pale eyes had him trapped, and Adam found himself moving through the crowd as if pulled by an invisible string. When he was close enough, he reached for a seductively swaying hip. The touch of a hand on the back of his neck encouraged him to move even closer.

They moved together for a while, sliding their bodies against each other but in no hurry to make it anything more than dancing. They simply let the pleasure of touch build on itself. The feel of his partner's body against his was electric.

Adam was about to ask if they should find the "bathroom" when the man asked, "Care to go upstairs?"

Adam hesitated. "Isn't it members only?" He figured that was a simple way to change the subject without having to turn the guy down.

"I can bring a guest if I want to."

There went his easiest excuse. His reluctance must have shown on his face because the man asked, "Not your thing?"

"Not really," Adam admitted.

"Ah" was the only reply, but Adam heard the disappointment in the word.

"Sorry."

"It's okay."

Truthfully, Adam had never given kink much thought. He'd heard about it, read a little online, but he'd never considered putting what he'd read into practice.

They kept dancing, but the mood had changed. Adam felt it in the air, and he didn't like it.

"I wouldn't need a…safeword or anything, would I?"

The man's smile was like a warm spring day. "That would depend on how involved you want to get. If you just want to check it out, you'll be fine without one. Say the word at any time, and we will leave."

Adam drew in a breath, steeling himself. "Okay. Lead on."

The smile widened into a grin. Taking Adam's hand, the

man led him through the crowd. There was a door at the back of the club framed by a pair of imposing bouncers, but the guards didn't hesitate to let them through. Adam and his escort climbed a flight of stairs and entered a completely different universe.

Leather was everywhere. Leather and skin. What Ash had said about indecent exposure was right. There was more bare skin here than Adam had ever imagined seeing in his life.

Once his mind made it past the wardrobe, he took in the rest of the details of the room and what the people in it were doing. A sharp slap yanked his attention to a large stage where a man was tied to what appeared to be a giant X. Another man stood behind him with a whip of some kind. It was short with a bunch of tails. As Adam watched, the second man raised his arm and brought the instrument down on the already-rosy ass in front of him. The recipient of the lashes moaned in pleasure.

"This is what you're into?" Adam asked.

"Among other things."

"Doesn't that hurt?"

"It can be a pleasurable kind of pain."

"I can't see how."

The slap came again, and the submissive's head fell back. His eyes were closed, lips parted in an expression of bliss. Adam couldn't imagine how the apparent torture could produce such obvious enjoyment.

"The only way to truly understand is to experience it." Hot breath tickled his ear with the words. "And the only way to do that is to be curious enough to give it a try. It's not easy to trust someone completely. I admire the men who are able to do so." His guide's attention had turned back to the sub as he finished speaking.

"I take it you're usually the one holding the whip?" Adam asked.

"Flogger," the man corrected, his eyes glued to the couple on the stage. "And yes."

Adam didn't know what to say, so he resumed his visual exploration. Various tables and booths surrounded a bar to his left. The seats were filled with men watching the demonstration. One man in particular caught Adam's eye. He wore leather from head to toe while another man knelt at his feet in nothing but a black G-string and a dog collar.

"That doesn't appeal to you?"

Adam hurried to change his expression as he answered. "Not really."

"Why?"

Adam scowled at him, offended by the question, but his host seemed truly curious. Maybe they were both trying to understand a perception not their own.

"It looks like he's the guy's pet"—Adam gestured to the submissive—"a dog, not even human."

"He is quite human, and I assure you he is treated as such. Better even. Some Doms like subs who are trained for puppy play and the like, but Dillon is not among them. You might even say both Dom and sub worship each other in that relationship."

"Sorry," Adam said. "I didn't know he was your friend."

"I did ask for your opinion."

"Are you into that?"

"Puppy play? No."

"I meant the whole collared, half-dressed, and kneeling thing."

The charming smile returned. "Sometimes. You have to admit, Michael looks beautiful like that."

Adam looked again. "I don't know. I can't get past the dog collar."

"Not all collars look like that." He glanced around the room for what Adam assumed to be an example. "See the man in the white T-shirt?" He nodded in the direction of his gaze, but the man wasn't difficult to find, as he was one of the few not wearing black. "The chain around his neck is a collar."

Adam's brows furrowed. "But it looks like a necklace."

"It's supposed to. When he goes into work or out on the street, it appears to most people as ordinary jewelry, but people in this community recognize it for what it is. More importantly, the man who put it there and the submissive wearing it know what it means."

"You make it sound like a wedding ring."

"It can be. Just like a wedding band is a symbol of a commitment between two people, a collar is a commitment. The vows may differ, but the promise is as strong and as binding. Maybe even more so."

"Oh." Adam hadn't heard those details before. He still didn't like the dog collar, but he tried to picture the man wearing it in a new light.

"Would you like to see more of the place?"

"There's more?"

Amusement dancing in his eyes, Adam's new acquaintance said, "Much more." With that, he grabbed Adam's hand and led him deeper into the club where Adam saw more of the BDSM scene than he could have ever imagined.

Harte's dance club filled the entire first floor of the building, but the rest of the club was spread out over three floors with space for any scene a person could devise. There was a small schoolroom, a doctor's office, a small library, and even a playground, though the swings were not the type found in someone's backyard. There were private playrooms for those who didn't want an audience and public alcoves for those who did. Toys, furniture, and props were supplied in every room, and signs indicated that if you needed something specific, all you had to do was ask. The place was a wonderland for kinky adults and, his host informed him, *absolutely* exclusive. Like Ash had said, the safety of the patrons was the highest priority.

After a whirlwind tour, Adam and his guide finally paused in one of the simpler playrooms. It had a cabinet, which Adam assumed was fully stocked with toys, lube, condoms, and props, but what caught his attention was the big X standing against the far wall. It was the same as the one the submissive on the stage had been strapped to.

"That's called a Saint Andrew's Cross."

"Why?"

The question was answered with a shrug. "Does it matter? Most people don't come here for history lessons."

"I suppose we're in the wrong room for that."

The tease went over well, and Adam was gifted with a smile. "Yes, that was the floor above us."

Adam made his way over to the cross to get a closer look. There were attachment points on each of the X's limbs where cuffs could be connected, but the cuffs were missing.

"Would you like to try it?"

Adam froze, suddenly nervous.

"I wouldn't tie you to the posts, but if you're interested in trying something, I have an idea I think you might like."

"Oh?" Despite his nerves, Adam wanted to hear what the man had to say.

"Let me ask you first, are you clean?"

Offended, Adam whirled to face him, then realized it was a completely reasonable question. No one had asked him so bluntly before.

"Yes," he said. "I'm always safe, and I get tested regularly."

"As do I. Now, if you're interested in doing anything, turn to face the cross again."

Adam hesitated. He didn't know what the Dominant had in mind and wasn't into giving over control to a complete stranger.

"I won't tie you up, and if you want to stop at any time, all you have to do is say so."

"You didn't make any promises about pain," Adam pointed out.

The Dom smirked. "Why? Would you like some?"

"No! I mean…that guy with the flogger…"

"You're right. My apologies. I promise I will not use any toy on you that would be painful."

That wasn't completely reassuring, but Adam was feeling reckless. "What do I have to do?"

"Turn back to the cross."

Adam did, and suddenly, there was heat at his back and a voice low in his ear. "I want you to line up your ankles with the posts and hold here with your hands." His arms were guided into place. "I'm not going to bind you, but you're not allowed to move. Make all the noise you want—beg if you'd like. I do enjoy that—but no moving. Can you do that?"

"What are you going to do?"

"Touch you," the man said simply.

"That's it?"

"Oh, I think that will be enough." As if to demonstrate, he skimmed his fingertips down Adam's neck, and a shiver ran through him. "I don't need anything more than my hands, wouldn't you say?" He caressed Adam's thighs and kneaded his ass through his jeans. "Maybe, a little of my tongue too?" he added, licking along the outer shell of Adam's ear.

Adam felt warm. "Okay. I can do that."

"And if you're a good boy and keep still, I'm going to fuck your brains out as well."

Adam's body responded eagerly to that, and he nodded.

"Good." The warmth at Adam's back disappeared as the man stepped back. "Now, take off your clothes."

Adam moved from the cross and unbuttoned his pants. "What about you?"

"I will when I'm ready," the Dominant said, heading to the cabinet and pulling out a bottle of lube and some condoms. He set them on a small table and dragged it closer to the cross. When he caught sight of Adam, he raised an eyebrow. Adam realized he'd stopped moving and resumed undressing.

"You know, this is my first time getting naked in a club— or outside of a bedroom, for that matter."

"Are you nervous?"

"A little."

"That's normal. If at any time things become uncomfortable, all you have to do is say so, and we'll stop."

"I know." Adam folded his clothes semi-neatly and set them aside before hooking his thumbs in his underwear and adding them to the pile. He stood naked, fighting hard not to cover himself. The Dominant pointed to the cross, and Adam moved back into position in front of it. It was less embarrassing to face the wall, but with his legs spread so wide, he was aware of how easy it was to access the most private parts of his body.

"What do you get out of this?" he asked, his nerves making him talkative.

"Having you at my mercy," came the reply. "It's quite a high. Intense and intimate." He kissed Adam's shoulder. "You're beautiful."

Warmth rushed through Adam at the compliment, and he turned to say something in reply, but was stopped midturn and made to face forward again.

"Uh-uh. No moving, remember? You're mine now."

Declaration made, the touching began. At first, it was gentle brushings that tingled and tickled. Featherlight, they were soothing, and Adam relaxed into the experience. Soon, the contact grew firmer as if his skin was being thoroughly explored. His arms, legs, back, and belly all received the attention of someone who wanted to learn every inch of him and what he liked best. Soft moans escaped him as the exploration continued, but they were nothing compared to the noises he made when the caresses reached his nipples. The sensitive nubs were teased with flicks and pinches, rubbed gently or barely at all. Adam had never met a man so creative with a person's nipples using his hands alone. His hips rocked, adding enthusiasm to the mix, but a sharp tap on his butt startled him, and he stilled.

"No moving," he was reminded.

The sting faded, but Adam was now focused, working hard to keep still as the man worked magic with his hands. He stroked him everywhere except the two places he wanted most.

"Please." The plea came out as a whisper even before he'd thought to voice it. He vibrated with his efforts, yet that focus was the only thing keeping him standing.

———

Oh, that sound was beautiful. Jesse kissed the boy's shoulder. Then he stepped back to admire the full picture of what stood before him. The young man trembled with effort, which only made Jesse want him more. His gaze traveled down smooth, creamy skin to a pert and clenching ass. His mouth watered at the sight.

He knelt and took hold of the perfect globes of Adam's ass, kneading the flesh and spreading them wide. The tight rosebud between them begged for attention, and he could not resist a moment longer. He teased at first, swirling his tongue around the inviting entrance before pressing inside. The boy wasn't the only one to moan as Jesse rimmed his new lover and happily nipped and licked to a litany of wordless begging. Finally, he traded tongue for a finger, and the body in front of him went taut.

"*Please*. More."

The plea went straight to Jesse's cock, and he worked swiftly, soon using two fingers, then three. Unable to wait any longer, he grabbed a condom and the lube from the table.

The young man quivered with desire and exertion. Jesse impaled him in one smooth thrust, pressing him against the cross with his body. He took a moment to bask in the pleasure of the tightness enveloping his cock, and the muscles clamped around him gradually relaxed.

"Remember," he said, his voice husky with need, "don't move, even now." Then he began to fuck in earnest. Deep thrusts worked the boy against the cross. His lover arched his back to give him better access, and he gratefully took advantage of the new position. Jesse rode hard, driving the boy to the edge of his pleasure and happy to make him struggle to hold on.

"Come when you like," he said, and the young man did, groaning with his head thrown back in bliss before collapsing against the cross. Jesse held him in place with his own body, waiting for him to recover. He grinned as he waited. He hadn't enjoyed a fuck like this in a long time.

———

When his mind cleared, Adam was grateful for the support. He shifted to stand but was prevented by the man's cock, which was still inside him and as hard as iron. Before he came to terms with what that meant, he was being pulled away from the cross and guided to his hands and knees on the floor.

"Push back on me," the man said as he started to pump again. Adam braced his hands as best he could on the floor and rocked back. They matched rhythm easily and pounded against each other. Their groans filled the room, and if Adam could have gone again so soon, he would have. Their rhythm fell out of sync when his lover quickened his pace for those last thrusts to orgasm. He pressed fully in against Adam as he came. After, they collapsed to the floor, panting.

"You did very well."

"I tried."

"That's all I ask for." The man brushed his fingers through Adam's hair. It was soothing. "I'd like to see you again."

The statement was unexpected, but Adam was pleased by it. "I'd like that."

"Good." The man rose to dispose of the condom and returned with two bottles of water. He handed one to Adam. "Drink up."

Adam did. He finished half the bottle, then set it aside and worked on catching his breath.

"Are you okay?"

"I feel like I've just run three hours on a treadmill, but I'll survive."

"You look well fucked, I'll grant you that."

"And whose fault would that be?" Adam teased.

"Oh, very much mine." His lover's gaze roamed his body as if inspecting his handiwork. That was when Adam realized he was the only naked person in the room. The Dominant's pants were open, though he'd tucked himself away, but aside from the need for access, he hadn't undone a single button of his clothing. Feeling vulnerable, Adam rose and began to dress.

"Are you sure you're okay?" the man asked again.

"Yeah. It's getting late, and I need to—" He almost said "search for a job" but stopped himself in time. He may have had sex with a stranger, but he didn't need to advertise how much of a loser he was after the fact. "Get up early tomorrow," he finished.

"Okay." Adam heard pants zipping. "I meant what I said though. I'd like to see you again."

Adam finished pulling his shirt over his head. "Yeah?"

"We can meet here. I tend to frequent the dance floor or the club on Saturdays when work doesn't interfere."

Sounded easy enough. They both knew the place, and it was public. "Sure."

"I'll see you on a Saturday then."

Adam went downstairs to find Ash and head home. It wasn't until they reached the apartment and Adam had taken a shower that he realized he didn't even know the guy's name.

TWO

"You got laid."

Jesse looked up. Leaning in the open doorway of his office was his best friend, Dillon Slade.

"Of course I did. Did you doubt it?" He poured a second glass of bourbon and carried the tumblers over to the big picture window stretched along one wall of his office. Lights flashed through the glass from the room below where a mass of gyrating bodies moved on the dance floor to music he and Dillon couldn't hear. When Dillon moved to join him, Jesse handed him his drink.

"Must have been good. You have that stupid expression on your face you get when your latest's been memorable."

Jesse laughed. "Well, aren't you astute. He was, by the way. Good, and one of those rarities called a surprise." The boy had melted like butter beneath his hands.

Dillon raised an eyebrow in interest. "How so?"

"He's not a sub, for one thing. I almost scared him off when I first suggested we go upstairs."

"What did you do with him then? You haven't gone vanilla on me, have you?"

"Oh no," Jesse reassured him. "Not at all. I simply gave him a gentle introduction to the wonders of kinky sex."

"How kinky are we talking?"

"Barely, by your standards. I had him stand against a cross and keep from moving while I teased him into begging me to fuck him."

"That's not a bad scene. I should try that to switch things up with Michael."

"I'm sure he'd appreciate it. Particularly the ending bit." Jesse tasted his whiskey. The burn of the alcohol felt good sliding down his throat. "I asked to see him again," he added quietly.

"Already? You're not leaving things to chance?"

"Well, partially. We didn't set a date, but I did bring it up."

"He must have been some surprise 'cause that's not like you." Dillon surveyed the crowd on the dance floor below them. "I say go for it. If he's that good of a fuck, why not make it a repeat thing? Better than taking a chance on someone who won't be up to par."

Jesse considered. "I suppose." He regarded his friend, and his brow furrowed. "Where's Michael?"

"Downstairs getting his clothing so we can go home."

"You let him go alone?"

"It took a lot of convincing, believe me," came a voice from the office doorway. Jesse turned to find Michael standing at the entrance, waiting for the men to acknowledge him. Unlike when Jesse and Adam had seen him earlier, the G-string was now covered by a smooth pair of black jeans and a T-shirt. The collar Adam had disapproved of rested above the crew neck of the top.

"I'm not surprised. Hello, Michael."

"Hi, Jesse," Michael said as he moved to his Dominant's side. Dillon wrapped an arm around the younger man's waist, pulling him close, and Michael leaned into him automatically. Jesse warmed at seeing the two of them together. It had been a long time coming, and Dillon deserved to be happy.

"You two are leaving already?"

"Michael starts classes on Monday, and we're still prepping for it."

This was news to Jesse. "You're going back?"

"I've decided to become certified as a personal trainer," Michael said.

Jesse gaped at Dillon in surprise. "And you're okay with that?"

"It was that or masseuse," Dillon grumbled.

Jesse laughed. To Michael he asked, "How did you come to that conclusion?"

"I hate sitting behind a desk and studying. I figured I wasn't going to like it any better as a job, so an office career was out. I like doing something physical and interacting with people. When I looked at certification programs, I saw personal trainer and figured I'd give it a shot."

Given Michael's previous profession, Jesse wasn't surprised he liked interacting with people. "I'm happy for you. I wish you luck."

Michael grinned. "Thanks."

"And what about you?" Jesse asked Dillon. "How are you handling this?"

Dillon shrugged. "I don't like anything that takes him away from me, which is all the more reason for him to have a job."

"You know," Jesse said thoughtfully, "I might know the perfect place for that job to be."

"Oh?" Michael asked.

"Yup. It's at a gym, and Dillon has a membership there."

Michael groaned. "Please don't ask me to be your personal trainer. Either of you. I don't think I could handle it."

Jesse laughed. "I'd love to watch you boss Dillon around for once. I think it'd be hilarious."

Dillon glared at him. "We'll deal with that when we get there. For now, let's get him certified."

"He's already signed up for the classes."

"That's not the hard part. The hard part will be leaving him alone when he's trying to do his homework."

"I have a feeling I'll be spending a lot of time in the library," Michael said.

"Oh no you won't," Dillon objected. "You'll do your homework like a good boy at home. I'll leave the house if it's necessary. The last thing I need is some scholarly nerd trying to hit on the hot guy in the library."

Jesse hid a laugh behind another sip of his drink, but Michael was also smiling indulgently.

"Yes, Master."

Jesse was happy for his friends, and for the first time, he wondered if it might be nice to have something like that for himself. Maybe one day far in the future, but maybe.

THREE

The club was packed as tightly as the last time Adam had entered. Bodies pressed up against each other, grinding to the drive of passion or the beat, sometimes both. As he waded through the mass and made his way to the bar, Adam wondered how he would find a man he'd met only once before and whose name he didn't even know. What if he wasn't here? What if he didn't want to see Adam again? A week was enough time for an impulse offer to become inconsequential.

He ordered a beer and let his eyes roam for a while. Eventually, Ash showed up and pulled him off his barstool to join in the dancing.

"I'm not going to let you sulk all evening," his friend shouted in his ear over the music.

"I'm not sulking."

"Yes, you are. Look, whether the guy is here or not, you're not going to waste your night waiting like some whipped dog. You're here to have a good time, and I'm going to make sure you do."

If only he knew what Adam had done the last time he was there… There hadn't been any whipping—on Adam, at least —but he had been reduced to panting like a dog while barely able to stand. It was an experience Adam wouldn't easily forget, and those memories kept his eyes wandering while he and Ash danced.

"Maybe he's not coming," Adam said later when his hopes had worn thin.

"Maybe," Ash agreed, though somewhat sympathetically.

"I'm going to head out of here. I'll see you later, okay?"

Ash seemed to be about to protest, but he didn't. Instead, he nodded, and Adam headed toward the front door. He was about halfway there when arms slid around his waist.

"Ash, what—" Adam's words cut off when he saw who was behind him. It was his mystery man.

"I've been looking for you all night," he said. "Mind if we move to a quieter end of the club?"

Speechless, Adam shook his head and followed him through the crowd. They headed deeper into the club and through a door Adam barely registered as Employees Only. After climbing a flight of stairs, they went through another door, and Adam found himself in an office. He whirled around at the sound of the lock turning, suddenly doubting his assumption the club meant safety.

"It's much quieter up here, isn't it?"

"Are we allowed to be up here?" Adam asked. This was different than being a guest of a club member. This was an official office with a gigantic desk and a full wall of windows overlooking the dance floor. Drawn by the sight, Adam wandered toward the glass, distracted from his own question.

"Wow, this is amazing."

"I thought you'd like it." The man slid his arms around Adam's body again and kissed his neck. "I'm glad you came."

"It was difficult to find you. I don't even know your name."

The man paused in his nibbling as if surprised by this. "My name is Jesse."

"Nice to meet you, Jesse. I'm Adam." It was awkward doing introductions while Jesse was pressed up behind him, but when he resumed kissing Adam's neck, Adam didn't care.

"Are you sure it's okay for us to be up here?" he asked again.

Jesse chuckled against his skin. "Perfectly fine. I have full permission to utilize this office for whatever purpose comes to mind. In this case, it's fucking." He punctuated this idea by groping Adam above his jeans. Adam's hips automatically rocked, arching back against Jesse who was already hard and wanting.

"I'm going to strip you naked and fuck you right up against this glass," he whispered in Adam's ear.

"I'm not into exhibitionism." Contrary to Adam's protest, his body liked the idea. His jeans were getting tight.

"You were downstairs," Jesse said. "Did you see any windows along this wall?"

Adam tried to remember but couldn't think of any.

"It's one-way glass. This way the floor can be monitored without anyone knowing."

Adam wouldn't have believed him so readily if he hadn't been in the club twice without noticing any windows. Jesse slid his hand into the front of Adam's jeans, which helped the argument.

"And before you ask—" Jesse banged on the window, and it sounded solid. "—the window's been reinforced. Trust me, it'll take a lot more than me ramming you into it to break."

Adam was out of objections. He'd never had sex in public, and he found the idea thrilling. Although no one would be able to see him, the window created the illusion he was out in the open for all the world to see. He was irresistibly tempted by it.

Taking his silence as agreement, Jesse was already unbuttoning Adam's shirt. Adam didn't stop him, but he did voice an opinion. "If we're doing this, you're getting naked too. It's not going to be like last time."

There was a slight hesitation to Jesse's hands Adam might have missed if they hadn't been on his body.

"Sounds fair," Jesse said before pulling off Adam's shirt and dropping it on the floor.

Adam wanted his hands on Jesse while he removed his clothing, but Jesse stopped him. "Put your hands against the glass."

Adam put his hands flat against the glass and felt the vibration of the club's music. The sensation distracted him, and before he knew it, he stood naked above a throng of people as Jesse caressed him everywhere he could reach, teasing his nipples and sliding over his skin.

"Clothes," Adam reminded him.

"Of course," Jesse said, and one of his hands disappeared to, Adam assumed, undo buttons while his other lazily stroked Adam's cock. When the hand returned, it was followed by Jesse's naked chest against his back. He shivered. Reaching back, he found the waistband of Jesse's pants and shoved. More skin pressed against him as they lowered. Jesse shifted, and the fabric was gone. He was slightly shorter than Adam, but his cock lined up perfectly with Adam's rear end. He nudged insistently against Adam, and Adam pushed back, wanting more.

"I'm going to fuck you right into this glass," Jesse said, his voice a low rumble in Adam's ear. Adam moaned, his own cock already dripping. True to his word, Jesse propelled him closer to the window.

Fear ran through Adam as the floor vanished from his sight. Though he believed the glass was sturdy, his instincts wouldn't listen to reason. His heart raced, and his panting wasn't only because of the gorgeous man pressed up behind him.

Jesse resumed caressing him, and Adam's alarm melted into the pleasure of the touch, making him harder as he swayed between the sensations.

"Jesse," Adam whispered.

"You like that?" Jesse asked. "You like being naked in front of all these people? On display for everyone to see?"

Adam's desire only increased from those words. Jesse's fingers brushed against Adam's hole, and Adam whimpered.

"Tell me, Adam. Tell me the truth, or I won't touch you here."

"Yes," Adam panted. "I love it. I love this. I love—"

Jesse drove two fingers into him, and Adam's words cut off in a groan. Where had the man found lube? Adam had no idea, but Jesse's fingers were slick and sliding in deep. Adam thrust back, making Jesse fuck him deeper.

"I'm going to make you scream so loud they'll hear you over the music," Jesse said. "They'll wonder where that noise is coming from, and they'll look right up here. Right at you."

Adam moved his hips faster, but Jesse abruptly removed his fingers from inside him.

"I think you're ready for me." Without waiting to see if Adam agreed—not that there was much need to—Jesse lined the blunt head of his cock against Adam's entrance and pushed in. He moved so *slowly*. Adam wanted to push back against him, make him move faster, but Jesse wouldn't let him. His hands were like iron clamps on Adam's hips, and any struggling was for naught. Slowly, so slowly, Jesse entered, then stopped. Adam hadn't noticed when his eyes had fallen closed, but now they snapped open as he cried out in protest. Jesse chuckled in his ear before slamming the rest of the way into him. Before the shock of the thrust could wear off, he was shoved against the glass, one hand pinning him to it as the other kept his hips angled out. Jesse pounded into him. His movements long, deep, and merciless.

Adam pressed his hands against the glass next to his face, bracing himself. He grunted with each drive of Jesse's cock, the cool texture of the glass soon heating up. Jesse changed his angle and moved in shorter strokes, beginning a relentless assault on Adam's prostate. He hit the gland again and again, moving too quickly for Adam to catch his breath between each thrust. Adam's grunts soon turned into one panting moan as he surrendered to the overwhelming sensation. Jesse changed pace again, his rhythm alternating, creating waves behind Adam's eyelids, and Adam never knew how long each one would build before crashing. He had almost forgotten his dripping cock for the sensations behind him when he felt a hand on his prick. With barely a touch, Adam's orgasm ripped through him.

Eventually, the whiteness of bliss faded back to the colors of the present. Adam was leaning against the glass, but it had long since become warm. He cracked open an eye, and all he saw was the long drop into the crowd below. He gasped, but Jesse's hands tightened reassuringly around him.

"It's all right. You're not going to fall."

Adam stood, taking his weight off the window. He felt a little better seeing the floor beneath his feet. He also noted a series of white smears on the glass. He turned to look at Jesse, but something in his ass stopped him. Jesse was still inside him, and he was hard.

"Did you think we were done?"

"I—" Adam swallowed. His throat was hoarse.

Jesse slipped out and let Adam turn to face him. "Brace your back against the glass," he ordered.

"You've got to be kidding."

Jesse raised an eyebrow, and Adam realized he was not.

"Jesse, I can't—"

Jesse stepped forward, pressing his body up against Adam's. The proximity made Adam move back against the glass.

"Put your arms around my neck."

Adam found himself doing as he was told even as he protested. "Jesse, this is—"

Jesse reached down and lifted Adam's legs. Instantly, Adam held him tighter, afraid of being dropped, but Jesse wasn't bothered. Who knew the man was that strong?

He maneuvered Adam to his liking, and before Adam

knew it, Jesse had sheathed his cock to the hilt inside him once more.

"Use the glass for extra support," Jesse said. "Keep your back against it. All I need you to do is move your hips with me. I'll take care of the rest." He must have seen something in Adam's face because he added, "You're not going to fall. I won't let you."

Before Adam could say anything, Jesse was at it again. He had to have been dying for release because his thrusts were now plainly driven with need. Sharp, snapping cracks of his hips had him working like a jackhammer inside Adam. Adam's ass would be sore come morning. He slid and his back stuck against the glass from his sweat, but Adam did his best to complement the movement of Jesse's hips with his own. Faster and faster, the other man moved, and Adam moaned in encouragement. He wanted to watch Jesse's face as he came, but Jesse kissed him instead, attacking his mouth with fervor as he pumped his load into the condom inside Adam. Spent, he rested his head on Adam's shoulder for a moment before moving back and letting Adam slide his legs down to the floor. Adam's ass felt weirdly empty as Jesse vacated it.

"Can you stand?" Jesse asked.

"Can you?" Adam asked in return.

"Touché." Jesse turned to pour two glasses of water from a jug on the desk.

"I'm surprised security didn't come barging in here," he said. "Even if the people downstairs didn't hear us, they probably would have."

"Who says the people downstairs didn't hear us?"

Adam knew Jesse was teasing, but he couldn't help glancing back out the window. Everyone was still grinding to some pulsing beat Adam couldn't hear.

"Why do you have access to this office, Jesse? It's too fancy for a fake setup, and I don't think the person who sits at that desk will appreciate the stains we left on the window."

"The stains *you* left on the window," Jesse pointed out as he stripped off the condom and dropped it into the wastebasket. "And I know for a fact he will appreciate them. I already do."

It took Adam a moment for his brain to catch up from the afterglow. "This is your office?"

Jesse nodded.

Adam took in the details of the room once again, but this time he really *looked*. There was a bar over on the right with a minifridge and an array of fancy bottles and glasses. Next to it stood a tall cabinet, but Adam had no idea what could be in it because everything office related was on the opposite side of the room. A bookcase and a couple of filing cabinets nestled in a corner to his left. Binders and books neatly lined the shelves of the bookcase, but one of the filing cabinet drawers hadn't been shut fully. The corner of a folder stuck out of it, the tiniest imperfection in an otherwise orderly office.

Jesse's desk sat in the middle of the room like a modern-day throne. A framed black-and-white photograph hung on the wall behind it. The picture was an extreme close-up of a man, the profile of his jaw and the upper part of his chest marking the boundaries of the shot. It was beautifully lit, but what caught Adam's attention the most was the collar around the submissive's neck, which had been colored in a warm burgundy. The photograph would have contained the only splash of color in the room if not for the flashing lights dancing through the windows from the club below.

One flash of a strobe brought Adam's attention to the plaque on the desk, which read *Jesse Harte* in golden block letters.

"Jesse Harte," Adam said incredulously. "This is your club?"

Jesse nodded again.

"No wonder you didn't have to worry about bringing a guest the other day."

"That's what comes to mind first? You're no longer worried about battening down the hatches against security?"

"Why didn't you tell me?"

"It was more fun not to." Jesse shrugged. "Besides, most people recognize my face. I'm surprised you didn't know or weren't told, at least."

"I'm not from around here, and the only person I know is the friend I'm crashing with."

"Would it have made a difference if you'd known?"

"I wouldn't have been as nervous about security," Adam replied.

"And that would have lessened the game. Either way, now you know. I hope my identity won't affect your desire to see me in the future?"

"No."

Jesse moved to embrace Adam. "I'm happy to hear it," he said before kissing him. "I do like the thought of memories of you in my office." His cock brushed Adam's thigh. Jesse was getting hard again. So soon? The man was incredible. "Think we can make some more at my desk?"

"What did you have in mind?"

"Oh...I'm sure we can come up with something," he said as he guided Adam backward. "You could ride me on my chair, suck me off under the desk, or..."

"How about I come up with the idea this time?" Adam interrupted him.

Jesse's eyebrows rose in interest, and Adam smiled.

"Let's see..."

———

Jesse was in his office, lounging with his legs kicked up on his desk. He could still see traces of white on the window where he had fucked Adam only hours before. The memory tempted him to light up a cigarette, but he'd quit years ago, and he wasn't going to start again just for a craving. Instead, he settled deeper into the chair, cradled by the warm leather, and let his mind drift back to earlier. He was lost in the daydream when the door opened, and Dillon walked in.

"I'm going to have to start putting something on the doorknob, so you don't barge in here when I have company," Jesse said.

"You could always lock the door," Dillon pointed out. Then he stopped and blinked in surprise. "You fucked him in here?"

"More than once," Jesse replied with a grin.

"You do realize you have office setups for something like that, right? You don't actually have to—" Dillon's voice cut off as he spotted the blurry marks on the window. "Against the window?"

"That was the first time. The other was at the desk."

Dillon gestured to an empty chair.

"That one's safe."

Dillon took a seat. "I take it you're still happy with him then?"

"I can't even begin to tell you. He hesitates, but he trusts me, and he's so *new* to everything. He won't be the lifestyle type, but there's so much potential, so much to explore that he has no idea about. I get a thrill thinking about what to show him next." He narrowed his eyes. "Don't look at me like that."

"Like what?"

"Like you know something I'm missing. Like you think there's more to this than just really good sex."

Dillon put his hands up defensively. "I didn't say a word."

"Not verbally but that doesn't mean you're not saying something."

"Do you think there's more to this than just sex?"

"I haven't thought about it. I've met the boy twice. It's not like I'm going to build a relationship out of two scenes in a nightclub."

They were both aware Dillon had built a relationship out

of two scenes at his house with a prostitute, but his friend didn't call him on it. Instead, he got up to grab some beers from the minifridge.

"Are you going to see him again?"

"Yeah. Next Saturday."

Dillon handed him a beer and didn't say anything more.

Grateful his friend was letting the subject drop, he asked, "How did Michael's first week of classes go?"

"They went well," Dillon answered as he took his seat again. "Now that he has a focus in mind, he's excited about it. He comes home every day with something new to share."

"That's great, but why don't you look as thrilled about it?"

Dillon sighed. "It's because I know he's worried about if he made the right choice. He doesn't want to get certified and then find out he wasted his money when he can't find a job."

"He can find a job. I told him that the other day."

"He won't let me help him pay for school. He's not going to let you hand him a job."

"I'm not handing it to him. He's going to have to apply and interview for it like anyone else. And if he doesn't want to work for me, I'm sure he'll be able to find a job elsewhere."

"I'm sure he can too, but it doesn't stop him from worrying."

"He's on the right path. He knows he is, but maybe you need to remind him."

Dillon sighed. "I will." He pushed up from his seat, taking a last swig of his beer. "And you should keep an open mind."

"About what?"

"You and this guy, the repeat fuck. It may not be anything right now, but you should see where it goes."

Jesse frowned. "I'm not dating him."

"No, but you are interested in somsthing. I say don't sweat the details and enjoy it. See what happens."

Movement out of the corner of his eye caught Jesse's attention. "Michael's here," he announced, grateful for the escape. "Have a good night, Dillon."

His friend rolled his eyes before setting the empty beer on the desk. "Night, Jesse."

Jesse waved to Michael as the couple left, and then he picked up his now-lukewarm beer. He frowned at it and set it back down again. "Keep an open mind, huh?" he said to no one in particular.

Maybe he would.

FOUR

Over the next six weeks, Adam and Jesse met up at the club every Saturday night. They never specified when they would meet but had a casual agreement to find each other in the crowd sometime after ten. From there, Jesse would lead Adam to a secluded area of the club and introduce him to his latest idea for fucking.

In the short time they'd known each other, Adam had begun to let go much more easily in Jesse's hands. He was less hesitant before each scene, and his enthusiasm was as fervent as ever. In relation to Jesse's experience, they played on the lighter end of things, but it made their encounters no less interesting. Anything pain related was off the table, but Jesse wanted to push things further than fucking in semi-public places. It was high time he discussed using safewords with Adam since it was getting harder and harder to keep things at a "no means no" level. He'd decided to bring the topic up when they met that night. He only hoped the idea wouldn't freak Adam out and undo all of the trust they'd built so far.

From his office window, he surveyed the crowd for any sign of Adam or the friend he usually arrived with. It was hard to recognize most people beneath the flashing lights, but

Jesse had become familiar with Adam's movements and was getting better at picking him out of the crowd. There was no sign of him.

Jesse checked his watch. Adam usually arrived by now. Was he not coming tonight? The idea didn't sit well with him, but he shoved the feeling away. Maybe Adam was running late. Besides, if they skipped a week, it wasn't a big deal. He was only noticing because it was the first time they'd skipped. That was all.

A knock on the door distracted him from his thoughts, and he called out, "Come in."

The door opened, and a security guard entered. "They're short a demo for the main room. Thomas just called and had to cancel. Who do you want me to ask to do it?"

Jesse scanned the crowd again. Still no sign of Adam. He pursed his lips thoughtfully. "Is Nicholas here?"

"I'm pretty sure I saw him. He's alone though."

"Good. See if he's willing to do it, and I'll demo with him. I'll meet him upstairs in ten minutes to discuss details unless you call me to tell me he's not up for it."

The guard nodded and left.

Once more, Jesse found his eyes straying to the mass below, but he forced himself not to look. He wasn't going to wait all night. Whether Adam came or not, Jesse planned on having an enjoyable evening. A part of him noted he'd have an even better time if Adam showed up, but Jesse told that part of his mind to sit in the corner and shut up. He went to the cabinet of toys in his office and pulled out his favorite flogger. He smiled as he ran the strands over his palm. It had been a long time since he'd played with it.

———

Adam was panting as he crossed the road and headed toward the line wrapped around the club. He was already running extremely late, and this would only make things worse. Was

Jesse waiting for him? Or had he found someone else to hook up with? Adam hoped for the former. He didn't want to have rushed all the way over here for nothing, and he didn't like the idea of Jesse fucking someone else. They hadn't said they were exclusive, but Adam wasn't the type to have sex with multiple people at the same time. He hoped Jesse felt the same.

When he finally made it inside, Jesse was nowhere to be found, and after twenty minutes of searching, he decided to try upstairs. Even if the bouncers wouldn't let him in, maybe he could convince them to find Jesse for him. Surprisingly, they let him in after asking for nothing more than his name.

"He's in the demo," one of the guards called after Adam as he headed upstairs.

Adam remembered the main room where the demos were held—he'd passed it often enough on his way to other areas of the club—so he followed his feet until they got him to where he was going. The room was packed. Doms were seated on every available space with a view, a sea of subs kneeling around them. Adam's initial scan of faces didn't reveal Jesse among the crowd, but there were too many people to be sure. It was also disturbingly quiet. A low murmur of conversation flitted through the room, but the tone was respectful, and Adam assumed the demo had begun. Curious, he turned toward it and found Jesse.

He was decked out in leather. Tight pants hugged the curve of his backside and the strong muscles of his thighs. He wore a vest with nothing underneath it and heavy black boots. Skin and leather were in abundance in the room, but when Adam saw the combination on Jesse, his mouth instantly watered. The appeal faded slightly when Adam noticed Jesse stood on the demo platform whispering inti-mately into the ear of a young man. The man stood in front of a Saint Andrew's Cross—Adam remembered the name from the first time he and Jesse had had sex—wearing nothing but one of those dog collars Adam had told Jesse he would never wear and the smallest G-string it must have been legally possible to wear in public. The submissive seemed at ease with Jesse, nodding to whatever Jesse said. Finally, Jesse stepped back and spoke loud enough for the room to hear him.

"Step up to the cross, Nicholas, and place your arms and legs in line with the beams." His voice carried, but it was focused for the ears of the man in front of him.

Adam couldn't stop staring as Jesse's order was followed. There were cuffs on the cross that Jesse attached to the submissive's wrists and ankles, making sure they were secure. Once they were in place, the man tugged a few times as well.

Jesse stepped back to survey the scene before speaking again. "Once we begin, you are not to speak until you come, and you are not allowed to come until I tell you to."

"Yes, Sir," Nicholas said.

"I will not touch your body with any part of mine tonight until we are finished. You will have no aid for release. You will only feel the kiss of my flogger, and you will come before I am finished with you."

The crowd stirred. Jesse's words weren't bringing only his submissive to arousal.

"Yes, Sir."

"Let us begin."

Jesse moved to a table where a dark-blue flogger lay. The laces were smooth and appeared soft from where Adam stood. Jesse ran the strands over his palm a few times before moving back behind his willing victim. He raised his arm and let it fall in a slow, easy rhythm, and Nicholas visibly loosened his shoulders as he relaxed into the scene. From an outsider's standpoint, the impacts didn't seem painful at all. The sub arched into Jesse's reach, rolling his head back as he allowed his eyes to drift closed.

The atmosphere of the room changed as the onlookers fell silent. The submissive's face had a peaceful expression as if he'd been lost to the sensations of the flogger. Jesse's focus was glued to the young man, watching as his ass turned pink and his body moved. It was as if the world had faded away and none of the crowd existed for the two upon the stage, not even Adam.

Nicholas's soft pants became louder as Jesse's rhythm increased. Tension built in the air as he moved faster and faster. Nicholas wriggled his ass with the impacts, but it was plain to see the movement was because of a tenting G-string instead of any true discomfort. The young man's panting became more desperate. He clenched his fingers above the cuffs and bit his bottom lip as Jesse hit him again and again.

"Ten more, Nicholas," said Jesse. "On ten, you come for me."

Adam didn't know if Nicholas would last for ten more strokes or if he could come on command, but he found himself counting in his head in anticipation as Jesse struck.

One, two, three…

The submissive clenched his jaw against what Adam could only guess was a groan.

Four, five, six…

He'd stopped wriggling, concentrating solely on following his Dominant's command. He bent his head forward and squeezed his eyes shut.

Seven, eight, nine…

Everyone could see the struggle, but Jesse didn't let up. Instead, he placed the tenth stroke right between the man's legs.

With a scream, Nicholas let go. He arched his back and opened his eyes wide as he came. He jerked through his orgasm, a moan drawing out of him as he finally finished and sank against the wood of the cross, looking spent and exhausted.

Jesse put the flogger on the table and came to stand behind him before sliding an arm around his chest and pulling the younger man back against his own body. He kissed Nicholas's shoulder and murmured to him quietly. Nicholas rolled his head back and closed his eyes as he smiled. Adam guessed he'd received praise.

Jesse supported the submissive as he released the cuffs. Then he guided him off the platform toward the back rooms. Again, Adam was left feeling like an outsider.

He jumped when someone tapped him on the shoulder. It was Dillon, the leather-clad Dominant with the dog-collared submissive Adam had seen the first night he'd been at the club.

"That took a lot out of Nicholas, so they're going to be a while. Want to get a drink while you wait?" Dillon asked.

It was kind of him to offer, but Adam shook his head no. "I'm gonna go. I have to go."

Dillon creased his brows in concern, but Adam wasn't sticking around to figure out why. He turned on his heel and bolted.

Once outside, Adam didn't know where he was heading. His familiarity with the town was limited, his attention being narrowly focused since he'd moved in with Ash. Somehow, he managed to find a park to wander in without fear of someone finding him before he was ready.

Once his pace had slowed, his brain began to function. What was he so bothered by? Jesse owned a BDSM club. Of course he was into stuff like that. He'd even told Adam so.

But Adam hadn't seen it before. Everything they had done together was kinkier than anything he'd ever done, but it wasn't like what he'd just witnessed, and the way Jesse had been so focused on the submissive in front of him... He'd never regarded Adam that way, and a part of Adam wanted him to. He wanted Jesse to look at him as if he were the only person in the world, but he wouldn't let Jesse strap him to a cross to get it. He wouldn't kneel at the Dominant's chair and wear a dog collar and nothing else in front of a room full of people. That wasn't in the cards for Adam.

But he couldn't stand by and watch Jesse do it with someone else either.

Adam's throat closed with the threat of tears, and he bit the inside of his cheek until the emotion had passed. What was he getting so worked up for? All they'd done was fool around. They weren't even in a relationship. But maybe Adam had wanted to be. Eventually.

The snap of a twig made Adam glance to the left where a happy couple was strolling through the park hand in hand. Not wanting to be seen, he started walking again. The park was getting crowded, and Adam soon left it behind.

With the choice of being miserable in front of strangers or possibly being miserable in front of Ash, Adam gave up on trying to find a space to be alone and headed toward the apartment.

"What are you doing home so early?" Ash asked when Adam entered. "Didn't you have a date with Mr. Entrepreneur?"

"I canceled it." Adam tried to avoid eye contact by focusing on hanging up his jacket.

"Why?" Ash asked, surprised.

"I didn't feel like staying at the club tonight, okay?"

Avoiding Ash was impossible, and as Adam tried to brush by to hide in the bathroom, his friend caught a glimpse of his face.

"What happened?" he asked, grabbing Adam's arm. "You look like you've been crying."

"I haven't been crying," Adam snapped. More softly he added, "I've been almost crying."

Ash pulled him down onto the couch. "You want to talk about it?"

"No."

Ash waited.

"I arrived later than usual," Adam said, "and figured he'd be upstairs by then, so I headed up."

"And?"

"I was right. He was upstairs. He was performing a demo with some sub on the platform, and I stood there and watched him as he made this guy come using nothing but a flogger."

Ash's eyes were wide. "Wow! That must have been fantastic!"

"Yeah," Adam agreed. "I have to admit it turned me on."

"So, what happened after?"

"Nothing. He took the sub somewhere, and I left."

"You *left*? Without a word to him?"

Adam nodded.

"Why?"

The words stuck in his throat, but he wasn't sure if it was more tears or the fear of voicing his feelings. "Because I wanted it to be me," he whispered. "Not the whole naked and flogging bit but the rest of it. When he was on stage, it was like the whole world had vanished. Nothing existed for him but that submissive. I've never had anyone look at me that way."

Ash sat back with a heavy exhale. "Neither have I."

"Is it wrong for me to want him to look at me like that?"

"Are you kidding? Everyone wants someone to look at them like that."

"Yeah but...I want him to *only* look at me like that."

"Have you talked to him about being exclusive?"

Adam shook his head.

"Sounds like you should."

"I can't."

"Why not?"

"Because I can't do what that guy did, and I can't ask him to give it up. Not when he obviously enjoys it so much."

"Oh," Ash said. "Well, that sucks."

"Yeah."

After studying Adam for another minute, Ash pushed himself up off the couch with a flourish. "I was planning on a classic movie night," he said as he headed into the kitchen.

He pulled out glasses and spoons, then rummaged in the freezer. "Luckily, you're home to join me. You would have missed out." He returned, waving a bucket of rocky road ice cream in Adam's face. "I would have eaten it all, you know."

Adam grabbed the tub from him. "Not if you wanted to live to see tomorrow," he threatened.

"We'll see about that, mister. Grab the top DVD on the floor next to you and pop it in?"

Adam leaned over and found the indicated stack of DVDs. He picked up the top one, Marilyn Monroe's *Some Like It Hot*, and did as he was told while Ash brought the cups, silverware, a quart of milk, half a bottle of rum, and the blender over to the coffee table.

"Might as well make it a party," he said with a grin.

Adam smiled, the weight of his confession lifting in his friend's presence.

With spiked rocky road milkshakes and some good movies, it ended up being a pretty good night.

FIVE

Adam had never shown up. Jesse had searched for him after he'd taken care of Nicholas, but the boy was nowhere to be found. Disappointed, Jesse had returned to his office for a drink. There was no longer a reason to stay sober for the evening.

He had just poured himself a glass at the bar when the door opened, and Dillon walked in.

"Do you have a GPS tracker on me or something? You always know when to show up for a drink."

"I'm guessing you didn't see Adam."

Jesse put down the bottle of Jim Beam. "He was here?" Did his voice really sound like that? He cleared his throat. "You saw him?"

"He saw the demo," Dillon said. He took a seat in one of the chairs, stretched his long legs in front of him, and folded his hands across his stomach. "I think it freaked him out."

"Then why didn't you stop him? Why are you sitting there if he needed someone?"

"I tried. I offered to get him a drink while he waited for you, but he bolted. I wasn't going to run after him. That would have only freaked him out more."

Jesse sighed and moved to sit at his desk, his drink forgotten. "Do you think he'll be back?"

"You could ask him. You have his number, don't you?"

"Yes." He and Adam had exchanged numbers a few weeks after they'd started seeing each other and it had become clear their meetings were to be a consistent thing. So, why hadn't Adam called to tell Jesse he was running late? Then again, why hadn't Jesse called to find out what was up?

He knew the reason. He wasn't used to calling hookups, and he'd never called before, so he hadn't thought about it.

"Are you going to call him?" Dillon asked.

Jesse should. He should make sure Adam was okay. Whether they would fuck again in the future was another matter. Unfortunately, that was something Jesse really wanted to know.

"Yeah, I'll call him. I only hope he picks up."

———

Adam didn't pick up. Though a pang went through him every time Jesse's number displayed on his caller ID, he made a point not to answer the phone. For a while, Adam debated getting a new phone number, but that felt like too dramatic a step to take. Instead, he focused on getting a job. He was long overdue and took to the idea with a vengeance. It was also high time he found his own apartment, but he recognized his determination as primarily a means to avoid Jesse.

He spent full days searching for help wanted signs, and when he had no more applications to send out, he went to a gym. The fees would bankrupt him before long if he didn't land a job, but he needed something to keep his mind from wandering. Running himself ragged on a treadmill or lifting weights helped to distract him. Nights, on the other hand, were a more difficult matter. Adam kept his brain occupied by marathoning full seasons of TV shows until he drifted off in exhaustion.

It didn't help that Jesse called or texted him constantly. Seeing the name "Jesse Harte" on his caller ID only made Adam's emotions more restless. He wavered between keeping his resolve and giving in and picking up the phone. Eventually, the calls lessened, and after a while, his resistance was rewarded with silence.

Three weeks after the messages had stopped, he received a call from his parents. When the phone rang, Adam was so shocked by the caller ID he stared at the phone long enough for the call to go to voicemail.

He was still standing there when Ash came into the kitchen. "Was that your phone again?"

Adam nodded slowly like his head was moving through molasses.

"I thought he'd given up."

"It wasn't Jesse."

"Who was it?"

"My parents."

Ash appeared as surprised as Adam felt. Ash was the first person Adam had called after his parents kicked him out of their house for being gay. He'd told his friend the whole story over a cheap bottle of tequila. After discovering the freedom of college and learning to be on his own, he'd decided to come out to his parents. It had been a difficult decision, but he'd wanted to be honest with them and not have to worry about keeping secrets. Instead of welcoming the news or even hesitantly accepting it, they had insulted him and told him to get out and never step foot on their doorstep again. He and Ash had regretted the tequila in the morning, but the pain had been nothing compared to the feeling of his parents' disgust.

"What did they want?"

"I don't know. I didn't answer."

"Good," Ash said and shoved Adam out of the way of the coffeemaker.

"They left a voicemail."

Ash paused. "Do you want me to listen to it?"

Adam hesitated.

"You could delete it," Ash suggested.

Adam's shoulders slumped. "I can't. A part of me wants to know why they called." He held the phone out to him. "The pass code is 4582."

Ash took the phone from Adam and pushed the appropriate buttons. Adam waited anxiously while the phone rang and Ash worked through the menu. He watched as his friend listened to the message, but Ash's face betrayed nothing. Finally, Ash hung up and handed back the phone. "They want to see you. They say they want to talk."

"They don't sound angry?" Adam asked.

"Not on the message, but who knows what they want to talk about? You should listen for yourself. Maybe you'll get more out of it than I can."

Adam listened to the message, and it was as Ash had said. At least they weren't screaming he was a "goddamned faggot" and to get his "pansy ass" out of their house.

"Are you going to call them back?"

Adam sighed. "I'll think about it."

Whether it was better than thinking about Jesse Harte, Adam couldn't say.

SIX

The phone call from his parents stayed on Adam's mind. He couldn't imagine them wanting to reconcile after the way they'd kicked him out, but for what other reason would they call him? The question kept circling around and around in his head, overshadowing memories of Jesse.

Except at night. When he was alone in bed, he'd remember Jesse's heat, his touch, and the best sex he'd ever had in his life. He wanted to feel that again, but then he'd remember the flogging scene and why amazing sex was all that could be between them, and that wasn't enough.

The thoughts whirling in his head kept him in a melancholy funk, which Ash was only willing to put up with for so long. "That's it," he said one night when it was clear Adam was going to spend it sitting on the couch yet again, "we're going to the club."

"You go, Ash. Have a good time."

"No. It's one thing to give up on a man because you can't handle his lifestyle, but it's another to give up on life entirely. Besides, it's Friday. Who says he'll even be there?" When Adam didn't answer, he added, "You've got twenty minutes to change into something fabulous, or I'm dragging you there in your pajamas. Now *move*."

When Ash was in a stubborn mood, there was no arguing with him, so Adam got up with a sigh. Twenty minutes later, they were out the door and on their way.

The club was as packed as expected. They threaded their way through the crush to get some drinks before joining their fellow dancers. Adam glanced up at the smoky glass hiding Jesse's office from view. If Jesse was there, Adam hoped against hope he wouldn't be able to find him.

He was beginning to have a good time, losing himself to the music, when Ash's face went from happy and animated to a fantastic semblance of a panicked rabbit. Adam knew Jesse stood behind him, yet he was surprised when he turned and saw him. He'd forgotten how good-looking Jesse was. The sight of him took Adam's breath away. There was a stretch of silence before Adam remembered his manners.

"Hello, Jesse."

"Can we talk?"

Adam hesitated, then nodded. Ash seemed worried and a little apologetic as Adam walked away.

Jesse led him upstairs to his office and shut the door to give them privacy. Unfortunately, it wasn't for the same reason as last time.

"I called you," Jesse said.

"I know."

"What happened? Dillon told me you came to the club but ran off after my scene."

"I... I didn't feel like staying."

"You could have let me know."

He was right. It had been terrible of Adam to cut off communication without a word. "I'm sorry."

Jesse stepped closer to him. Adam couldn't help being drawn to the other man's presence.

"What happened? Did I do something wrong?"

"No! I...I just..." He was being pathetic. "I don't think we're right for each other."

A crease appeared between Jesse's brows as he furrowed them in confusion. "Right for each other?" he echoed.

Adam took another breath, this time for the courage to continue. "I saw the demo. You were so…into it. It was amazing. That sub was amazing. I could never do that kind of stuff for you."

"We've talked about this," Jesse said. "I'm not pushing you to be any kind of sub for me, Adam. I've never asked you to be."

"I know," Adam replied. "It's just…I could never be in that position. No matter what, you'd always have to look for that somewhere else."

"And I do. If your concern is safety, rest assured I always play safe."

Adam shook his head. "I'm not worried about that. I…" He licked his lips as he tried to find the words.

Jesse stepped forward, placing a hand on his shoulder. "I love the things we do. You get a little kinky with me, and we have a lot of fun. I don't need to be a full-out Dom all the time. I'm not always looking to play that role, so I don't want you to think there's something lacking when we get together. If I wasn't happy with the way we were fucking, I wouldn't keep looking for you in the crowd out there. Besides," he said, "it's not like we're dating, so there's nothing to worry about."

Yes. Of course. Jesse was free to find what he needed wherever he wanted to. Adam didn't have to be enough for him. Which meant Adam would never be enough for him. So much for talking about exclusivity.

"Right." Adam's throat felt tight. He cleared it and asked, "Do you have any water in here?"

His expression must have given something away because Jesse frowned. "Have I said something to upset you?"

Not trusting his voice, Adam shook his head. "Just thirsty."

"Okay," Jesse said, though he didn't appear convinced. He

went to the minifridge below his office bar and pulled out a bottle. "Here," he said and handed it over.

Adam took the time to drink and swallow three times before he put the cap back on. By then he'd shoved his disappointment down far enough Jesse wouldn't see it when he looked at him.

"Are you sure you're okay?"

"I'm fine. Too much dancing without a drink."

Jesse must have believed him that time because he stepped closer and slid his arms around Adam's waist. "Man, I've missed you."

Adam's heart fluttered at the phrase, but he felt a pang at the same time. He couldn't stand being a casual fuck for Jesse any longer. He should pull away, but the sensation of Jesse's arms encircling him had Adam leaning into his warm body, and when Jesse kissed his neck, Adam's cock stirred. He had to walk away, but before he did, would it be so bad to give in one last time?

"Fuck me, Jesse," Adam whispered. "Fuck me so I'll never forget it."

His words affected Jesse as well. His cock grew harder against Adam's thigh, and Adam shifted his hips to better accommodate him.

"You're such a tease," Jesse said.

"Not a tease. Not when I plan to follow through."

"Really now? And what did you have in mind?"

Adam was tempted to have Jesse press him up against the window again, but he put that thought aside. He wanted something new, something memorable. Something to carry with him when he walked out of the club forever.

"On the roof," Adam said.

"You want me to fuck you on top of the building?"

"Why not?" Adam asked, stepping back to look at him. "Don't you have access?"

Jesse rolled his eyes. "I've created a monster."

Adam grinned. "You love it."

Jesse's smile was just as bright. "Yes. I really do." He walked to the phone on his desk and pushed a button on it. There was a click, and a deep bass voice responded.

"Yes, Harte?"

"Seb, do you have the key for the roof-access door?"

There was a moment of silence before the voice answered. "Tobias has it. I can get it from him if you want."

"Please do. Just unlock the door and leave the key for me, will you? I won't want to be disturbed for a couple of hours."

"Got it. I'll have it ready for you in ten minutes."

"Thank you." Jesse hung up and turned his attention back to Adam. "The roof it is. Will we be needing anything besides lube and condoms?"

Adam hadn't formulated any ideas after the location had popped out of his mouth. "I don't think so?"

Jesse's expression was mischievous. "Seems like you aren't too sure. Maybe we should find a few things just in case."

Adam's body flushed with arousal as he considered the possibilities. "Sure." Thankfully, his voice was steady, even if the rest of him vibrated with anticipation.

"Sure," Jesse echoed. "I'll look around and see if there's anything we might need." He pulled the lube from his desk drawer and two more bottles of water from the fridge. Then he went to the cabinet in the corner of the room and rummaged through its contents. From his angle, Adam couldn't see what was inside, but he didn't want to spoil the surprise.

After what appeared to be much deliberation and change of mind, Jesse exclaimed, "Ah yes! This!" and pulled out a long cord of black rope. He turned his head and trapped Adam with a seductive smile. "I'm going to tie you up."

Adam almost came right then.

<hr>

Being tied up for sex brought to mind images of fuzzy handcuffs, four-poster beds, and things Adam had seen pictured on product boxes in sex stores. There would be no bed on the roof, but the fantasies that skittered through his brain as they headed upstairs were of a similar nature. The closer to the roof they walked, the more interesting the positions in his mind became, but he couldn't begin to imagine what Jesse had planned.

The air was cool when they stepped outside, but not cold enough to worry about, especially when there would be plenty of body heat to go around soon enough. The key had been left hanging on the door handle, and Jesse took it before closing the door behind them.

"I think your employees have an idea of what we're getting up to," Adam said.

"Of course they do. Why else would I be up here?"

"I meant because of that." Adam pointed to the big picnic blanket spread out on the tarred roof. Bottles of water and a second blanket were placed neatly beside it.

Jesse laughed. "That was considerate of them." He moved to the blanket and added their water bottles, lube, condoms, and the coil of rope to the pile.

"Oh no," he said when Adam moved to join him. "The only way you're getting over here is if you're naked." He moved to lounge on the blanket and looked up expectantly.

"You want a show?"

"Why not? It's a great angle."

Adam slid off his top shirt.

"Slowly, please."

Adam rolled his eyes but continued at a slower pace. The T-shirt came off next, followed by his boots.

"Can I at least stand on it, so my feet don't freeze?"

"They are not going to freeze, but if you insist..."

Adam stepped onto the blanket after pulling off his socks —something only burlesque dancers could make look sexy— and unbuttoned his pants. Jesse was fully invested in this part of the show. His tongue snaked out over his lips, and he leaned forward a little.

"Still like the angle?" Adam asked him.

"Not sure. Take off the pants and then I'll decide."

Adam pushed his pants down, doing his best to keep his underwear on. One side got caught and slid down to reveal his hip bone, but the rest of his modesty remained intact. After stepping out of the heavy fabric, he turned back to Jesse.

The Dominant's eyes were locked on Adam's hip. He pushed himself onto his knees so he could run his fingers over Adam's skin there. Adam's body tingled where Jesse caressed. When Jesse licked in the crevice where his hip met his groin, Adam's knees almost buckled, and he moaned.

Jesse chuckled. "Mind, they can hear you this time if we're not careful. No soundproofing out here."

When he licked Adam's hip again, Adam didn't give a flying fuck what people heard as long as Jesse continued. Jesse hooked his fingers over the waistband of Adam's underwear and slid them down ever so slowly. Each inch he revealed was covered in kisses, licks, and small bites. He never touched Adam's cock, but by the time Adam was naked, it was as hard as a rock and dripping.

"Oh yes," Jesse said. "A very good angle." He leaned back and took hold of the rope. "Are you okay? Not cold or anything?"

"Do you really think I could be cold right now?"

Jesse laughed. "No, I guess not."

Adam watched as Jesse tied a complicated pattern of rope from the back of Adam's neck, down over his body, and around his cock and thighs. Then he had Adam kneel on the floor with his head and shoulders resting on the folded blanket so his ass stuck up in the air. When Adam breathed, he felt each crisscross of the rope on his body.

"Are you okay?" Jesse asked as he finished tying Adam's wrists to his ankles.

"Yeah, I'm okay."

"You sure you don't want something else under that shoulder? You're going to be in this position for a while."

"I'm okay, Jesse. If I need something, I'll tell you."

There was a pause before Jesse continued moving. Adam wondered if he'd asked the sub Adam had seen him with similar questions and how often. Was it easier to trust someone like Nicholas in things like this, or was it just Adam Jesse didn't trust? It didn't matter. It was just sex after all, right?

There was warmth at Adam's back as Jesse leaned over him and traced Adam's ear with his tongue. "I'm gonna fuck you like this." His voice had taken on that deeper quality it did when he was fully turned on, and Adam wished he could see Jesse's cock or feel it against him. He knew how hard it would be, but he wanted physical proof.

He wasn't going to get any. Instead, the warmth disappeared, and Adam heard the pop of the lube bottle opening before Jesse's fingers spread his ass wider. There was a rush of air on his hole, and Adam yelped. Jesse chuckled and blew on it again.

"What the fuck are you doing?"

"Teasing you," Jesse said as if it was perfectly obvious. It was, but then he started shifting ropes and making another knot.

"What are you doing now?"

"You'll see."

It wasn't long before Adam did. As soon as Jesse released the rope, Adam shifted to figure out what he'd done, and a cry escaped him. Little points of pressure pressed against his perineum and it felt like a noose was cinched around his cock and balls.

"What—ah!—did you do?"

Jesse chuckled again. Adam wondered if the man was a sadist. Waves of sensation flooded through his body, and he couldn't tell his fingers from his toes anymore.

"You feel this?" Jesse nudged something small between Adam's cock and his balls.

"Yeah," Adam panted.

"That's a knot. It'll move every time you do and stimulate you. And this." He tugged, and the rope around Adam's balls tightened for a moment. "And this too." The rope around the base of his cock tightened briefly as well. "Nothing will stay too tight, but any shift will change the pressure. I was going to put one against your hole, but I'd rather be in there instead." He dragged his finger between Adam's ass cheeks. It went bump, bump, bump as it traveled over his perineum up to his hole. "Those are more knots. Whenever I push into you, they'll move too." His hands came around to caress Adam's chest, and the skin already singing praises to the light breeze made Adam want to cry. "Everywhere on you. I've taken every inch of your skin and made it an instrument for me to play." He rubbed Adam's nipples, making his hips squirm, which only made the knots rub against him more. "That's it," Jesse coaxed. "Keep it up, honey. You're gonna cry before I'm done with you. You're gonna cry and love every minute of it."

Adam already was. Moans and gasps flooded from his lips, and all Jesse was touching were his nipples. Endless, gentle circles that seemed hotwired down to his cock had Adam rolling his hips and moaning from the resulting sensations. His cock was beyond dripping. A steady stream flowed from its tip, begging for touch, for release, for *anything*.

"Please, Jesse," Adam panted. "Fuck me, please."

"Nope. I'm not ready for you yet."

He had to be. There was no way the man wasn't in as much need as Adam was, yet he had the iron will to resist. Tears rolled down Adam's face, and Jesse leaned forward to lick them up.

"Yes, my sweet. Enjoy it for all it's worth."

Adam's moans were constant now. His hips never stopped moving from Jesse's teasing, and sweat had broken out all over his body. The cool air only made for worse teasing as it danced over his weeping cock and emphasized the rope lines on his body.

"Please, Jesse. Oh god, please, fuck me." Adam's voice grew louder as he begged.

He heard the smile in Jesse's voice as he leaned over to speak low in his ear again. "No," Jesse said, and Adam sobbed.

"Please. Please..." The plea became a mantra, over and over, the only word Adam could say, the only word he could think. Unable to do anything else, Adam surrendered to the onslaught. He lost himself in the sea of sensations, no longer able to focus on where they were coming from or even notice if he was still begging. He barely registered the nudge of fingers against his asshole or the coolness of the lube as it was rubbed inside him. He arched into the familiar burn as Jesse's fingers entered him, working and stretching.

Jesse's hands braced his hips and stopped them from rocking. There was pressure against his entrance, different and bigger than the small knots that had been torturing him. They still tortured him as Jesse entered with a smooth, deep thrust.

Adam's back arched, and the ropes pulled, making him cry out. His throat was raw, but the sensation washed away again as Jesse finally began to move. Adam felt his rhythm and the response from the ropes, but he floated among it all, only somewhat registering the movements. He focused on Jesse, the connection of their bodies holding him to the Earth, and rocked his body in response. He worked with Jesse, bringing them both pleasure until Jesse sped up. His pace increased, and his fingers pressed hard against Adam's hips, desire and need building and building until Adam felt Jesse climax inside him. His body clamped around Jesse, not wanting to let go, and they rested for a moment together.

Jesse's hands brushed soothingly among the ropes, and Adam's wrists were released from his ankles. He stayed still as other knots were undone and the rope was gently unwound from his body.

His neck twinged from the angle he'd kept it in, but he remained as he was. Jesse's soothing hands eventually coaxed his body to unfold. He lay on the blanket while Jesse used his talented hands to massage blood back into proper circulation and convince tense muscles to relax. Finally, he covered Adam with a blanket.

Jesse pressed his warm body against Adam's, his strong arms wrapping around him. Adam had no memory of coming, and if there had been any evidence, it must have been cleaned because he felt none, yet he drifted off to sleep feeling safe and satisfied.

SEVEN

Jesse hadn't known how much he'd missed Adam until he'd spotted him on the dance floor. At first, he hadn't believed his eyes. His heart had jumped into his throat, and he'd counted to ten to make sure he wasn't seeing things.

He'd gone down to meet him with barely a thought of what he'd do when he got there. Anything had been on the table, from talking to grabbing the young man and fucking him with the whole crowd watching. He was quite proud of himself for keeping it together, and now he was on the roof of his club with Adam beside him. It had even been Adam's idea to come up there.

Jesse smiled. Adam had come such a long way since they'd met, and their time apart hadn't ruined anything. All the boy had needed was space, and now he was back.

Jesse ran his fingers through Adam's hair to reassure himself the sleeping form next to him wasn't an illusion. The silky strands didn't vanish, but once he'd started touching Adam, he couldn't stop. He was sure Dillon would say he had a stupid expression on his face, but he didn't care. He watched Adam sleep for a few minutes until a soft breeze reminded him of how late it was getting. The blanket may have felt warm, but he wouldn't risk Adam getting sick right after they had been reunited.

"Adam," he called softly. "Adam, you have to wake up now." Although what he said was true, he wasn't in a hurry to leave.

———

"Adam."

It took a minute for Adam to register the name was his.

A hand smoothed the hair back off his face as the voice spoke again. "I don't want you to catch cold. You can nap in my office if you want, but we shouldn't stay out here any longer."

Catching cold wouldn't be a problem. There was a warm body pressed next to him, and a blanket covered him. He shifted in protest, and the brush of fabric against his bare thigh made him wake up a little more. He remembered where they were and what they had done.

"Oh..." Adam groaned.

"Shh," Jesse said. "Your throat is probably sore. Drink this."

Jesse lifted Adam's head and brought a bottle to his lips. Adam took small sips, and the water soothed his throat.

"We have to get up?"

"Yes. You don't want my employees to come up here to check on us and find you naked, do you?"

"Why would they come up here?"

"I asked them for the key, remember? They would at least make sure we haven't been locked out all night."

Adam groaned again and pushed himself into a sitting position. Cool night air rushed in to attack him, and he bundled up in the blanket, stealing it from Jesse. The other man was clothed. He could deal.

"It's gotten cold out."

"For a man who's recently had his brains fucked out, yes. I'm sure the dried sweat on your skin isn't helping either."

"I need a shower."

"I would gladly help you with that."

Adam glared at his grin, but he liked that idea. "Where are my pants?"

Jesse handed them over along with his shirt and shoes. "We'll head down to my office and drink something warm. You should get the chill out of your bones before you head home."

Home. That's right. Adam had come here with Ash, hoping never to see Jesse again. He had even made the decision this would be their last time together. A shared shower didn't fit into that plan, which was disappointing but necessary.

He finished getting dressed and followed Jesse downstairs. No matter what, warming up with a cup of coffee and not getting sick sounded ideal. He also had to end things with Jesse before he left. He wouldn't be a jerk and disappear like last time.

When they returned to the office, Jesse locked the door and dumped the blankets on the couch before heading to the coffee maker. In a few minutes, he'd set the machine to brew. Still feeling the chill from outside, Adam followed the blankets onto the couch and covered himself with them.

"Are you okay?" Jesse asked.

"Yeah. Just cold."

Jesse sat down beside him and put his arms around him. Adam knew he should pull away, but he couldn't.

"That was...intense," Adam said.

"You were amazing."

"Do you do that a lot?"

"Do what?"

"Tie people up until they lose their minds, then fuck them."

"I have done something like that before, yes," Jesse said.

"I like to push people to their limits, overwhelm them with sensation."

"Is that what you did in that scene with the sub?"

"Yes. Though Nicholas is also a masochist, so he enjoys different kinds of sensation than you do."

Adam's stomach twisted. Did it matter, that difference? Did Jesse want someone who liked pain? From what he'd learned, the flogger didn't necessarily have to be painful, but would something like that be enough for Jesse?

Adam shook himself from his thoughts. "How do you know how far to push?"

"Knowledge and trust mostly," Jesse replied. "I'm practiced in things like this, but I also read your reactions and trust you to tell me if something is wrong."

Jesse trusted him. That made Adam smile.

"You make me sound like a sub."

"Technically, you did submit to me just now," Jesse said. "I wouldn't consider you a sub, as you've stated that's not your thing, but what we did had major elements of a scene, and the fact you put yourself in my hands was a great display of trust. Not to mention you let go of everything while I teased you. I saw it. Didn't you feel it?"

Adam recalled the moment when he was floating among sensation and understood what Jesse was talking about.

"That's called subspace. Not everyone achieves it. Not everyone believes it exists."

"It was definitely different."

"Did you enjoy it?"

Panic seized Adam. Alarm bells were ringing in his head. Was Jesse trying to turn him into a sub? He didn't want that. He wasn't going to be one of those guys who knelt on the floor in a dog collar. He wasn't going to let someone dictate what he could and couldn't do. He was strong. He was independent. He could think for himself. He wasn't—

"I didn't raise my son to be some goddamned faggot. Get your pansy ass out of my house."

Adam stood up.

"I enjoyed what we did," he admitted, "but it's not going to happen again."

Confusion marred Jesse's beautiful features.

"Like I said before, we're not a good match for each other," Adam continued. He didn't want Jesse to speak. If he spoke or touched him, Adam would lose his nerve, and who knew what he would do or say then? "I can't give you what you want, so I think it best we end this now."

He put up a hand in case Jesse was going to say something. He couldn't tell because he was no longer looking at him. "You're an amazing guy, Jesse. I—" No. Too much talking. "I have to go."

Adam grabbed his jacket and left. It would have been a smooth exit, but he fumbled with the office door lock, and the frustration when it didn't open smoothly brought tears to his eyes. They were hot and stung, blurring his vision and making his exit more difficult.

"Adam?"

Jesse calling his name didn't help matters, and he worked harder to get the door open. Once he did, he ran through it, fighting to keep his vision clear and his eyes dry as he stormed through the hallway and out of the club.

Once on the street, the tears came forth like a deluge. They streamed down his cheeks as he made his way back to Ash's place. Thankfully, Ash was either in bed or not home. He didn't want to see him yet. He didn't want to deal with any kindness his friend would extend or any insult he would offer to Jesse in his honor. Adam curled up on the couch and stuck a pillow in his mouth to muffle his sobs when they came. Tomorrow, when Ash asked why his eyes were red and swollen, they would talk.

EIGHT

Jesse stared at the open door as if expecting Adam to reappear through it. When his confusion finally turned into an instinct to run after him, it was already too late. The boy was long gone.

What had gone wrong? He paced his office, reflecting on their roof scene. It had been hot, and afterward, Adam had slept so peacefully beside him. Even as they'd returned to his office, things had been running smoothly. It was only when Jesse had brought up the topic of subspace Adam had freaked.

Jesse stopped pacing. He closed his eyes with a sigh as he realized what he'd done. Opening them again, he went to his desk phone and dialed Dillon's number.

"You up for a drink?" he asked when his friend answered.

"My place or yours?"

"I'll be over in ten, if you don't mind."

"I'll have the whiskey ready."

Jesse hung up and called Seb to inform him he was leaving and where to reach him if necessary. Then he threw on his jacket and headed to Dillon's.

The door opened before he knocked, and he and Dillon

made their way to the living room where the promised bottle and two tumblers waited on a side table.

"Where's Michael?" Jesse asked as he took a seat on the couch.

"Upstairs taking the opportunity to get ahead in his reading," Dillon said. He sat in the wingback chair opposite Jesse. "I thought you might like to be alone for this one."

Jesse sighed. "I fucked up."

Dillon patiently waited him out in silence.

When they came, the words tumbled out of Jesse's mouth in a rush. "Adam showed up at the club today. I asked him if we could talk and took him to my office. He asked me to fuck him on the roof, so I took him up there, tied him up, and did it." His face softened as he remembered Adam's begging. "It was beautiful, Dillon. He completely let go."

"So, what happened?"

"We went back to my office because I didn't want him catching cold. I thought everything was going well. We were talking about the scene, and he seemed to like it, but then I mentioned subspace, and he panicked. He ran out of my office as if the hounds of hell were chasing him."

Dillon got up to fix their drinks while he waited for Jesse to continue.

"He's petrified of being a sub," Jesse explained. "I've told him repeatedly I don't need him to be one. I'm not trying to force him into being one, but the slightest hint of the topic makes him freak and run."

"Do you think he's a sub?" Dillon asked as he handed Jesse a glass.

"I think he likes submitting to a scene. I'm not sure he'd ever be into something focused mainly on D/s, but he does get off on what I do to him. He likes following what I tell him to do, even when he's scared or hesitant, and when he finally lets go, he does so completely, but it's only in the scene. He will never wear a collar, and he will not be a submissive outside of sex." He couldn't say "outside the bedroom" since they'd never been in one.

"So, he only has a problem when you're not fucking."

"He's hung up on the fact I'm a Dominant and he's not a submissive. At least, that's the excuse he keeps throwing at me."

"Well, you do own the biggest BDSM club in town. It creates a particular image of you as a Dominant."

Jesse sighed. "I know, but this is the first time it's getting in the way."

"Look, from the sound of it, you two have excellent chemistry, but he obviously needs some time to figure things out for himself. If he can't get over his fears and come to terms with what he wants—whatever that may end up being—it will never work with the two of you. You're going to have to give him some space."

"I already did that," Jesse snapped.

"Stop being a brat. You know it wasn't enough time for him. You have to be patient."

"But what if…what if he doesn't come back?"

"Then you'll have to show him it isn't submission that you want from him."

Dillon was right. It wasn't the power he wielded as a Dominant Jesse needed from a partner. It was the trust. He thought back to his scene on the roof with Adam. The sex had been hot as always, but afterward, Adam had slept in his arms without a care in the world, sated and peaceful. The trust Adam had placed in him not only to tie him up but to make him fly and bring him back down safely again was more powerful than any orgasm. It was an exchange of gifts, and it had never felt as potent as it did with Adam. Adam's reluctance to let go made his ability to do so even more precious. Jesse wanted to cherish that as well as the man who impressed him every time they were together.

"How do I do that when all we've ever had is sex?"

"There are these things called words, Harte. Try them sometime."

Jesse glared at his friend. Then he sighed. "You're not going to call me on this? Tell me how obvious it was and how long you've known?"

Dillon shook his head. "I don't have to, but believe me, I will. I'm saving that for when I can truly enjoy the moment."

Jess rolled his eyes and went back to his drink. The "I told you so" hung in the air, loud and clear between them.

NINE

This time Ash didn't try to get Adam to go back to the club after a few weeks had passed. They spoke the morning after Adam "broke up" with Jesse, and then the topic was never mentioned again. Adam was relieved. He didn't want to talk about it. He didn't want to get caught up with mulling over the situation and wondering if things could have been different. He had broken his own heart, and there was no one else to blame, no reason to think on it further. As for Jesse, Adam would have to forget about him.

But how did he forget a man like Jesse Harte? At night in the dark, thoughts of Jesse were inescapable. He'd remember the way Jesse had touched his skin and the heights he would push him to before he came. His own hands were unsatisfying in comparison, but every night, knowing the outcome, Adam fell into fantasy and worked his body until he achieved a disappointing release. Even during the day, Jesse would come to mind. The trace of his voice would tease Adam's ear; the smell of his skin would tickle his nose, and Adam would find himself turning, searching, then scolding himself for the attempt.

He became desperate for distraction. One of the jobs he'd applied for, a position doing data entry for a production company, came through, and he began working constantly. He gladly took any extra hours they were willing to give. He told them he wanted to learn as much as possible to become more efficient, but the truth was he would do anything to keep himself from thinking of Jesse. His coworkers were only too happy to add to his workload as he was new and doing grunt work anyway.

Even with his busier days, Adam still went to the gym. In the hope he would pass out after his shower and not dream of Jesse, he ran on the treadmill until his legs turned to water beneath him. Ash worried he was overworking himself and only became more so when Adam announced he'd found an apartment and was moving out.

"Come on, you're happy to have your privacy back. You can bring guys home again," Adam teased.

"As appealing as your argument is, that's not the point. I'm worried about you, Adam. You haven't been taking good care of yourself."

"I'll be fine. Really."

"We'll do lunch? Once a week?" Ash asked. "If we lose touch because you move out, I will never forgive you."

"You just want to be a mother hen, but yes, we'll do lunch." Adam hugged him.

"Who else is going to check up on you?" Ash asked as he hugged Adam back.

"Oh, that reminds me. My parents called again. They're planning on coming in next month, and I agreed to meet with them for dinner."

Now a new worry clouded Ash's face as he asked, "Do you want me to go with you?"

"Nah, I'll be fine. I'm an independent adult now. Besides, if they get to be too much, I'll leave. I'm planning on sticking them with the bill either way."

Ash laughed. "That's my boy."

———

"Are you enjoying the high life now you don't have to tiptoe when you get home?" Adam teased Ash on their first lunch date after Adam had moved out.

"Darling, I always enjoy the high life," Ash said with a wave of his hand. "Though it is nice not having to worry about being loud anymore."

"I feel sorry for your neighbors."

Ash shrugged. "And what about you? Have you stopped thinking about him constantly?"

"No," Adam admitted, "but I'm handling it better."

"Good. Then it shouldn't make a difference he was asking about you on Saturday."

"What?" Adam exclaimed.

"I haven't heard anything directly, but he's been asking around about you, trying to find out where you've been and how you're doing."

"No one knows me but you. How is he going to find out anything? It's not like my coworkers hang out at Harte."

"You never know," Ash said with a wink. "And you're not as invisible as you think. You're a hot piece of ass, and it's only gotten better since you've been going to the gym."

"It's not like I've been back to the club for anyone to see it."

"Honey, the people who go to the club are the same people who go to the gym. It's not that big of a world out there."

Adam picked up his drink as he considered this information. Jesse was looking for him. Why? More importantly, did Adam want to be found?

"What do you want me to do?"

"What do you mean?"

"You're going to get wrinkles if you keep furrowing your brow like that," Ash said. "I meant, if I see him, do you want me to tell him anything? Do you want me to tell him to fuck off and stop asking about you?"

Adam opened his mouth to answer, then realized he didn't have one and shut it again. "I don't know."

Ash nodded as if he'd expected that. "When you figure it out, let me know."

He was still trying to figure it out when he went to sleep that night, which might have been the reason for the dream he ended up having. In the dream, he lay naked on a four-poster bed, limbs outstretched and bound to the posts. Jesse knelt between his legs, lazily jacking his hard cock and gazing down at him with a smile that told Adam he liked seeing him this way.

———

"Next time I'll blindfold you," Jesse said. "We've never done that before." He shifted, and a thin leather strap appeared in his hand. "But we haven't done this either." He held Adam's cock steady as he snapped the strap around its base. Instantly, the pressure of Adam's aching erection intensified, and he moaned.

Jesse's smile widened, and Adam knew the man wasn't even close to finished with him. Jesse reached for the bottle of lube on the bedside table and slicked his fingers. He slid his knees beneath Adam's thighs and raised Adam's ass so he could access it better, then began working him open. Adam was about ready to beg when Jesse pulled his fingers out. Adam hoped his cock was next, but the blunt object that pressed against him wasn't what he wanted. Jesse slid it inside and wiggled it around until Adam gasped in surprise.

"There we go," Jesse said.

The plug must have been designed to curve right on a man's prostate because that was where it settled. Holding it against Adam with a finger to make sure it didn't slip out, Jesse reached back out of Adam's sight with his other hand. Adam wondered what he was going to do next when an intense vibration from his ass answered the question. Adam groaned as the toy jackhammered against his prostate without stopping. His groans turned into moans, which were followed by begging as his cock ached more and more.

"Jesse. Jesse, please. Let me come. Please."

"You can come any time you want. Multiple times if you want. The toy isn't going to stop until it runs out of battery."

Oh god. *Adam moaned. "I-I can't. The strap. I can't."*

"Yes, you can," Jesse said. "If you want it bad enough, Adam, I'm sure you can do it."

Adam wanted to kill him. He wanted to cry. He wanted it to go on forever.

According to Jesse's words, it probably would.

———

He woke to the sound of his alarm clock, entangled in sticky sheets. After peeling back the damp fabric, Adam stood on wobbly legs and headed into the shower. He had never come that hard from a dream. Hell, he had barely come that hard from sex in real life unless it was with Jesse.

———

As the days wore on, the dreams continued. No matter how exhausted Adam left his body before bed, they would still come. He was wasting as much money on laundry every week as food, but what worried him more was the nature of the dreams. He had ended things with Jesse because he couldn't be a submissive for him, yet every time he closed his eyes, he saw images of Jesse in Dominant positions over him. He'd even dreamed of being flogged by him.

Adam wouldn't kneel for Jesse in public wearing nothing but a dog collar, but the more he thought about it, the more he had to admit Jesse had been leading him every time they were together, and Adam had followed, not only without complaint but with anticipation and excitement. Yet the idea of being labeled a submissive still scared Adam. If he gave in to the role, it might prove he was weak, and above all he wouldn't be weak. He wouldn't prove his father right.

With the tumult of thoughts swirling in his mind, he wasn't in the best state to have dinner with his parents, but the evening they'd chosen had arrived. In the hours leading up to the meeting, he found himself constantly rubbing his clammy hands over his thighs. The last time he had seen them was the day they'd kicked him out. Though his mother had been kind and cheerful on the phone, he had no idea what they wanted from him. He wasn't sure what he wanted from them either. He was caught between a desire to show he was better off without them and wanting to prove he was a good son, worthy of their praise.

He dressed casually but made sure to look his best. He wouldn't give them an excuse to find fault in him. The only thing he couldn't keep them from disapproving of was something he couldn't change, not that he would have even if he could.

He arrived at the restaurant on time, yet they were already waiting for him.

"I put in our name," his father said as Adam approached. "They said it would be a fifteen-minute wait."

"How was the trip down?"

His mother relaxed at the sign of small talk, though his father was the one who answered. "We came in on Thursday after the morning rush-hour traffic."

"The ride was pleasant," added his mother. "Lovely weather for it."

"I'm sure," Adam said. "It's been nice and sunny out lately."

A waiter came out, calling his father's name, and they followed him inside. They were seated in a booth, Adam's parents on one side and he the other. He imagined he was in front of a firing squad.

"So…" his mother began, then lost her courage. Adam hoped any potential blowups would hold until after dinner. His nerves had burned through what little he'd been able to eat earlier in the day, and he was hungry. "Do you have a job?" she finally asked.

"Yes, I'm working for a production company doing data entry. It's a low-rung job, but it pays for rent and food."

"So, you have your own apartment," his dad said, his voice polite but gruff.

Adam's hopes for a peaceful dinner dimmed. He took a deep breath before answering. "Yes, it's about two blocks from here. It's small, but it's enough for me, and everything runs when I need it to."

"Oh, I couldn't imagine not having hot water or dealing with leaks and such," his mother said. "Are you sure you're doing okay?"

Adam blinked in surprise and searched for his voice for a moment before he was able to answer. "Uh, yeah. No problems like that, Mom. The place is nice, really."

She didn't seem satisfied with his answer, but she let the subject drop. It felt strangely comfortable to call her "Mom" despite how long it had been since he'd used the word.

"How's your garden?" he asked in an effort to keep the conversation going.

"Oh, don't get me started!" she began. "I had ordered the Henry Hudson tulips, and they brought me Red Hunters! Can you imagine? You have no idea how many phone calls I had to make before they would fix it."

Oh yes, Adam did. He had seen her in action many a time. His mother could be formidable when she wanted to be, and when it came to her garden, she took no prisoners.

"It worked out in the end," she continued with a satisfied lift of her chin. "They gave me the Henrys, and they let me keep the Hunters for free."

Adam smiled. It was so like her. "That's great, Mom."

He glanced at his father, who sipped a glass of water, stone-faced. He wasn't much of a talker, but Adam felt the tension radiating from him. His father wanted to say something but wouldn't until he was ready. In the meantime, Adam was left to sit and stew.

Luckily, the waitress came to take their orders, and Adam was given a five-minute reprieve as they all scrambled to figure out what they wanted to eat. Once she was gone, the peace of the moment shattered like a dropped vase as his father asked, "Are you still gay?"

"Uh, yes."

His father nodded to himself like he had expected this. He took a deep breath and pursed his lips as if he'd come to some sort of resolution. "I'm not going to say anything about your lifestyle. I don't approve of it; I don't understand it, but it's your choice. You're an adult now and can make your own mistakes, but you are our son, and I will not lose you over something so frivolous. Your mother's been a mess since you left. You can imagine what that's like to live with."

Adam could, and he wouldn't wish that on anyone, but he was too busy trying to sort through his feelings to sympathize. His parents were coming around, no longer angry and trying to forget their only son, yet his father's words were daggers to Adam's heart. He still saw Adam as disgusting and was probably only there out of a sense of duty and because of his mother.

"We want you to come home," his mother said.

"What?" That was enough of a shock to cut through the rest and get a response. "Are you kidding? You're the ones who kicked me out!"

His father glared at him, silently cautioning Adam to lower his voice before he caused a scene.

"Well, it was something of a shock," his mother pointed out. "I had so been looking forward to a daughter-in-law and grandchildren."

"Look, son, we understand you want to be on your own now. We just want you to know our door is open."

It hadn't been Adam's choice to be on his own. He had happily been going to college when they'd cut him off and kicked him out between semesters. He hadn't been thinking of independence yet. He had been focused on taking advantage of college campus life and getting his degree, but now… now Adam couldn't imagine going home even if he was to go back to school again. And as for their open door, Adam heard the truth in his father's voice. It wasn't open for *if* things didn't work out for him but *when*.

Adam felt hurt, angry, and confused. He wanted to scream at them or cry or *something*, but he knew it would be useless. He was too emotional to talk about this calmly, and they wouldn't hear him if he made a scene. It would only make him seem more like a child. He forced his emotions back and said, "I'll keep it in mind." It was a lie. He wouldn't take them up on their offer even if the world caved in on him.

His mother beamed. "And you'll visit." It wasn't a request. "Every boy needs a home-cooked meal once in a while, no matter how old he gets."

The idea of eating his mother's cooking again made Adam's mouth water, but he wouldn't be able to sit through conversations like this to get it. Even for her apple pie.

The waitress returned with their predinner salads, which, to his relief, silenced the conversation for a while. For once, Adam was grateful his parents didn't like to talk while eating.

Somehow, they made it through the rest of dinner without any more outbursts. Most of the conversation steered away from uncomfortable topics, but occasionally, a comment grated on him. His mother may have "accepted" the fact Adam was gay, but that hadn't stopped her from playing matchmaker in her head.

"Susan Catalano will be home for the holidays. You remember her, don't you, Adam? She had a crush on you when you were little. It was so cute how she followed you around that one summer. I'm sure she'd be happy to see you."

"Isn't she the girl who pushed me in the pool before I could swim?"

His mother laughed, as if his almost drowning were an amusing anecdote. "She's all grown up now and studying to be a nurse!"

"Good for her." The only thing Adam remembered about Susan was a bright-pink bathing suit. Still, he wished her well.

His mother's other attempts to fix him up were less subtle.

"I'd love for you to meet some of the nice young ladies in our neighborhood. One moved in across from the Andersons' and another right on the corner. Such pretty girls."

"Mom, I wouldn't be interested."

His mother waved her hand. "Oh, you never know, dear."

Adam sighed loudly.

"It'd be nice, Adam," his father interjected, "if you'd at least keep up appearances when you're home. There's no need to flaunt your lifestyle and give the neighbors the wrong impression."

The comments made dinner hard to swallow, but he forced himself to stay quiet and eat, reminding himself the nightmare would be over soon. Needless to say, Adam was relieved and itching to run after his father paid the bill and they were saying their goodbyes on the sidewalk.

His mother gave him a big hug, and Adam couldn't help hugging her back. He had missed her hugs.

His father put his hand on Adam's shoulder and held it as he regarded his son appraisingly. "You look good," he finally said. "I guess if you're going to be gay, at least you're not some pansy weakling who lets other guys push you around." He gave Adam a quick hug, barely touching Adam with more than his arm, then turned to lead his wife away.

Adam stood watching until they caught a cab and drove off before he turned and headed toward home. He planned on filling a mug with a very stiff drink when he got there.

Remembering he'd promised Ash he would visit after dinner, he altered his course toward his friend's apartment. Ash was worried his parents would say something to upset him and with good reason. Adam was sure his friend would have something alcoholic to indulge in while he relayed the details of the evening.

He was right. Ash offered to fix them both a rum and Coke as soon as Adam arrived, but as he recounted his story, his friend skipped the frivolities and poured a few fingers of straight vodka into two glasses.

"Your dad is still disgusted with you being gay, but he's going to allow you to do so anyway?"

"Yup. It's my mistake to make, he said." Adam took a sip of the drink, letting the sharp bite of alcohol burn down his throat. "He congratulated me on being a man about it though. I guess he approves of me going to the gym since it means I won't be a"—Adam made out air quotes with his fingers—"pansy weakling who lets other guys push me around." He sighed. "If only he knew."

Ash's lips pressed together tightly, and Adam knew he was holding back from bringing up Jesse. Granted, Adam had done it first, so he couldn't blame Ash for running with the topic, but his friend refrained and took the conversation in a different direction.

"How about I go to the gym with you tomorrow? It's not like I need the exercise, but I guess I could give it a shot."

Adam blinked at him in surprise. As far as he knew, Ash had never set foot inside a gym. He wouldn't have been surprised if his friend had been allergic to them. "Seriously?"

Ash shrugged. "Who knows? Maybe I'll find a cute guy and get his number."

"Okay."

And so, bright and early the next morning, the pair stood before a multitude of exercise equipment and a crowd of sweaty bodies—many of which, Ash was happy to note, were attractive.

"What do you normally do here?" he asked Adam as he surveyed their options.

"Uh...the treadmill mostly. Occasionally weights for some upper body work, and there's a pool."

"How exciting," Ash said sarcastically.

They were lucky enough to find two treadmills next to each other. Having never used one before, Ash let Adam set both machines to a programmed workout routine, and they began with a casual warm-up.

"This isn't so bad," Ash said.

"This is the warm-up."

"I know. I'm trying to stay positive. It's either that or debate whether the exercise or the boredom will kill me first."

"Thank you," Adam said. "I know how much you're hating this."

"Good. You will be paying me back for this hell I am about to go through for you. This is *not* charity."

"I understand."

"And you're going to figure this thing out about Jesse. You can't keep running. Whether you want to be with him or not, running is not the solution."

"I know."

"Good."

Ash didn't say much after that, focusing instead on the increasing treadmill speed. He made it through a half hour of the routine before he called it quits. Adam was surprised he had held on for that long, but a sufficient supply of eye candy had helped to motivate him. He didn't complain when Ash stumbled off the treadmill, fumbling with the controls until it stopped.

"That's it," Ash panted. "My good-friend quota has been maxed out for the week. I'll be by the smoothies. Find me when you're done." With that, he swayed off in the direction of refreshments and healthy snacks.

Adam shook his head with a laugh and kept running. It felt good to push himself after the night before. The weight of his father's words had stayed with him like clinging mud in his mind, even after a good scrubbing in the shower. They had been enough to stifle even the most erotic of temptations, and for the first time in weeks, Adam had woken without stained sheets. He was glad Ash had made sure he'd come to the gym because he likely would have skipped his workout to wallow in the disappointment of his parents yet again. Ash had saved Adam from that once before, so he deserved any revenge he wanted to inflict.

Adam was so focused on his newly returned motivation for exercise he didn't notice when someone got on the machine Ash had vacated. He did notice when the person's pace matched his, but he chose to ignore it.

"Hey," said the newcomer.

Adam kept running. He wasn't interested in being picked up, especially not today.

"You're Adam, right?"

It was harder to ignore the guy when he obviously knew his name. Adam would kill Ash if this was his idea of revenge.

"Jesse's boyfriend?" the man prompted.

That made Adam stumble. He fell into the handrail and clung to it as he scrambled for purchase with his feet. The other guy leaned over to stop his machine and helped Adam stand.

"Hey, are you okay?"

"Yeah," Adam lied, pushing the man's hands away. "I'm fine."

"That was some tumble. Are you sure you're all right? I didn't mean to startle you like that."

"It's nothing. Just missed a step, that's all."

"You okay to continue?"

"Actually, I'm done," Adam said. "I've got to meet a friend. He's waiting for me."

He grabbed his water bottle and towel and practically ran to the smoothie station. Ash was sitting at a table chatting up one of the gym's personal trainers.

"Thinking of signing up?" Adam asked as he slid into an

empty chair and stole a sip of Ash's smoothie. Peanut butter and blueberries. Ew.

"Maybe."

"Well, I'm done for the day. Figured you wouldn't mind heading home, but if you're busy, I could always catch up with you later."

Ash's brow furrowed. "You never leave this early."

"I'm not feeling it today. Are you staying or heading home with me?"

"Um..."

Adam understood Ash's hesitation. The man was gorgeous.

"Here," the trainer said, pulling out a business card from who-knew-where and sliding it across the table to Ash. "Give me a call sometime. My work and personal number are on it."

Ash smiled. "Sure."

With a few more pleasantries, the trainer left.

"Well, I know what number you're going to use when you call him," Adam said once they were alone and heading toward the locker room.

Ash waved away his teasing. "What happened? You were perfectly fine when I left you on that horrible contraption."

"I..." Adam's voice trailed off when he caught sight of a familiar couple by the locker room door. The younger man was dressed this time, but the thick black line of the dog collar stood proudly above his T-shirt.

"We meet again," Dillon said when he and Ash came near. "Adam, right?"

"Yeah," Adam said, distracted by the submissive's neckwear.

"We've never been properly introduced. I'm Dillon. This is Michael."

The younger man smiled charmingly and stuck his hand out, snapping Adam from his distraction. "Nice to meet you."

"Uh, nice to meet you too," Adam said, taking his hand and shaking it.

"Eh hem," came a voice from behind him.

"Oh, this is Ash. He's a friend of mine."

"Pleasure." Ash leaned forward to shake hands with Dillon and Michael.

"We were just leaving," Adam said. "I don't want to keep you from your workout."

"See you around," Dillon said.

"Yeah. See you."

Adam watched as the two men headed off into the crowd.

"Hello? We're leaving, right?" Ash asked.

"Yeah," Adam said, finally turning to head into the locker room.

"That's Jesse's friend, isn't it? The one you told me about?"

Adam nodded.

"And that was his lover, I presume?"

"Submissive."

"Well, that was obvious," Ash replied. "They seemed really happy together."

"What makes you say that?"

"The way they looked at each other. How they stood together. It's like any sort of space between them is nonexistent. I'd like to find someone like that."

"Even if it meant wearing a dog collar?"

The shocked expression on Ash's face made Adam think his tone had been harsher than he'd meant it. "It's not all about dog collars and kneeling," Ash said.

"I know, but I can't get that part out of my head."

"Obviously. Come on. Let's get home and shower. You need a drink, and I know just the place to get one."

———

The club Ash took him to that evening was the usual affair with a line of people outside waiting to get in, pulsating lights and music beckoning through the doorway, and a crush of bodies gyrating on the dance floor once they were inside.

Adam had been anxious on the ride over, but this would be good for him. It was time to move on and try again. A few drinks and some dancing helped. Plus, the place wasn't under Harte ownership, so he could relax about bumping into Jesse.

"Having a good time?" Ash asked.

"Yeah." Adam nodded to emphasize his answer, not sure if he would be heard over the music.

Ash made a gesture, then wove through the crowd toward the bar. Adam let him go with another nod and kept dancing. Before he knew it, a tall blond man with a dazzling smile had taken Ash's place.

"Care to dance?" the guy asked. He was broad in the shoulders and looked like a bodybuilder with warm, brown eyes and a square jaw. He looked nothing like Jesse, so Adam smiled back at him. "Love to."

They worked with the beat, and the stranger wasted no time closing the space between them. Adam slid his arms around the man's neck and pressed their bodies closer together. The friction between them soon became too much for the dance floor.

"Want to get out of here?" Adam's dance partner asked.

Adam didn't like the idea of leaving with a complete stranger, but he had no qualms about finding a private space for a while. "Bathroom?" he suggested.

The man nodded, took his hand, and led Adam through the crowd toward the back of the club. They went through a door marked Restrooms and into a hallway. Once the door closed behind them, the music diminished by half, and the relative silence was deafening. The stranger turned and pressed Adam against the wall; he massaged Adam's cock with his hand through his jeans while his mouth moved to claim Adam's. Returning the kiss fervently, Adam ground his hips against the man's palm, wanting more. It had been so long since anyone had touched him. He felt like a starving man. Adam grabbed hold of the man's shirt and crushed his mouth against his lips, opening his teeth to invite the man's tongue in deeper.

They fumbled their way into a stall. Adam shoved the door closed, but it bounced back from the force, and he had to push it again before locking it. There was no way either of them were getting naked, but the need for skin-on-skin had Adam roaming his hands everywhere they could reach. The man returned the favor by lifting Adam's shirt and tweaking his nipples. It sent an electric shock straight to his groin. In a flash, he remembered stronger sensations, endless passion bound in ropes. He kissed the man harder to chase the memories away. It worked for a while.

Eventually, the stranger pulled a packet of lube from his pocket and said, "Turn around," an order Adam would normally be only too happy to comply with, but the break in their passion left him open to hesitation, and it flooded in readily. Panting, he leaned against the side of the stall. This wasn't what he wanted.

"I can't."

The man frowned.

"I'm sorry," Adam said. "I can't do this."

There was a moment of disbelief written plainly on the guy's face before he said, "Fuck. That's not even a tease."

Adam didn't say anything.

"Shit." The man pulled the stall door open and stormed out.

Adam was slow to follow. He took a moment to splash some water on his face before leaving the bathroom to find Ash. He wanted to go home.

TEN

"Do you want me to go?" Dillon asked from the office doorway.

Jesse was lost to a pile of paperwork and hadn't noticed his friend's arrival. He looked up in surprise. "What time is it?"

"Seven thirty." It was one of Michael's study nights, and Dillon had gotten into the habit of dropping by Jesse's office for a visit to avoid distracting his sub from his homework.

"I lost track of time. Come on in. Grab us some beers while I put this away." He set about clearing his desk while Dillon grabbed the drinks and took a seat. When Jesse was done, he turned his attention to his friend. "Something on your mind?"

Dillon sipped his beer, clearly considering his answer. "I saw Adam at the gym today," he said finally.

Jesse almost choked on his drink and put the bottle down as he carefully swallowed. "Oh?"

"He was there with a friend. Apparently, he's a member, and he's been going there for a while now."

"I had heard. How did he look?"

Dillon shrugged. "He seemed fine for the most part. He

was a little wary when he saw me, but I guess that's not a surprise."

"Is he…" Jesse's voice trailed off, but at Dillon's expectant expression, he shoved aside his hesitation. "Is he seeing anyone?"

"Harte, he was ready to rabbit at the sight of me and Michael. Do you really think I had the opportunity to find out his dating status?"

"I know. It's just…I should never have let him run out of here. I shouldn't have let him go."

"We both agreed he needed the space," Dillon said. "It wouldn't have worked if you hadn't."

"But how much space is enough? I—" He swallowed and gave in to the confession. "—I want him, Dillon. I don't want anyone else to have him. He's mine."

Dillon tilted his head and smirked. The expression on his face plainly stated how this was the moment he'd been saving his "I told you so" for. Jesse glared at him. "Shut up."

Dillon laughed.

Jesse sighed and asked, "What do I do?"

"If you can't wait any longer, go and speak with him."

"But what if he turns me down again?"

"That's the chance you take."

Jesse frowned. "This sucks."

"Yes," Dillon agreed, "but when it's right, it's worth it in the end."

ELEVEN

Life continued, as it was wont to do. Adam filled his days with work and the gym. On weekends, he and Ash went clubbing. The personal trainer hadn't lasted long—Adam hadn't expected him to—and although it was selfish, he was glad Ash was free to accompany him for evenings of dancing, drinking, and scouting for hot men. Still, something about their outings left him unsatisfied.

He'd flirted with a few guys, but any time he considered trying for anything more, it always felt wrong. Something would be missing, or the temptation felt forced. When he mentioned this to Ash, his friend said, "Welcome to the wonderful world of finding the right man. It's a bitch. Good luck."

After that, Adam decided not to worry anymore.

———

Adam had seen Dillon a few times since they'd first bumped into each other at the gym, but they never did more than nod at each other and continue on their way. If Michael was there, the younger man would add a smile and a wave to the mix, but that was the extent of their interaction. Therefore, it came as a surprise when Dillon struck up a conversation in the locker room one day. Granted, they were alone, but they could have ignored each other like perfectly civil almost-strangers.

"You seem to be doing well," Dillon said.

Adam froze while hanging up his towel. Blinking himself back into motion and silently cursing himself for being so stupid, he shut the locker door and turned to face Jesse's friend. Dillon stood at a locker three doors down from his. He had a pair of sweatpants slung low on his hips and a towel around his neck. The rest of his bare skin was slicked with a thin sheen of sweat from recent exertion. The first time Adam had seen Dillon's muscles, they'd been encased in leather and impressive. Now, revealed in their full glory, he found it hard to detach his eyes from them and look at Dillon's face. His mind was in the gutter too often lately.

"Uh," Adam started, trying to remember how to use his voice. "Yeah."

"You haven't been to the club lately. Is everything okay?"

"Sure. It just isn't my thing."

Dillon nodded. "I had wondered. You seemed freaked out the last time I saw you there."

That had been the night of the flogging when Jesse had done the scene on stage with Nicholas. Unbidden memories of that night flooded back to Adam, and he found the looseness of his sweatpants useful, if not fully helpful.

"Yeah, I hadn't expected that. It put things into perspective for me."

Dillon kept a steady gaze on Adam's face, and Adam felt himself blush a little. Thankfully, the other man wasn't looking down.

"It was probably overwhelming," Dillon said.

"Definitely a surprise," Adam admitted.

"Did it scare you?"

Adam's brows furrowed. "In what way?"

"In any way. People who aren't into kink probably

wouldn't have liked it. Others who are can sometimes be surprised and possibly frightened by the realization they do like it."

Adam narrowed his eyes. "You think I liked it?" he asked, though he already knew the answer.

Dillon pointedly dropped his gaze to Adam's crotch, then looked back at his face with an eyebrow raised.

"You think I'm a sub," Adam said.

"It's not my place to label what you are or aren't. Only you can decide that."

"Did Jesse ask you to talk to me?"

Dillon appeared surprised. "No."

Adam felt stupid for asking and bit the inside of his cheek.

"He does ask about you though. He's worried and wants to know you're okay."

"What are you going to tell him?" Adam was sure Dillon would tell Jesse exactly what he thought.

"I'll tell him you're well enough. It's your choice what you do with your life, not his. He knows that. He may not like your choice, but he'll have to live with it."

"He shouldn't worry about me so much," Adam said.

"That's his choice," Dillon replied. "You'll just have to keep on ignoring it."

———

Adam was quiet that night when he and Ash met up for dinner. Too many thoughts were going through his head to keep up a good conversation.

"What's up?" Ash finally asked him.

"Have you ever done the submissive thing?" Although they were in public, and normally he would have waited until they'd left to talk about it, the topic had been on his mind too much to ignore.

Ash shrugged. "I've been spanked a time or two. Played a

couple fantasy scenes and the like. It's not my cup of tea as an everyday thing, but yeah, I like it."

"How do you…give up control like that to someone?"

Ash studied his face for a moment before replying. "You never gave up control to Jesse?"

Adam thought over all the times he'd been with Jesse, from the first time when Jesse had told him to keep still against the cross to the night he'd tied Adam up on the roof and every one in between. "Yeah," he said. "I did. A lot."

"What's the difference between that and submitting to him for a scene he plans for you? I'll tell you something, Adam. In a relationship like that, it's the submissive who has the power. The Dominant may make all the rules and decisions, he's the one who's in charge, but it's the submissive who's put him there, and it's the submissive who can make it all stop."

Adam had never thought of it that way. "I don't want to seem weak."

"Do you know how much strength it takes to submit? It's easy to tell someone what to do. It's a lot harder to purposefully let someone else take control."

Adam remembered Jesse's words the first night they met. *"It's not easy to trust someone completely. I admire the men who are able to do so."* Maybe he'd been thinking about this all wrong. "I still can't see calling myself a submissive."

"Then don't!" Ash snapped. Though his voice was low, Adam flinched, hoping they wouldn't catch the attention of the people around them. "It's a label, Adam, like everything else. You don't need to use it if you don't want to, but don't make a freaking *word* your excuse for dumping a guy who was obviously good for you. If I were Jesse, I'd be so pissed if I heard you right now."

"You are pissed," Adam said. "Your eyes are going to get stuck like that if you keep glaring at me that way."

Ash took a deep breath and let it out slowly. "Look, whether you were doing the right thing or not, I figured it was your decision to make, but I'm beginning to wonder if you're thinking you made a stupid move when you dumped him."

Adam didn't reply. He didn't have an answer he was willing to give.

———

After his conversation with Ash, Adam's mind was permanently tuned to the radio station of all things Jesse Harte. He thought about him constantly, daydreaming of all the things they'd done together as well as many things Adam was coming to realize he wanted them to do together. He kept bracing himself before turning corners, afraid he'd see Jesse and torn between whether that would be a good thing or not. Adam wasn't sure if he was ready for what would happen between them, but he was beginning to think he'd been too harsh to push Jesse away so fast. He considered stopping by the club but was too scared to go. A couple times he'd come close but wound up talking himself out of it before getting anywhere.

Adam was lost in those thoughts again, his hands crossed at his waist, ready to lift his shirt over his head, when he had another visitor in the gym locker room.

"You're doing well," came a voice from beside him. For a moment Adam thought the speaker might be Dillon again, but the Dominant had already voiced his concerns, and this didn't sound like him anyway. His heart jumped into his throat as the voice registered, and he recognized it. He closed his eyes and swallowed before closing his locker and turning.

"Jesse," he said, his voice a whisper.

"Dillon told me you were doing okay, but I had to see for myself."

Well, that answered the question as to what he was doing there. That also left Adam without a question to ask, so he didn't say anything. The silence stretched, and Adam didn't know how to break it.

Finally, Jesse spoke again. "I'm sorry."

"For what?"

"For not telling you there was no one else. I haven't fucked anyone else since our first time together. I didn't want to."

"And that sub?"

"He's someone I've known for a long time. We've scened together often, but he understood sex was off the table that evening."

"Why didn't you say anything?"

"I didn't think it mattered. I didn't realize I had to. I should have seen it. I should have known what you needed to hear."

"Now you're sounding like a Dom."

"I am a Dom, Adam. I've never lied to you about that."

That fight-or-flight response seized Adam again. Jesse must have caught sight of it in his face because he moved to block Adam's way to the door. "Don't leave," he said. "I'm not going to force you to do anything you don't want to. I just came to talk."

"So, talk," Adam said, not trusting himself to say anything else.

Jesse took a seat on a bench. Adam sat on the one beside it, keeping space between them. That way he could breathe. He could think. He needed to be able to think.

"I miss you," Jesse said, and Adam almost fell off his bench.

"You miss me?"

"Yes. I miss touching you, kissing you, talking with you."

"We didn't really do much talking."

"I'd like to change that."

"Now you sound like you want to date me."

Jesse didn't deny it. Adam stared at him in surprise, but he wasn't ready to believe him.

"I want you, Adam." Jesse kept his eyes locked on Adam's as he stood. "I've never wanted anyone more."

This wasn't good. Adam was at a disadvantage being lower than Jesse, but he couldn't find the power to stand. When Jesse stood in front of him, he was trapped. He sat frozen as Jesse leaned forward, bringing their mouths closer together. He didn't touch Adam, but then again, he didn't need to.

"Come back to me," Jesse whispered. Then he kissed Adam.

An electric shock shot through Adam's body with the kiss. His cock instantly throbbed, and his skin felt as if it had just come up for air for the first time in forever. It was a gentle press of lips, yet Adam felt it more than anything else he'd ever experienced. When Jesse pulled back, Adam found himself following. He realized what he was doing and stopped. Jesse gazed into his eyes, searching for something, but Adam was again at a loss for what to do or say.

"If you'd rather, I'll go and never bother you again," Jesse said, "but I wanted you to know the truth."

Adam's voice wasn't working, nor was any other part of his body that needed his brain to function. Jesse took that as a silent rejection and frowned, obviously disappointed. It hurt to see that expression on his face. When he turned to go, Adam's heart raced.

"Wait."

Jesse stopped. When nothing more came from Adam's lips, Jesse turned to look back at him. Adam still couldn't find the right words, but he didn't need to. Whatever Jesse saw on his face was enough. Before Adam knew it, he was lying back on the bench with Jesse leaning over him, their lips pressed together in a hungry kiss. Adam clutched at Jesse's back as if it were a lifeline. He ached for more than a kiss. He ached for anything Jesse was willing to give him.

"I'm going to fuck you right here," Jesse growled in his ear. "I don't care if someone comes in and sees us. I'm going to keep fucking you until you scream my name or pass out."

"Yes," Adam panted, pulling the man even closer. He didn't care if anyone saw them. He needed this. He needed Jesse. The man's touch alone left him more satisfied than any self-induced orgasm he'd had lately.

"Take off your clothes," Jesse said.

He stepped back to give Adam enough room, and Adam yanked his shirt over his head then lifted his hips as he tugged his sweatpants down and off his legs. He sat there, naked, looking up at Jesse and completely unconcerned with the possibility of someone walking in and seeing him like that.

"Fuck me. Please," Adam begged.

Jesse smiled, and a shudder ran through Adam. He knew that look. It was the one Jesse had whenever he was planning something devious. Adam would beg for a lot more before Jesse was finished with him. The promise in Jesse's eyes made Adam smile as well. This was what he'd been missing.

Jesse pulled his own shirt over his head and off and then dropped it on the floor beside them. He fished a tube of lube and a condom out of his pocket and set them on the floor beside Adam before shucking off his jeans and dropping them.

Adam fingered the condom packet. "Confident, were you?"

"Hopeful," Jesse said. "Would you rather I hadn't come prepared?"

Adam gazed up at him, naked and gorgeous, his erect cock standing proudly. Adam wanted to put his mouth around it and suck until it released the taste of his lover on his tongue. He wanted Jesse inside him, and he didn't want to wait. "Prepared is good."

Jesse glanced around, and Adam pushed himself up onto his elbows, trying to figure out what he had in mind. Jesse went to one of the shelves and grabbed a pile of fresh towels before returning to the middle of the room. After opening them, he laid them out on the floor. Then he turned back to Adam and answered his unasked question.

"If someone comes in here while we're fucking, I want them to have a good view."

He had to be kidding, but with Jesse, Adam could never be too sure.

"Come over here," Jesse said as he sat down on the towels. "And bring the lube and condom with you." He had left one towel folded. He fluffed it and placed it behind his head before lying back on the floor. Adam picked up the supplies and moved over to him. Jesse held out his hand, and Adam took it as he knelt beside him. He pulled Adam closer, and Adam leaned forward to kiss him. Jesse slid his free hand over Adam's back to tease his hole, and Adam whimpered.

"Lube?"

He handed the tube to Jesse, and it wasn't long before the man's finger returned, this time prepared. He pushed in to one knuckle, but Adam wanted more. He tried to shift to give Jesse better access, but Jesse refused to relinquish the kiss.

"Help me," he said between kisses.

"I'm trying," Adam said.

He shook his head. "You do it."

Ah. Adam reached back to where Jesse's finger rested frustratingly inside him. Adam pushed the finger deeper, but it only went a little farther, nowhere near deep enough. Adam tangled his fingers with Jesse's, getting lube on them. Finally, Jesse guided Adam's hand back to his ass, and Adam worked a finger inside himself. He pressed it deep and groaned against Jesse's mouth.

"Put in another," Jesse said.

Adam did, working carefully but hastily, wanting Jesse's cock inside him more than the fingers. He drove his fingers in and out in deep strokes. Jesse's hand rested on his, not guiding but feeling what Adam did with each movement. It wasn't long before Adam's hips moved, wanting more.

"Three?" Jesse asked.

Adam nodded and slid the third digit into his hole.

"I wonder if you could get more than that inside you."

Adam shivered. Like a tease for his suggestion, Jesse dipped the tip of a finger inside him. It wasn't much of an addition, but it made Adam gasp and move faster. His cock dripped, making Jesse's belly wet where it slid against him. No longer concerned with kissing, Jesse gripped Adam's ass and pulled him higher so he could push his finger fully inside Adam.

"That's four." Jesse grinned.

Adam groaned.

"Fuck our fingers. Come on. No reason to stop now."

He was right. Adam had been moving his hips all along, and now he kept them moving, fucking four fingers for the first time in his life. Together they were thicker than Jesse's cock, and the space felt tight. Adam relaxed his body and rode them, enjoying the new sensation, but it didn't last for long. He wanted something deeper inside him, and their fingers only went so far.

"Please, Jesse. Fuck me."

"I am."

"With your cock."

"No."

Adam stopped moving. "What?"

Jesse chuckled and looked down at Adam's hips. Both of their fingers were plunged deep inside him. Jesse wriggled his, and Adam squirmed.

"Please," Adam said. "Why not?"

"Because you're going to do it." He gently removed his finger from Adam's body, and the others followed. Jesse grabbed the condom and tore it open, then eased it down his beautiful cock and slicked it up with lube. He hissed as he stroked it, and Adam figured it must be throbbing as badly as his own.

"Ride me, Adam. I've told you how much I want you. Now show me how much you want me."

Adam hesitated. This was more than just a fuck. Jesse didn't move while he waited. He could easily have teased Adam, and Adam would have been on him in an instant, but he didn't. This time it was fully Adam's decision.

Adam straddled Jesse's body. Taking hold of Jesse's cock, Adam lined it up with his disappointingly empty ass and slid down as far as he could go. His eyes closed instinctively, and he wriggled, taking a moment to truly believe it was Jesse inside him.

Jesse's hands skimmed over Adam's thighs, and Adam opened his eyes to look at him. There was a different kind of smile on Jesse's face now, one Adam had never seen before. It was achingly beautiful, and Adam leaned forward to kiss him.

"Yes," Jesse said, and Adam agreed.

He sat up and moved his body, fucking himself in long, deep strokes, enjoying the glide of Jesse's cock inside him and the feel of it filling him up with each thrust. After a while, Adam changed the angle and made it hit his prostate, building tension in his cock and making him moan from the pleasure. Jesse let Adam have his way, folding his hands behind his head and watching.

Adam didn't try to put on a show for him. Instead, Adam gave him what he'd asked for and showed Jesse how much he wanted him, how much he had wanted this. Jesse only intervened when Adam was getting close to coming. Without warning, there was a viselike grip on the base of his cock, and it startled Adam into sitting down hard. He glared at Jesse, panting in frustration.

This time, Jesse's smile was the mischievous one Adam was familiar with. He glared at Jesse, knowing exactly what was in store. Jesse's grin only widened at Adam's expression.

Whatever the true definition was, or whatever Jesse might

say to the contrary, Adam was convinced the man was a sadist.

"Keep going," Jesse said.

"How can I keep going when you're holding my dick like that?"

"I'll move my hand with you. I don't want you coming before I'm ready."

How the fuck was the man not ready? Jesse could be ready to explode and still not come for another hour. Adam had no idea how he did it.

He tried pushing himself up again, but the pressure building in his balls was a distraction, and his limbs were getting tired. Adam had done a full workout before Jesse had shown up, and fucking him felt like running a marathon on top of that. Jesse saw his struggle and was happy to help.

"Here," he said, taking hold of Adam's hip with his free hand. "Let me."

Jesse snapped his hips, ramming his cock up and down in short thrusts. The man knew Adam well by now and hit that spot of pleasure with every move. Adam moaned consistently, completely forgetting there was a gym full of people outside. It was all he could do to hold himself in place for Jesse's assault. His eyes rolled back into his head as pleasure enveloped him, and he tried to buck his hips, but the steel grip on his cock and his hip held him in place. Adam was helpless to do anything but take the pleasure and ride with it.

"I-I can't..." Adam protested. His brain shut down, and he was no longer able to form any sort of sentence, let alone a complete one. Nothing but moans escaped his lips, one for every thrust, and he couldn't have kept them back even if he'd had the sense to try.

The hand on his cock was no longer still but stroking, and it all became too much. Adam's hips were free, and he snapped them fast, wanting to both ride and escape the overwhelming sensation until, finally, he screamed with release. Pearly white strands decorated Jesse's chest and belly. Adam had enough awareness to feel Jesse pumping into the condom before he collapsed atop him. Tingling sensations ran through his entire body as he lay panting. Jesse's arms wrapped around him, and Adam listened for a while to his lover's breathing against his ear.

"You didn't scream my name," Jesse said after a while. "And you didn't pass out."

All Adam was capable of doing at that moment was breathing, so he didn't answer.

"We'll have to try again before we leave."

"Jesse!" Adam exclaimed, pushing up from his chest and gaping at him in shock.

"Or that could count," Jesse decided.

Adam sat there panting for a few more minutes. "I might die if we did that again so soon," he said finally.

"Oh, come now. We've had better. You passed out on me the last time."

"That doesn't strike me as a reasonable goal for sex."

"Well, you didn't actually pass out, but you were too exhausted to move and fell asleep on me."

That was true. "That's what I have to look forward to in the future? Sex until I'm too tired to move?"

"Would that be so bad?"

Adam didn't answer. There was no need.

"Does this mean we have a future?" Jesse asked.

Adam opened his mouth to say something, though he wasn't sure what it was going to be. Instead, he hesitated, and his usual excuse returned. "I'm not going to be some sub who will perform with you on stage, Jesse. I won't be going with you to parties in dog collars and standing naked before other people."

"I know."

That surprised Adam. Jesse had to have known, but he seemed so sure about it as if it were a simple thing.

"But you like that kind of stuff," Adam said.

"Yes, I do. I also like a lot of other stuff, if you haven't noticed."

Adam sighed. "I want to give you what you need, Jesse, but I can't."

Jesse laughed, sliding his arms around Adam and then pulling him back down onto his chest. "Baby, you already do."

When they were finally able to move again, they hopped into a quick shower—Adam had to fight Jesse off with a washcloth before they were done—then got dressed. Adam wondered why no one had walked in on them and attempted to prepare himself for the gym version of a college walk of shame, but when they exited the locker room, the gym was empty.

"What the… Where is everyone?"

"Oh, didn't I tell you? I own this gym," Jesse said. "In fact, I usually come here to work out, but I couldn't while I was trying to respect your desire for space. If I'm at all out of shape, it's completely your fault."

The man wasn't at all out of shape and probably had a fully stocked gym in his home. That made Adam wonder what Jesse's home even looked like.

"You own this gym?"

"Yup. I offered free drinks at Harte to everyone if they cut their workouts short today so we could close early. They didn't seem to mind."

Well, that meant the next time Adam went to Harte or the gym, he'd be embarrassed. Great.

"You're going to be a lot of trouble to date, aren't you?" Adam asked.

"I have no idea what you mean," Jesse protested innocently.

Adam shook his head. It was useless to try to run now. He'd already done that and ended up right back where he'd started. At least he wasn't afraid anymore. This time he knew he was right where he was meant to be.

LIMITS AND STAKES

ONE

It was spring break, and Daniel Stone was enjoying a full week of student-free days. Dressed head-to-toe in tight black leather and itching to play, Daniel entered the Lock & Key. The club wasn't as big as the one he'd been a member of before moving to Georgia, and membership wasn't as exclusive, but it was well-recommended, and the staff kept an eye out for the patrons. Most of the members seemed to be well-versed in the lifestyle as well, enough to give him the confidence that, if he were to play with someone, they would at least know what they were doing or say something if they didn't.

The club was a sufficient distance from where he worked, so he didn't have to worry about being spotted as a familiar face outside of the scene. A BDSM club in a college town was not where a professor wanted to be found, no matter how liberal the residents claimed to be. A five-hour drive and the expense of a hotel room for the week was a worthy price for freedom.

He ordered a bottle of water and scanned the crowd for potential company. A small group of men caught his eye. Two of the three he disregarded immediately, but the third, a lean blond in the skimpiest pair of leather shorts he'd ever seen, held his attention. He was unable to tear his gaze from all that pale skin or the way the leather hugged his perfectly round bottom.

The boy was obviously new to the scene. There was uncertainty in his movements, but he was doing his best to keep up the conversation. Daniel had full confidence the young man would succeed. Anyone brave enough to go out in public in shorts like those could hold a simple conversation.

When the group moved toward the bar, Daniel finally saw the young man's face. He froze in surprise. Of the students crowding Georgia State University campus, he now faced the one he'd wanted to avoid the most, the one he wanted to forget. Against his better judgment, he intercepted the group.

"Chris," he said.

Chris Owen looked up at him, startled. His eyes widened in recognition, and his mouth fell open.

"Pr—" He stopped himself just in time. "Mr. Stone."

Relief flooded through Daniel. He preferred to keep his daily life separate from the club and was glad it would remain that way.

"You know this kid?" asked one of the men. He stood too close to Chris for Daniel's liking.

"Yes." Daniel resisted the impulse to claim anything more. He had no right to claim anything, but his instincts wouldn't let him back down completely. "My apologies for the interruption. I wasn't aware Chris planned to be here today."

The stranger scrutinized the young man, paying particular attention to his neck. "He's not marked."

"I'm instructing him," Daniel said. Well, he had been. For half a semester, he'd tutored Chris in advanced calc, but that had changed after winter break. Either way, the details didn't apply here. He clutched at straws with half-truths, but he couldn't help himself. He wanted to know why Chris was there and what he had in mind. He wanted to keep the boy safe.

He wanted to keep him.

No. He's a student. You promised him two months ago nothing would happen between the two of you, and now you're trying to put a collar on him? Get a grip, Stone!

"Of course, he's free to choose who he goes with," Daniel added, attempting to pull himself out of the hole he'd been digging.

The other man looked at Chris expectantly. Chris flickered his eyes back and forth between them, seemingly lost on how to answer. Daniel put a hand on his shoulder.

"You can continue to the bar as you were, or you can take a tour of the club with me. Which do you want to do? There is no wrong choice."

"I..." Chris's gaze locked on Daniel's. "I..." He swallowed. "I want to go with you."

There was a *tsk* from behind Chris, but Daniel ignored it. He also did his best to ignore the sense of triumph running through him.

"Follow me," he said and headed toward the bar.

"I thought we were going for a tour."

"One step at a time, boy." Daniel ordered another water, then scanned the room for somewhere to sit. When the bartender put the drink on the counter, Daniel left it for Chris to pick up and led the way toward the table he'd found. He was glad to hear the crinkle of plastic as Chris followed. The seating he'd chosen had a semblance of privacy. Daniel took the chair against the wall and gestured for Chris to take the other.

"Now, I take it this is what you meant about trying new things over spring break?" he asked.

The boy flushed red. "I... Yes. I've always wanted to come here and finally worked up the courage to do it."

"You did more than that." Daniel dropped a pointed glance in the direction of Chris's shorts.

The color in Chris's face deepened. "You're not gonna tell anyone, are you?"

"I believe a person's private life is their own business."

"Thanks."

Daniel took a sip of his water. After a moment, Chris did the same. Daniel caught himself staring when Chris licked his lips. He'd kissed that mouth.

The small details of that moment were forever embedded in his mind. One evening during winter break, they'd come across each other outside the math building on campus. He couldn't recall why they'd lingered. All he remembered was huddling in his coat against the winter chill and then not caring about the weather as he became entranced by the puffs of air dancing between them as they spoke, the rosy color on Chris's cheeks, and the sparkle in his clear blue eyes. There had been silence all around them when the conversation had hit a lull and a pull, an irresistible urge had driven him to kiss a student. Granted, Chris was a grad student and not in any of Daniel's classes, but Daniel had been his tutor at the time. Even if he hadn't, Chris was still a student at the college where Daniel worked, and that wasn't something Daniel was comfortable with. Recklessness led to trouble, and so he'd pulled away. Yet here was that face again, looking at him so openly as if the kiss had never happened and Daniel hadn't ruined an innocent student-teacher relationship.

He mentally shook himself from his reverie. "Did you have anything in mind when you came here tonight, or was getting through the door the main goal?"

Chris's blush deepened. "That seemed to be a big enough goal to start with."

"Now that you've accomplished it, what do you plan to do next?"

———

Was Professor Stone offering to do a scene with him? That was impossible, especially after the way the man had reacted to their kiss during winter break.

It had been sweet, the kiss. A chaste press of lips against

his as the snow had fallen around them. There had been a moment of perfection when the kiss had broken, and they'd gazed into each other's eyes, but it had only lasted a few seconds. Once the mistake had registered, Professor Stone had left him standing alone on the sidewalk. The rejection had hurt, but it hadn't been a surprise, and the memory of the kiss had warmed Chris for the rest of the vacation.

After winter break, Professor Stone had taken the time to apologize and reassure him nothing inappropriate would ever happen between them again. His earnestness had driven the point home deeper than the initial rejection, and Chris had left the professor's office with a heavy heart.

He'd liked the kiss, loved it in fact. It had been the focus of many a late-night fantasy, except his dreams never ended with just one kiss. His imaginings had been one of the reasons Chris had plucked up enough courage to come to the club for spring break. He wanted to find someone who would make his fantasies come true and take his mind off Professor Stone. So far, the plan hadn't worked.

"I've only made it to the bar," Chris said. "Maybe I should see the place before deciding?"

"I did say I'd lead you on a tour. Drink some more of your water, and then we'll begin walking."

Walking would be tough. Chris had known the tight shorts would do little to hide any sign of arousal, but he'd figured he'd be around strangers, and it wouldn't matter. Now he was not only in front of someone he knew, but the man across from him was the very source of his nighttime fantasies. Keeping a calm exterior was already proving impossible, and Professor Stone was bound to notice.

Chris drank slowly, trying to relax, but the view across the table had the opposite effect on him. He'd seen Professor Stone every day while on campus. The man always dressed in a flattering suit, but tonight he was encased in skintight leather pants with heavy black boots and a black T-shirt that appeared painted on. The attention of his intense brown eyes didn't help either. Giving up, Chris put down the bottle.

"Ready?"

Chris nodded. There was nothing to be done, so he might as well get it over with.

Professor Stone rose from the table and turned from him. Chris followed, thankful to hide his embarrassment a little longer.

———

The tour went by in a blur for Daniel. He tried his best to inform Chris of the options the club offered, but the look of wonder and wide-eyed interest on the boy's face distracted him at every turn. Chris had sported an erection the entire time they'd been together. The lifestyle definitely appealed to him. It took everything in Daniel to remember a tour was all he'd offered. To do anything more would break the promise he'd made to Chris after winter break.

He ended the tour in one of the private playrooms. After ushering Chris inside, Daniel closed the door behind them. "What do you think of your first BDSM club?"

"It's..."

Daniel didn't need to hear the rest. He already knew what Chris would say.

"I can't wait to do it all," the young man said dreamily.

"No reason you shouldn't, but don't try to do everything all at once. A scene doesn't have to be complicated to be satisfying, and it can be dangerous to do something like that, especially in the beginning. When you find someone you trust, who you know will take care of you, I'm sure you'll have a great time figuring it all out."

"And what about you?"

Daniel blinked, thrown by the question. "What about me?"

"You came here for your spring break too. What were you hoping to find?"

A sub who could get my mind off you. "You don't have to worry about me. I'm not in a rush."

"You were planning to find someone to scene with tonight, weren't you?"

Daniel shrugged. "The night's still young."

"Would you do a scene with me?"

Daniel forced himself not to hesitate before answering. "I like to have sex with my subs, and you already know I don't have sex with students."

"Technically, I'm not your student," Chris pointed out. "What's our school policy on that anyway?"

"Strictly speaking, relationships aren't against the rules," Daniel admitted. "Though they are strongly frowned upon, and there is a massive amount of red tape centering on the potential abuse of power."

"Do you have to have sex in your scenes?" Chris asked. "Would you consider doing something that didn't include sex?"

Daniel was tempted to give in, but he didn't reply.

"You said I should find someone I trust to do a scene with," Chris added. "You're the only one in this building who fits the bill, and I'd rather learn from you than try something with a complete stranger."

Damn. The kid had a point. Daniel would make sure no matter what they did, Chris would be safe, and he had to admit the thought of Chris doing a scene with someone else didn't sit well with him. "No sex."

Chris's grin switched on like a lightbulb. "No problem."

"You're going to do what I tell you and not complain if I don't push you as far as you want to go. I make the rules. If you don't like that idea, we can stop this right now."

"No, I like it."

"Good. Now, tell me what you've been fantasizing about whenever you've thought of coming here."

Chris furrowed his pretty brows. "What?"

"Tonight, your main goal was to get through the door, but before then, back when you didn't yet have the courage, what did you imagine would happen once you were here? What is it about this place that turns you on more than vanilla sex in a bedroom with your boyfriend?"

———

If Professor Stone didn't want Chris thinking about sex, he was doing a pretty poor job of keeping things platonic. Images flickered through Chris's mind, making his tiny shorts tighter by the second. Heat rushed to his face and down his neck. He bit his lip and stared down at the table to avoid the other man's gaze.

"That. What did you think of just now?"

Chris swallowed. "I was thinking… I sometimes imagine being put on my knees to…suck someone off."

"Someone you know or a stranger?"

He swallowed again. "Someone I know."

"Good. What else do you imagine?"

It was easier to answer the questions if he didn't think about what he would say before he said it. "I imagine being tied up."

"With what?"

"Cuffs or rope or something. I don't usually focus on specifics. It's being bound that I think about."

"Anything else?"

"Spanking."

Professor Stone lifted his eyebrows. "Spanking?"

"I…I want to try spanking."

"As a punishment or for pleasure?"

"P-pleasure."

Chris's face burned. He licked his dry lips and did his best to ignore that his shorts were now stretched to their limit.

"Pick a safeword."

The shift in topic distracted him from his embarrassment. "Red."

"*Red* and everything stops. *Yellow* and I'll slow down so you can get your bearings, and we can discuss what happens next. Agreed?"

Chris nodded.

"Out loud please."

"Yes, Sir."

"Good. Now, don't move."

Chris stood still as Stone moved around him. His eyes strained at the corners of their sockets, trying to follow the other man's movements, but he didn't dare turn his head. He wouldn't waste this chance by not listening to directions.

Was this really happening? He'd been so embarrassed when sharing his fantasies, not because of the fantasies themselves, but because he was hard-pressed not to admit Professor Stone had been the man in them. Stone had dominated Chris's mind since their first meeting. Their kiss had only solidified the face in his dreams. Now the man was here, in the flesh, and going to do an *actual* scene with him. Chris hoped he didn't come before they even began.

Chris's attention snapped back to the present when something heavy dragged across the floor. A weird-looking bench had been pulled to the center of the room.

"You're going to kneel with your knees here"—Stone pointed to one end—"and your hands here." He pointed to the other. "Once you're in position, I'll strap you down. That way you'll stay where I want you even if you move. Even though you'll be tied down, you *won't* move unless I tell you. Do you understand?"

"Yes, Sir."

"Good. Now, come here."

Chris placed his knees on the pads meant for them, then lowered his body down onto the bench. Stone nudged him with his knee, making Chris shift until he was satisfied with his position. He buckled Chris's wrists and ankles into cuffs attached to the wooden frame. After Chris's limbs had been trapped, more straps were placed over his waist and upper back. His thighs were bound in a similar fashion, effectively making Chris immobile.

"How is your first experience with bondage?"

Chris rolled his eyes up to try to look at the other man. "Restricting, Sir," and not as engaging as he'd imagined.

Gentle fingertips brushed over his spine, startling him, but the straps kept him firmly in place. He wiggled more, discovering his body's range of mobility. He had none.

"Oh…"

"Now you're beginning to get it," Stone said, sounding amused.

He walked behind Chris, and Chris strained to hear any hint of what would come next. He gasped when fingertips plucked at the waistband of his shorts. The thin fabric was peeled back and tucked in at the crease where his butt met his thighs. Cool air brushed his skin, drying sweat he hadn't been aware of and making him feel how exposed his rear end was to another man's whims. The shorts also trapped and bound his cock just as much as the rest of him.

———

Chris's skin was so beautiful and white as if it had never seen the sun, let alone the kiss of a flogger or paddle. It was a perfect canvas waiting to be decorated, and Daniel was eager to do so.

He took out the paddle he'd stored in his back pocket. The smooth, polished wood had warmed from where it had been waiting. Though he would much rather use his hand and give Chris a proper spanking, he wasn't ready to cross that line. He glided the paddle over Chris's bottom, making small circles with it.

"What—?"

"This is a paddle," Daniel answered. "We're going to see if

you like it. Depending on how much you do, you may not be sitting comfortably tomorrow."

Chris's ears turned pink. "Yes, Sir." He was so easy to read.

Daniel rubbed a little longer, listening to the boy's breathing to gauge how nervous he was. When the time felt right, he pulled back and swiftly brought the paddle down on one cheek.

"Oh!" As Daniel let the initial sensation sink in, Chris added, "That's not so bad."

"No, one isn't bad at all. I'm warming you up first."

He brought the paddle down on the other butt cheek. Chris didn't comment in the pause this time, so Daniel started a slow rhythm, as he'd said, warming the boy up evenly. He wouldn't hit Chris hard, but by the time he was done, the layer upon layer of blows would definitely have an effect.

He liked the idea of Chris thinking of him every time he sat down. He had to admit, there were a lot of things he enjoyed the thought of when it came to Chris.

Grunts accompanied each impact, and it wasn't long before they turned into soft moans as the heat spread and Chris's ass became more sensitive. His hips twitched in their bonds, and Daniel was sure Chris wanted to come. Daniel didn't want to push him into begging yet but continued for a few more blows before stopping. Chris remained braced for another impact for a moment. Then he exhaled and deflated on the bench. Daniel came around and sank his fingers into the boy's blond locks.

"That was very good, Chris. You did amazingly well."

Chris smiled, but Daniel stopped him when he tried to speak.

"No, just rest. That is all you need to do right now. Rest and feel."

He stood for a while, running his fingers through Chris's hair until the submissive began to doze. He put the paddle away and grabbed a tube of Arnica from the cabinet, along with a blanket and some water. The water he placed on the floor in front of Chris. He quickly undid the buckles and laid the blanket gently over the boy's upper body, leaving his rear end clear for Daniel to doctor.

A hiss and a moan greeted his efforts, and he chuckled. "You seemed to like your first paddling."

"Yes, Sir. I—"

"Talk but don't move, boy. I will slap your rump if you move before I tell you to."

Chris stilled. "It was intense. I always knew it would be intense, but I didn't… I didn't know *exactly* what it would be like, what kind of intensity."

"I'm guessing it was a good one."

"Oh, yes. Though next time…could you use your hand?"

The idea appealed to Daniel, but they had only agreed to the one scene. Doing anything more would be reckless. Still, he couldn't turn the request down flatly. "If you're a good boy, we'll see."

Chris was quiet as Daniel finished with the Arnica and drew the blanket down to cover the rest of his body. He appeared boneless but happy, and it made Daniel smile. The younger man would enjoy his week here, trying new things and learning about the scene. Daniel wanted to be the one to show him those wonders. When he thought of someone else in that position, his happiness turned sour. Could he be the one to show him? The idea went well beyond the line he'd set for his relationships with students, but perhaps he could bend the rules just this once? As he'd told Chris earlier, it wasn't against regulations to fraternize with students, only frowned upon.

"Drink up," he said, handing Chris the water and taking a seat on the floor beside him. "That was a simple scene, a taste, if you will, of what this lifestyle could offer you. There is a lot more than you'll be able to encounter in a week's vacation, but if you're interested in trying things out, I'm willing to offer you a broader introduction. Something that will give you enough experience that, when you come here in the future, you'll know what to ask for and where your limits may be. Would you be interested?"

As it was evidently forgotten, Daniel took the water bottle and placed it back on the floor before it spilled. Chris's eyes were glued to him, barely noticing the action.

"Yes. Yes, Sir, I would definitely be interested in that."

"Remember, there would be no sex involved. If that's something you're hoping for this week, you'll be sorely disappointed."

"That's okay! I don't mind at all."

Daniel's lips pursed into a frown. "Don't interrupt," he scolded. "I also do not do things by halves. If we are going to do this, you will be my sub for the week. That means exclusively mine. You will do as I say, when I say it, and you will not be doing anything with anyone else. The only other people involved in what we do will be people I bring in, if I so choose, and what we do will also be up to me, though I will be hearing more of your fantasies and ideas. I will not let this experience go to waste by not exploring something you want if we can do it, but the final decision on when, how, and if it happens is up to me, understand?"

"Yes, Sir," Chris said quietly.

"What's the matter?"

"Are you really going to bring other people in?"

"Depends on what we're doing. Have you ever had a fantasy that included exhibitionism?"

"I, uh..." Chris's face colored.

"When it comes to something like that, I would discuss with you first about what may or may not happen and who would be involved. No one will touch you if you don't want that. Part of the reason I'm putting an official claim on you for the week is so everyone will know they do not have permission to do anything to you unless I let them."

Chris exhaled and relaxed. "Oh. Okay."

"Do these terms satisfy you?"

The boy nodded. "Yes, Sir."

"Good." Daniel stood. "We'll discuss specifics tomorrow when your head isn't muddled by a recent paddling. Can you get up?"

Chris carefully pushed himself up from the bench, realizing too late that sitting on his heels was a mistake. He winced. "I think I can stand."

Daniel offered Chris a hand up, then wrapped the blanket around him. He smirked. "You might want to look in the mirror when you get back to your hotel."

An answering smile beamed at him. "I'm looking forward to it."

"By the way..." Daniel gestured with his chin toward Chris's crotch. It was covered by the blanket, but he knew there was an erection beneath the fabric. "You're not allowed to touch that tonight. Take a shower, but if I find you've come before I see you tomorrow, there will be consequences."

Chris's lips parted in surprise, but whatever protest he may have voiced remained unspoken.

"You're mine for the week. I may not be having sex with you, but I still own every part of you for the rest of this vacation. Your dick included. No coming without permission, Chris. Got it?"

The boy's cheeks had turned pink, but he was still beaming as he said, "Yes, Sir."

"Good boy. Did you bring clothes to go home with?"

"Yes."

"I do hope they're soft," Daniel teased. "Meet me at the bar here at eight tomorrow night. Don't forget to eat something before arriving."

"Yes, Sir."

"Good. Now, off with you before I spank you once for the fun of it."

Chris scampered off without any more prompting. As they parted, both men were still smiling.

<h1 style="text-align:center">TWO</h1>

Chris spent most of the following day remembering the events of the night before. He still couldn't believe Professor Stone had done a scene with him, and he practically vibrated with excitement over the fact there was more to come.

When it came time to get ready, he ran into a dilemma. He didn't know what to wear. Yesterday's shorts were filthy, and he didn't want to repeat himself anyway. Could he wear a pair of black jeans? What if Professor Stone was expecting something slutty like yesterday? He spent so much time worrying that he ran out of time to eat before he left. He grabbed his darkest jeans and the mesh shirt he'd once worn to a dance club and threw them on. He hoped a large fry from a nearby fast-food place would count as "eating something."

He arrived on time and found Stone sitting at a table in the main club room, finishing what appeared to be a delicious dinner. Chris licked his lips as the last of the meat loaf and potatoes disappeared into the other man's mouth. He wished he'd had more than french fries before arriving.

"I didn't know they served food here," he said as he approached the table.

Stone eyed him over the rim of a glass of water before answering. "Besides some light snacks and drinks, they serve dinner here from seven to eight. It gives the club an excuse to open earlier than other clubs in the area."

Chris figured the term "club" didn't refer to only the BDSM kind as there weren't that many around. He'd researched all those he could find within a reasonable traveling distance from the university. This one had struck him as the best choice since it was well-rated and far enough to keep him from bumping into anyone he knew. Except for Professor Stone apparently.

"I'm glad to see you're punctual." Stone pushed his empty plate away and sat back in his chair. He gestured for Chris to take a seat.

"I always try to be," Chris replied.

"Good. I don't like wasting my time waiting for boys who are late. Did you eat?"

"Some."

"What do you mean by 'some'?"

"I had some fries on my way over."

Stone frowned and gestured to a passing waiter. "Could you bring another plate of meat loaf and a glass of water, please?"

The waiter glanced at Chris before answering, "The kitchen is closed, but I can probably nuke something."

"Reheated leftovers will be fine."

With a nod, the waiter left.

There was a heavy silence after the server had gone. Finally, Stone spoke.

"When I tell you to do something, I expect my order to be followed to the best of your ability. Mistakes and inability are acceptable. They are a part of learning and growing. Half-heartedness is not. Do you understand?"

"Yes, Sir." Chris bit the inside of his cheek. How badly had he messed up? Would the scene be canceled for tonight? What about the rest of the vacation?

He needn't have worried. Having made his point, Stone

said, "Good," and slid a piece of paper across the table. "I want you to look at this and see if anything stands out."

"What is it?" Chris asked as he turned the paper over.

"It's called a checklist. We're not going to fill the form out completely, but I want to go over it with you. I need to know if there's anything you absolutely do not want to do or something you would really like to try. I figured the checklist might inspire you since it will likely mention things you've never considered."

He was right. As he scanned the list, Chris's eyebrows scrunched more and more.

"If there's anything you don't understand, let me know, and I'll tell you what it means."

"Like saran wrapping?"

"That's a form of mummification," Stone explained. "The saran is used to immobilize a person by wrapping their whole body in it."

"Why?"

"The arrangement gives the bound person a feeling of complete helplessness. It can also be coupled with sensory deprivation and sensation play."

Chris pursed his lips. "I'm not sure I'd like that."

"We can leave it off the list. You can always change your mind as you learn more about the scene and your limits and interests."

Chris, distracted by the possibility of a future with Professor Stone, missed his next question.

"I'm sorry, what?"

"Does anything else stand out?" Professor Stone repeated.

"Uh, I don't think watersports are going to be my thing."

Stone laughed. "Okay, what else?"

———

Daniel was patient and gentle as they worked over various things on the list, and gradually, Chris relaxed and opened to the conversation. By the time they were done, Chris had also finished the meat loaf Daniel had ordered.

"How do you feel about exhibitionism?"

"I would rather not get arrested for it," Chris said, and Daniel smirked.

"No, but if I were to flog you on the club stage in front of everyone, would you like that?"

"Maybe," Chris answered with a shrug.

Daniel leaned over, pitching his voice low. "What if I made you stand on that stage while I slowly peeled every inch of your clothing off your body and made you stand naked for an audience?"

Chris swallowed and shifted in his seat. His voice was slightly breathless as he repeated, "Maybe."

The thought turned Daniel on as well. He took a drink of water to cover the reaction. By now he had a solid grasp on where his temporary sub's interests lay and where they could work with his own. Their interests meshed very well, too well in some cases.

"We've established there will be no sex in our scenes," he said. "This includes intercourse, oral sex, and mutual masturbation, but you will often be naked for them. I will also use touch to stimulate a reaction from you at times. I need to know that, if at any time things become uncomfortable for you, you will tell me immediately. This does not mean everything will have to stop, but we will discuss what's happening and how to fix the problem. Everyone has limits, Chris, and it is our duty to respect them." Daniel wondered if he was reassuring his submissive or himself with this speech. "I want to give you an introduction to something I think you'll enjoy, but neither of us will have a good time if one of us is truly uncomfortable. Understand?"

Chris nodded.

"Good." He pushed back from the table and stood. "You can keep the list if you'd like, but now it's time for practice instead of theory."

The boy's face immediately brightened, and he abruptly stood, shoving the checklist into his jeans pocket. Daniel smiled as he picked up the bag of supplies he'd brought with him from his hotel and led the way to the private room he'd reserved for them.

Once they were alone, he hesitated. He'd already established nudity would be involved in their scenes. Might as well get them both used to it. "Strip," he ordered.

Chris blinked in surprise but proceeded to take off his clothes. Daniel's eyes were glued to the blond as he undressed. He'd looked forward to this, though he knew he shouldn't. He was sure this whole scenario would end up being a big mistake.

When Chris peered at him questioningly, jeans in hand, Daniel said, "You can put everything on that table there. Folded please."

Chris complied, leaving a neat pile of fabric where instructed and his shoes beneath the table. It was only after he faced Daniel that he blushed.

"No," Daniel said when Chris moved to cover his erection. "I want to see all of you." He swore the boy became harder after he said that.

"How is your ass feeling?" he asked as he walked a slow circle around the sub. Chris was perfection. His lean body was smooth, virtually flawless, except for a small scar on his left shoulder. Daniel wondered where it had come from. Chris was mostly hairless, and where hair adorned him, it was a dusting of pale-blond wisps that matched the nest of curls surrounding his eager, pink cock. Daniel's mouth watered at the sight of it.

"Fine, Sir," Chris answered.

For a moment, Daniel had to backtrack to remember his question. "Still sore?"

"Not too much."

"Good. Have you masturbated since you left here last night?"

"No, Sir."

"You didn't touch yourself at all?"

"Only a little to wash, Sir."

Daniel's mouth curved again. Chris was so honest.

"Have you ever played with your nipples, Chris?"

"Sir?"

"When you jerk off at home, do you ever play with your nipples for more sensation?"

"Sometimes, Sir."

"Are they sensitive?" As he asked, Daniel stepped close and rubbed his thumbs over the pert pink buds. Chris squirmed.

"Yes, Sir."

"Do you think you could come if I rubbed them like this?"

The boy turned crimson. "I'm not sure, Sir. I've never tried."

"Shall we find out?"

"If...if you'd like, Sir." Chris was leaning into his touch now, pushing against his thumbs for more sensation. Daniel stopped moving and let him go.

"I think we can find a more interesting way of doing this. Move to the center of the room, please."

While Chris did as he was told, Daniel released a thin rope from a cleat on the nearby wall. The line of the rope extended up to the ceiling and looped through a pulley above Chris's head. Once the ends hung next to Chris, Daniel pulled a pair of cuffs and a few other props from his bag. He hadn't known what he would need for the scene tonight, so he'd brought a bunch of options. With the idea he had in mind, he'd be able to use quite a few of them. He smiled as he returned to the waiting submissive. They had barely begun, and Daniel was already enjoying the scene. It had been way too long since he'd had time to indulge.

"Put your hands behind you."

Chris did as he was told, and Daniel buckled his wrists into the cuffs. The leather was soft, worn in, and the cuffs were held together by a clasp that could swiftly be undone if necessary but was out of reach for Chris.

"Do you see these?" Daniel asked, holding up a thin chain with small clamps at each end. The clamps had screws in them, and Daniel squeezed them open to show how they worked. "These are called nipple clamps. I am going to put them on you. I will not make them incredibly tight, but they will be intense. Remember to breathe."

Without waiting for a reply, he placed the first clamp on Chris's left nipple.

"Oh my god," Chris said.

"Here comes the second one."

The second made Chris's eyes roll back into his head, and his knees threatened to buckle. Daniel steadied him until he was sure Chris could stand on his own.

"Like that?" he asked.

A moan was Chris's only reply, but a sharp tug on one clamp refocused his attention. Daniel tied one end of the rope to the center of the chain, then took up the slack until it was lifted from Chris's chest. He pulled a little more to show Chris what it would feel like if the chain were pulled before relaxing it again.

Chris swallowed and closed his eyes. Daniel let him experience the sensation as he tied the free end of the rope to a small fishing weight. With his eyes on Chris, he lowered the weight until it pulled at the chain. Chris gasped. His eyes opened, and he watched as Daniel added a second and a third weight. The weights were light when held in a person's palm, but their combined pull on the tender buds turned Chris's moans to groans, and his hips wiggled. Satisfied with the effect of the setup, Daniel lifted the weights for the next step in the scene.

"Open your mouth," he ordered.

Chris did, and Daniel placed a stretch of rope between the boy's teeth.

"Bite. Good. Now, don't let go. You are the only thing

keeping the weights from dropping and pulling on those clamps, and if they fall, it won't be a gentle tug like last time."

Chris's jaw tightened around the rope.

"Good. Say red."

Chris struggled to figure out how to do that, but he eventually sounded the word "red" around the rope. The rope was thin enough the word came out clearly.

"Now say yellow."

"Yellow."

"Good. If you need to say those words at any time during the scene, I want to make sure I can hear them. Now..." Daniel's smile turned wicked. Oh, how he loved teasing a sub like this. "We're going to play a game. All you have to do is keep from dropping the weights. My job is to make you drop the weights. If I quit playing with you before you open your mouth, you win. If not, I do. We'll decide on the prizes later." The terms weren't fair, and the expression on Chris's face made it clear he didn't like them. Daniel grinned then headed to his bag.

"Let's see..." He selected a few toys and made sure to keep them out of sight as he returned.

He started with a feather duster. The touch was light and tickling, and it startled Chris, but beyond a hiss sucked between his teeth, the boy remained still. He moved the soft feathers from Chris's hip, along his lower back, and around to the front of him. He played them over Chris's stomach and danced them around his tortured nipples. Chris moaned, his hips rocking again. Daniel loved watching the struggle. A bead of liquid adorned the head of Chris's cock like a silent plea, but it was the one area he would not touch. He completed a circle around Chris, and once out of sight, he switched to something new.

The next sensation was sharper. Daniel walked the small, prickling spikes of a Wartenberg pinwheel across Chris's back, down over his buttocks, and behind each leg. He rolled the wheel over Chris's stomach and down his thighs, paying particular attention to the inside of them as that made the submissive squirm the most. At one point, he glided the sharp spikes over the sensitive skin of Chris's perineum, and the boy's moans turned to pleas. Chris's eyes were entreating as well. Daniel's smile only grew wider.

"You'll have to beg a lot more than that before I'm done with you."

He returned to his bag and rummaged again. He grabbed a roll of tape, some lube, and a vibrating plug. Kneeling behind Chris, he put the tape on the floor and spread some of the lube over the plug he'd chosen. It was a beginner plug. As Chris was new to all of this, Daniel thought it best to start small. Besides, it wasn't the size that would make the toy effective.

Once the plug was slick, he slid the tip of it up and down the crevice of Chris's ass, acquainting him with the new toy. At first Chris stiffened, but soon his hips were rocking as if trying to guide the plug to a specific place. Daniel slid the plug down and circled Chris's opening, steadily swirling but with no pressure.

A pleading groan escaped his submissive. "Please," he was sure the sound meant.

Daniel made him wait a little longer before dipping the tip of the plug into Chris's body. Chris gasped, and Daniel checked to see if the game was over, but no, the rope was still in place. He pushed a little harder, working the plug in and out in longer strokes each time.

It wasn't long before Chris's hips were moving in counterpoint, and the plug sank deeper until it was all the way in. Daniel pushed at the base to make sure it was properly seated then sat back to appraise his work. The plug was a light pink, a small tint against the creamy white of Chris's skin. His eyes followed the wire attached to the base down to the remote waiting patiently in his hand. He hit the first button.

"Oh!" The weights dropped slightly when Chris exclaimed, but he caught them before they could fall fully.

Disappointed by the recovery, Daniel pushed the second button, and the vibrations on the plug increased. Moans greeted this new pace, and Chris's hips made small circles as if trying to shift the plug deeper or to a place it couldn't quite reach.

Chris's struggle entranced Daniel. He could have watched for hours, but they were a long way from that level of play. Instead, he hit the third button, making the vibrations as fast as they could go before taping the remote to Chris's leg and moving around in front of him.

Chris's teeth were clenched tight around the rope, both to keep from dropping it and because of the struggle against pleasure. His moans had turned into grunts, and his cock leaked. Daniel was sorely tempted to lick the stray drops and taste his submissive, but that option was off the table. Instead, he admired the full picture he had created.

Chris panted, and his balls were pressed tight against his body. Drool had begun to slide from the corners of his mouth. He tried to wipe his mouth on his shoulder.

"Leave it," Daniel ordered. "You will not hide any sign of struggle from me."

Chris blushed, but he did as he was told.

Daniel brushed a hand over Chris's cheek. "Wonderful."

He pulled a single clamp from his pocket and held it up so Chris could see it. "I'm going to put this on you. I'm not going to tell you where, but after I do, I'll come around to take the rope from you. If you can keep from dropping the rope, you will have won. Understand?"

Chris nodded.

"Good. Now look at the ceiling for me. You will not look down until I tell you."

He waited until the order had been followed, then knelt to place the clamp against the tender skin behind Chris's balls. He let it close, and the boy cried out. A series of moans echoed from Chris as Daniel left the clamp in place and rose.

He was happy to see Chris still staring at the ceiling and the rope still in place. He took hold of it.

"Let go."

It took a moment for Chris to comply, having focused so hard on keeping his jaw shut. His teeth parted, and Daniel took the rope from between his lips. He slowly let the weights lower, gingerly adding their pressure to the clamps on Chris's nipples.

"Oh..." Chris moaned. "Please. Please, I can't take it anymore."

Daniel caressed Chris's damp skin as he moved behind his submissive. He stepped close but kept his own straining erection away from Chris's bound hands. He stroked the sides of Chris's body and reached around to the clamps on both nipples.

"This will hurt when I take them off. The blood will return, and the sensation will be overwhelming." He couldn't resist kissing the boy's neck as he added, "If you come from this, it will please me greatly."

Without waiting for a reply, he opened the clamps and let them swing free. Chris screamed as blood returned to his nipples. Daniel gently rubbed the tender skin. He teased Chris to a series of pleas, groans, and wiggling hips. Before either of them expected it, Chris's body spasmed and come shot across the room, decorating the floor in pearly ropes of white.

He collapsed against Daniel, spent and boneless. Daniel lifted him up and laid him on the table. Turning him, Daniel unhooked the cuffs and removed the last clamp. He lowered the speed on the vibrator to medium, then, after a moment, to soft. Finally, he turned it off, though he left the plug where it was.

He covered Chris with a blanket and prepared to wait until his submissive was ready to return to the present world and his Dominant's care.

Chris was floating, and a gentle hum thrummed through his body. He relaxed into the sensation and let himself be carried along by it for a while. Eventually, the buzz faded, and he returned to earth. He opened his eyes and found he was lying on the hard surface of a table. A warm blanket covered him, and soothing hands ran through his hair.

"Welcome back."

Chris shifted, but the hands pushed against his shoulders and kept him lying down.

"There's no reason to get up. Relax and enjoy the moment."

Chris did, though he needed to ask, "I came, didn't I?"

"Did you forget?" Professor Stone asked wryly.

"No, I just…thought it might've been a dream. I've never come like that." He shifted, and something poked inside him. "I—"

"The plug is still inside you. I will be exchanging it for another without a remote attached, but I'd like you to remain plugged for the rest of the evening. The cuffs will stay on as well."

Chris moved one of his hands and noticed the cuffs were, indeed, still buckled around his wrists.

"Why?" he asked.

"To remind you that you belong to me. And because it pleases me to think of you struggling with something in your ass while you do mundane things."

"Do you often leave things in your sub's asses throughout the day?"

There was a moment of silence before Stone answered. "On occasion. There are also chastity belts, which I have used, cock rings, and other such implements. I do like leaving something on my sub at all times. It's one of my kinks."

Chris could get used to that, and he realized, for at least a week, he was the one Professor Stone would be leaving things on.

"How are you feeling?"

"I'm okay. Feeling more rested and able to stand on my feet again."

"Before you do that, turn and lie on your back." Stone moved to his bag as Chris did as he was told. He returned with lube and a small white plug.

"I'm keeping things small for now as this is new for you, but don't think that means you won't feel it." He folded the blanket back from Chris's legs. Again, Chris felt exposed and vulnerable with only his chest covered by the blanket. Stone maneuvered his legs and placed his feet flat on the tabletop.

He carefully removed the tape from Chris's leg and slid the vibrator out. Chris felt surprisingly empty once it was removed, but the touch of cool lubricant and the new plug soon replaced it. Stone slapped Chris on the thigh. "Okay, time to get up."

"What now?"

"Now we're going to get something to drink."

Chris lowered his feet to the floor. The plug felt weird as it shifted with his movements, always reminding him of its presence. He wrapped the blanket around himself as he stood, wondering if he should dress or if Stone wanted something else from him. Stone appeared to be wondering the same thing.

"Just your jeans," he said. "We'll put the rest with the coat check. It should be safe there."

Chris grabbed his pants. Bending to put them on was an experience with the plug inside him. Stone chuckled before asking, "Have you ever had a plug inside you before?"

"No. I bought one but never got around to trying it."

"Why not?"

"Too afraid of someone walking in on me. My roommate runs on sporadic hours, and I don't feel comfortable doing it when he's home. He doesn't always knock before barging into my room."

"You could always try it in the shower. Sneak some lube in with you, and you'll have all the privacy you need. Unless, of course, your roommate walks in on you there as well?" Stone raised an eyebrow with the question.

"He doesn't."

"The shower it is, then. When you return to your dorm after vacation, try it. Play with it and see what you like. You can also try wearing it under your clothes like you're going to do now, but you'll need to be aware of what lube you're using and how long it will last if you do that. We can talk about that later if you have questions. For now, let's see if there's anything going on in the main room. Ready?"

Chris quickly zipped up his jeans, grabbed the rest of his clothing, and nodded.

Stone led the way from the room and down the hall to the coat check where they dropped off the unnecessary clothing. Back in the main room, Stone took a seat at a table and gestured for Chris to kneel on the floor next to his chair. He leaned over to speak quietly to Chris. "We'll be here for a while. As this is your first time kneeling for me, you're going to do your best not to fidget. It will be uncomfortable, and your feet will probably fall asleep, but I expect you to do your best. If it truly becomes too much, you will let me know."

"Yes, Sir."

"Good boy." Stone relaxed in his chair, turning his attention to the rest of the room. He called over one of the house subs to order a bottle of water with a straw and a cup of decaf coffee. When the drinks were delivered, he opened the bottle and slid the straw inside. Turning to Chris, he instructed, "Back straight, please. Hands clasped behind you. Yes, like that, and you might want to uncross your feet." He lowered the bottle so Chris could take a drink before setting it back on the table.

"So, what do you want as your reward?"

Chris blinked. "What?"

"Your reward. You won our game, and I said you would get a prize. What would you like?"

Chris thought about it for a minute. He didn't know what he could and couldn't ask for, so he went with the first thing to pop into his head. "Ice cream."

"Excuse me?"

Chris flushed red and looked down at the floor. "Ice cream," he whispered.

He wasn't sure if Stone heard him, but the man read his mind anyway.

"Ice cream. Well, that's not what I expected, but it's certainly doable. Do you have any particular kind in mind? Are we talking about a sundae run or something from the supermarket?"

"Chocolate chip, please, but that's all I have in mind."

"Ice cream… I'll have to see where we can get some."

He gestured toward the center of the room where two men were getting ready to put on a demo. From the amount of rope coiled on the table next to them, Chris guessed it would be a rope bondage demonstration, but he had a hard time concentrating on the presentation when Stone appeared so deep in thought.

"If I decide to quiz you on this, you'll be in trouble if you don't pay attention."

Immediately, Chris's eyes snapped back to the demo. He didn't think he'd be tested, but he couldn't be sure. He didn't want to take the chance of displeasing Professor Stone again. As the exhibition continued, he was easily pulled into it. The complicated knots and patterns were fascinating.

He barely registered when Stone called over the house sub again and whispered in his ear for a while. The waiter nodded, then left. Chris found it curious when he didn't return, but it wasn't his job to worry. Instead, he wondered if Professor Stone would ever tie him up like the guy on stage. He hoped the answer was yes.

THREE

After the demo, Professor Stone led the way into another private room. As soon as the door closed behind them, he ordered, "Strip." He didn't wait to see if Chris would comply. As Chris removed his jeans, Stone took a stool from the corner of the room and moved it to the center.

"Place your jeans, folded, on the table over there; then come here."

Chris did as he was told. Stone turned him around and pressed on the back of his neck until he bent over and rested his chest on the stool. Chris bit his lip, thinking of all the possibilities the position could be used for.

"I see you enjoyed the demo." Stone's voice was low and seductive in his ear.

There was warmth at his back, and Chris imagined the man leaning over him. His cock twitched, making his erection bob against his stomach. "Yes, Sir."

He felt pressure against his hole and gasped when the plug inside him rubbed over his prostate in eye-rollingly delicious ways. He moaned.

There was a chuckle against his ear. "You seemed to like this as well. We'll have to play with it more another day."

Chris let out a whimper when the plug was removed. He hadn't expected the feeling of emptiness to be so strong.

"Stand up."

Chris did, trying to hide his frown, but the other man caught it. He caressed the side of Chris's face.

"You're mine to do with as I please. I get to fill you, and I get to keep you empty. Both of those sensations are reminders of me. Understand?"

Chris nodded.

"Good. Take a seat on the stool. You can hook your feet if it will make you feel more secure. You need to be balanced without your hands."

Chris hopped up on the stool and shifted until he felt steady. Once he was in place, Stone took his hands and connected the cuffs behind his back. Though he hadn't moved, Chris hooked his feet, as suggested, for extra security.

"How are you feeling?"

"Steady, Sir."

"And your body? Everything feels fine?"

"Yes, Sir."

"How about these?" Stone teased Chris's nipples, and Chris squirmed on the stool.

"Uh." Chris searched for words in his uncooperative brain.

The tease turned into a pinch. "Well?"

"F-fine, Sir," Chris said, his hips rocking from the sensations as they continued.

"They still seem a bit sensitive."

"Y-yes, Sir."

"I'd say your nipples are wired straight down to your cock, but we know that already since you came from me teasing them earlier today."

Chris nodded.

"I wonder if you can do that again," Stone mused.

A knock at the door interrupted them, and the teasing stopped.

"Don't move."

As Professor Stone answered the door, Chris wondered if he would let the person in. He bit his lip and hoped they would remain alone.

Stone didn't take long. He opened the door, said, "Ah, thank you," and closed it again. When he turned to Chris, he held an ice cream cone.

"Chocolate chip, as requested."

Chris's worry vanished, and he smiled. "You bought me ice cream."

The older man laughed. "You asked for it."

"Yeah, but…"

Stone lifted Chris's chin with a finger. "If you deserve a reward, I will give it to you, and if I ask you what you want, you'll get it."

"Yes, Sir," Chris whispered. "But how will I eat my prize with my hands behind my back?"

Stone's lips curved into a wicked smile. "Just because it's your reward doesn't mean I can't enjoy it too." He held out the cone. "Don't miss a drop now."

Professor Stone planned to feed him the ice cream? Chris leaned forward and took a tentative lick.

"If that's how you eat ice cream, it'll end up on the floor before you're finished. Don't think I'm letting any drop be wasted."

Given all the things that could have happened in the room before they'd entered, Chris wasn't taking any chances. Catching sight of a stray drop, he hastily leaned forward to catch it on his tongue. He took a long lick up the side of the ice cream, filling his mouth with the delicious taste of vanilla.

He swallowed and asked, "You're enjoying this?"

The man laughed again, and his eyes made a pointed voyage down and back up Chris's body. "Absolutely."

Chris's face heated, and he resumed eating the ice cream. He licked a few more times to keep the treat from dripping. He returned his attention to Stone as he chewed a few chips.

The man's eyes were locked on Chris's mouth. Swallowing, he kept watching as he leaned forward to lick again. He moved slowly, and Stone tracked him the whole way.

Curious, Chris looked down as he sat back to swallow again. Professor Stone was hard. Wanting to please the man more, he took his time leaning forward again. He teased the ice cream before taking some on his tongue to eat. A grunt of approval came as the result of this performance.

"You've missed some."

Chris furrowed his brow. Nothing was amiss. Then he saw it. He'd neglected the other side of the cone, and the ice cream now dripped over the back of Stone's hand.

"I suggest taking care of this if you don't want to eat it off the floor tonight."

Chris was more than happy to do so. He leaned forward once again and took a long swipe. His taste buds exploded with the flavor of vanilla and Professor Stone. With a soft moan, he didn't bother to sit up but set about cleaning the rest of the man's hand. Next time he was granted a reward, he'd ask for Professor Stone's body covered in ice cream. He'd love to lick the creamy sweetness off every inch of him.

"You seem to be enjoying yourself."

Chris nodded as he licked his lips, chasing stray drops to savor every moment of this newly improved treat. "Yes, Sir. Would you like some?"

"Perhaps later. You enjoy it for now."

Chris returned to licking the cone. He enjoyed himself so much he startled when Stone dipped his finger into the ice cream. The digit slid into the other man's mouth, and Chris whimpered. The next scoop was held toward Chris, and he didn't hesitate to open his mouth and wrap his lips around the treat. Once he'd captured the finger, he was sure to suck any trace of ice cream clean before letting it go again.

"Your mouth is sin on an angel's face," Stone said as he fed Chris more ice cream. In answer, Chris teased the digit with his tongue as if it were an ice-cream-covered cock instead of a finger. He lost himself in the fantasy, making love with his mouth until the touch of cold on his thigh startled him into opening his eyes. A drop of ice cream had fallen on his leg.

"You better clean this up before the next one is on the floor," Stone advised.

Chris licked the rebel drops that threatened to fall from the cone. Stone swiped his finger over the one that had fallen and held it out to Chris. His hand had been *so close* yet so far from Chris's cock that Chris began to ache with need. Before he knew it, the word slipped from his mouth. *"Please."*

The finger remained steady in front of his face. "No."

Chris closed his eyes. He wanted to fall to his knees for a true taste of the man in front of him, not this ice-cream-covered tease. He felt cold at his lips and licked obediently, but the ice cream didn't concern him anymore. He wanted something else entirely.

"Please." It came out as a whisper.

The ice cream vanished from his mouth. "Look at me, Chris," Stone ordered.

Reluctantly, Chris opened his eyes.

"The only thing either of us will eat tonight is this ice cream. Do you understand me?"

Chris grudgingly nodded. "Yes, Sir."

"Good."

The ice cream returned, and Chris dutifully licked at it. He preferred the moments when Stone fed him directly, instead of when he licked at the cone. He savored the fingers when they were offered. Still, a seed had been planted, and despite the agreement of no sex for the week, Chris decided he would somehow find a way to have Professor Stone's cock between his lips before the vacation ended.

———

"You did well," Daniel said. "Not a drop on the floor."

Chris licked his mouth clean. "Thank you, Sir."

Daniel kept space between them as he unclasped the cuffs, but he paused before removing them.

"Where are you staying?" he asked.

"In a hotel right down the road," Chris replied. "The uh…"

"The Morton?"

"Yes."

"Good. I'm in room 203. We'll head there tonight, and I'll put a different pair of cuffs on you. They'll stay on for the rest of the week. In fact, I'll collect you from your room each night in case I need you to wear anything specific before we get here, and we can carpool to the club together."

"Yes, Sir. I'm in room 245."

Daniel unbuckled the cuffs. He could have left them on. The only difference between them and the ones he had in mind were the color, but the blue ones he'd removed were the ones he used for scenes with strangers. The red ones he would use on a submissive of his own.

He'd promised that he'd be Chris's Dominant for the week. He should treat him accordingly. That's why he was switching to the red cuffs. It didn't mean anything more than that.

That's what he told himself as he took hold of Chris's wrist, trying to ignore the feeling of wrongness he got at the sight of uninterrupted skin. "We'll fix this when we get to the hotel." He let go and put the cuffs on the table next to the plug to be disinfected. "Go get dressed."

The faster they got out of there, the sooner he could put his real mark on Chris.

———

That night as he lay in bed, Daniel replayed the scenes from the evening in his mind. Chris was so beautiful, so responsive. He was dangerous. Daniel had come way too close to giving in to the boy's begging. He'd practically felt those luscious lips around his cock and ached from the need of it.

Even the simple act of putting his cuffs on Chris when they'd arrived at the hotel had been torture. The strips of red-and-black leather fit him so perfectly. Daniel had no idea how he'd convince himself to remove them when the week was over.

One thing he was sure of, there was no backing out now. He couldn't stand the thought of Chris submitting to someone else, and he couldn't imagine finding someone else to play with while he was here. He supposed if they did this, they might as well go all the way. Within the limitations of their agreement, of course. He'd told Chris he didn't do things half-heartedly.

Daniel smiled as an idea came to him. He was still smiling as he fell asleep thinking of Chris and tomorrow.

FOUR

The next morning, Professor Stone called to tell Chris he would meet him at his room in one hour. Chris had showered but waited for him to show before getting dressed. When he opened the door in nothing but a towel, he thought Stone looked pleased.

"Where are the clothes you have with you?"

"I put them in those two drawers."

Stone opened the indicated drawers and rifled through Chris's clothing. His lips pursed; then he drew himself up without selecting anything.

"What do you say about doing a scene outside of the club?"

"Sir?" Chris asked.

"There's more to this town than a kink club. And even if you're not in the club, things can still be kinky. Would you like to see what it's like to play in an everyday setting?"

That could be fun, but would Chris have to do things like laundry or—god help him—cook? He wasn't into domestic submission. "What would that entail?"

"There's a deli down the block that makes fantastic sandwiches. We'll stop there for breakfast, then do a little shopping. Afterward, I'm thinking we could catch a movie and maybe take a hike if the weather stays nice. For dinner, we can return to the club and see what else we'd like to do for the evening. What say you?"

Chris was relieved chores weren't on the list, and he was happy to spend the day with Professor Stone, but the plan didn't sound very kinky. He couldn't help feeling disappointed. The more he thought about it, the more it sounded like a date. When he thought about it that way, the disappointment vanished.

"Okay."

"Now if there's anything that makes you feel uncomfortable, you will speak up. You still have your words, and I expect you to use them if necessary. I won't get offended, nor will it ruin the rest of the vacation. Understand?"

The topic of safewords confused Chris, but he answered, "Yes, Sir."

"Good. Now, slip on a pair of jeans and a shirt. No underwear and bring a jacket in case it gets chilly. I need to get a few things from my room. Meet me there when you're done." And with that, Stone left.

Chris was still baffled by the plans for the day, but he did as he was told. He shoved his wallet into his back pocket before grabbing his jacket and room key and heading over to room 203. He knocked politely and entered after he heard, "Come in."

Professor Stone was rummaging through an open suitcase on the bed when Chris entered. "Come here," he ordered without looking up. "Drop your pants and lean over the duvet."

The command rushed straight to Chris's cock. Maybe this wouldn't be an ordinary day after all. He moved to stand next to Stone and unbuttoned his jeans. Letting them fall around his ankles, he braced himself against the bed and leaned over. Cool, lubricated fingers worked quickly to relax and stretch him; then something blunt eased into his hole.

"This plug is bigger than the last one," Chris said with a grunt.

"Yes."

Chris clenched his teeth to keep from moaning when Stone jostled the plug to make sure it was seated properly.

"Do you think you'll need a cock ring?"

"A what—?" Chris choked on the question. "Why would I need one of those?"

"To keep from coming until I tell you to. You'll be sporting an erection either way, I'm sure."

"Uh…"

"I'll keep one in my pocket in case we decide to use it later. Stand up and button your pants."

Chris did as he was told. The rough fabric of his jeans was hell when it came to calming his erection.

Stone zipped up the suitcase, locked the tabs together, and set it in the narrow space between the bed and the wall. When he turned to Chris, he said, "Wrists, please," and swiftly checked the fit of Chris's cuffs.

Chris loved the feeling of having them on. They had comforted him like a security blanket while he slept, reminding him of Stone's claim on him even when they were apart.

"These will stay on all day. They'll be mostly hidden by your sleeves, but you'll be in public with them and people may see them. Do you think you can handle that?"

Chris caressed the leather. An involuntary twitch reminded him about the plug in his ass and his lack of under-wear. He would feel this way for the entire day and *in public.* His pulse raced, but his erection grew even harder.

"Yes, Sir."

Stone grabbed his coat and wallet. "Come along then. We'll take my car. No sense in walking to the deli if we're going shopping afterward."

———

Despite all the preparation, breakfast was perfectly ordinary —if eating an omelet across from a sexy Dominant in a room full of people while there was a plug up his ass and cuffs on his wrists could be called ordinary. Had anyone noticed the "bracelets" on his wrists weren't really bracelets or that he sat cautiously and wiggled his butt occasionally in his seat?

"Looking like a paranoid conspiracy theorist will get you more attention than those cuffs will," Professor Stone said casually before biting into his ham and cheese sandwich.

"What if someone sees?" Chris whispered.

"Would that be a problem?" Stone leaned forward, his eyes locked on Chris's. The intensity and possession in his gaze made Chris's heartbeat quicken. "Those cuffs state that you belong to me while you wear them. I could rip your sleeves off for the world to see them if I wanted."

Chris's heart instantly raced even faster, and his balls throbbed. He would love to be Professor Stone's, to have the man show the world Chris belonged to him in any way he wanted. He touched one of the cuffs with his fingers, realizing he already did belong to him, though only for the week. The time limit saddened him, and he sank back into eating his breakfast.

"Do you have a problem with me showing you off?"

Chris swallowed. "No, Sir."

"If I told you to take off your shirt right now, would you do it?"

Chris flushed at the question. He nodded. "Yes, Sir."

"You belong to me right now, Chris," Stone said. "Anything that happens to you will be because I want it to. No one will touch you or do anything to you unless I allow it, even you. Doing what you're told is all you have to worry about. Do you understand?"

"Yes, Sir."

"Good. Now, stop looking at the other patrons and eat your breakfast. I want to get going in the next ten minutes."

"Yes, Sir," Chris said again and continued eating his eggs.

Chris hadn't had any idea what the shopping part of their day might entail. Part of him had hoped, even though it was early in the day, they would go to some kinky store for toys, but for all he knew, that was just as likely as shopping for toothpaste.

What he hadn't expected was for Professor Stone to do school errands with him in tow. There were a few supplies the instructor needed for the rest of the semester, and he utilized this opportunity to be productive. Chris was disappointed in the turn of events, but feeling like Stone wouldn't have noticed at all if he hadn't been there was worse. He followed silently as the man searched the store for what he needed, and Stone seemed content to let Chris become invisible.

After the office supply store, they went to a nearby mall. Stone said he wanted to pick up a new suit, but they would also browse. Chris expected to be neglected like before, but as they window-shopped, Stone asked for his opinion and prompted conversation. Chris was bewildered by the contrast between the prep they'd done that morning and the ordinariness of what they did now. He didn't complain. Spending time with the man gave him pleasure. He even thrilled when Stone chose a few of the things Chris pointed out to him. He couldn't wait to see the professor on campus in his new tie and know he'd purchased it after Chris had said it looked good on him.

Chris followed Stone's lead through the mall. He never suggested where to go or pointed out something to look at unless he thought Stone would like it. He did his best not to get carried away with shopping for himself, but when he caught sight of one of his favorite stores, he couldn't help stopping in front of the window.

"Would you like to go in?"

"Oh, we don't..."

Stone didn't wait for him to finish. He grabbed hold of

Chris's wrist and pulled him inside. They explored leisurely. Chris tried not to notice too much, lest he be tempted to try something on, but Stone wouldn't have it. He aimed for a rack with items from the window display and thumbed through them.

"What size are you?"

"Uh, small."

Stone selected something off the rack. "Well, look around. No sense coming in here if you're not going to try anything on."

Chris selected a few things, but sensing his hesitancy, Stone pushed him to add more until he understood it was okay to truly go shopping. By the time they headed to the changing room, both men's arms were full of clothes.

"Favorite store, I take it?"

Chris blushed. "Yeah."

They deposited the clothing in a fitting room, and Chris was left alone to change. It wasn't until he unzipped his pants that he remembered he didn't have any underwear on. He couldn't try on clothing without underwear. What if he didn't buy them? He'd have to put the clothing back on the rack, and someone else might try them on after him. He frantically tried to remember if there was an underwear store nearby. If he bought something to wear just for trying on the clothes, that would be okay.

"You didn't get buried under that mound of clothing, did you?" Stone's voice cut across Chris's thoughts.

"N-no, Sir."

"Then what's the problem?"

"I..." Chris tried to remember if there was anyone else in the changing room or if anyone had come in while he'd been thinking. He wasn't sure, so he bit his lip, not wanting to say his concerns aloud.

"Change into the clothes, Chris," Stone ordered. "We have a movie to get to."

"But, Sir, I..."

"Now."

Unable to defy that tone of voice, Chris continued changing. He could always buy the one outfit and refuse to try on the rest. Once dressed, he unlatched the door to his stall and stepped out. He headed for the three-way mirror at the end of the room. Stone sat in a chair next to it.

"That looks good on you," he said. "Fits well enough, but I think there are a couple that will be better."

"P—Sir, I..." Chris stepped close and lowered his voice to a whisper. "I'm not wearing any underwear."

"I know." Stone's voice was matter-of-fact and in no way a whisper.

"But...these clothes..."

"Try them all on, Chris. No exceptions."

Chris swallowed. "Yes, Sir." He turned and headed into the stall for the next outfit.

As Chris worked through the clothes, he found himself walking toward the mirror more to model them for Stone's pleasure than to check and see if they fit. The lack of a barrier between his body and the clothing made him feel naughty, and Stone's intense stare only made wearing each progressive outfit worse than the one before it. He ached by the last time he came out of the stall and found the chair next to the mirrors empty. He froze, not knowing what to do, or where the other man might have gone. He walked toward the mirrors as if going through the motions would magically make Stone appear. It didn't.

In the mirror he saw the nervousness on his face, but he was soon distracted by the outfit he was wearing. The ensemble was mostly made up of Stone's suggestions. They weren't his usual style, but they looked good on him and fit comfortably. He'd just turned to see how the jeans fit his ass when he caught sight of movement behind him in the reflection. He whirled and came face-to-face with Professor Stone.

"I didn't know where you went," he said lamely.

Stone held up a piece of clothing. It was a light-tan color

and appeared to be creamy soft. He stepped forward, reaching around Chris to help him slip on the jacket. Though he didn't touch any part of Chris directly, the smooth movement of the fabric over Chris's arms and the way he took the time to fix the collar and make everything lay correctly had Chris panting for breath.

"Sir. I'd rather not come in unpurchased pants."

"If you can come from this alone, I'll buy you the pants and anything else you want in this store."

A small noise escaped Chris's lips.

They turned to face the mirror. The jacket looked great and completed the outfit, but Chris's attention was fixed on the heat of the man behind him and the look in his eyes reflected in the mirror.

"I would fuck you right here and now if I could," Stone whispered in his ear.

Chris whimpered. He wanted to beg him to do so. Screw the rules. He hadn't wanted them in the first place, but if he complained, the moment would be over.

"Keep talking like that, Sir, and one of us will definitely purchase these pants," he said instead.

Stone chuckled against his neck. "Is that so?"

Chris jumped when hands fumbled at the button of the slacks. His eyes grew wide as Stone pull the zipper down. He moaned at the thought of Professor Stone taking hold of his cock. The idea was strong enough he didn't care when the man didn't. Instead, Stone caressed his ass, sliding his hand over Chris's skin, between his cheeks, and to the base of the plug Chris couldn't believe he'd forgotten about. Chris's knees weakened as the plug twisted inside him.

"Hold your pants up."

Chris grasped the fabric as Stone walked them backward into the tiny changing stall while still playing with the plug. When the door closed behind them, Stone ordered, "Hands against the wall and lean forward."

Chris did as he was told, letting the pants fall to his knees.

"Farther."

Chris leaned over more.

With another twist, the plug steadily withdrew from his ass. Chris whimpered, his butt feeling horribly empty. He gasped at the sound of a packet tearing. He ached for nothing more than the other man filling him with his cock. He held his breath and waited. Warm, lubed fingers circled his entrance before sliding in the stretched hole. They worked within him, getting him wet, then withdrew. A blunt object pressed against him, but it was only the plug again, re-lubed and settled back into place.

"Disappointed?"

"A little," Chris admitted.

"The day is nowhere near over. You might not get what you were imagining, but I don't think you'll be disappointed for long." A sharp slap on his butt followed. "Get dressed. Pick what you want from the pile—and don't worry about come stains—then meet me outside the dressing room. It's time to get a move on or we'll miss the movie."

Stone didn't let Chris pay for anything and insisted he pick out everything he wanted and not hold back. The bill was bigger than Chris normally would have gone for, but he couldn't argue with Professor Stone or lie to him. He also made sure the jacket Stone had picked for him was in the purchase pile along with the outfit that went with it. After the clothing was bagged and paid for, they returned to the car and headed toward the theater. Chris had no idea what was playing nor what kind of movies Stone watched, but he wasn't given a chance to worry as he was immediately sent off to get their snacks.

"Go buy us a bag of popcorn while I get the tickets. Nothing too big and no salt."

"What about butter?"

"Feel free, but if my hands get too greasy, I will not be pleased."

Stone handed him money and gave him a look when

Chris tried to protest. After returning the look with one of his own, he scampered off to buy the popcorn, vowing to find a way to return the favor. He bought the medium-sized popcorn, figuring it would be enough to share without being too greedy. He skipped the butter even though he wanted some. Greasy fingers and Professor Stone didn't match in his mind. By the time he had received his purchase, the other man was waiting for him.

"This okay?"

"That's fine. We're in theater three."

When they entered the theater, it was mostly empty. Stone chose a seat in the middle, and they had the area to themselves. Chris took a seat next to him and set the popcorn between them.

"Do you come to the movies much?" he asked.

"Not really, no. I don't have time for them lately, though I used to go often. A friend of mine always came with me."

"Why don't you go with them anymore?" Chris asked.

Stone's jaw tightened. "It was before I moved here," he said. Chris let the matter drop.

When the previews began, Stone took the bag of popcorn and settled it in his lap. Chris didn't think that was fair and didn't feel right reaching for it when the bag was practically between the other man's legs. After fuming for a few moments while he waited to see if the bag would be returned, he asked, "May I have some, Sir?"

Stone dug his hand in the bag and held some kernels out to Chris on his palm. When Chris went to take them, the hand closed.

"Put your hands on the armrests of the chair. You are not to move them until the movie is over."

Chris's lips parted in surprise. "But how—" He stopped short when Stone raised an eyebrow at him. Slowly closing his mouth, he placed his hands where directed. Once they were in place, Stone opened his hand, and the popcorn was revealed.

"How am I..." Chris's voice trailed off. Stone's hand was high enough for him to lean over and reach the popcorn with his mouth. Licking his lips in anticipation, he leaned forward, catching a few kernels with his lips and teeth, careful not to bite any skin while doing so. He chewed and swallowed, then collected the remaining kernels. When the hand hadn't moved after he finished eating his treat, he set about cleaning the salty taste of popcorn from Stone's palm. By the time he sat up, the movie was beginning. He settled in to watch the film, a smile on his face.

It was an action film. Chris forgot the name as soon as it started, but he got drawn into the adrenaline rush that usually came with films featuring big explosions and car chases. After a while, he noticed he was squirming in his seat more than usual. It took him a moment to figure out why.

A low hum of vibration was running through him, and it had nothing to do with the movie on the screen. The plug inside him was vibrating. The vibration increased, and he gasped, clutching the armrests of his seat. He strained to hear if the sound was audible to anyone else in the theater or if it was his imagination that made it so loud. Warm air by his ear distracted him, followed by Professor Stone's voice, the pitch low, a match to the sensation drumming into his ass.

"No one is watching you. No one can hear it. The only ones who know are you and me, so sit back and enjoy the ride, boy. I am going to have you moaning in this seat before the movie is halfway done."

Chris's eyes rolled back in his head, and he groaned. He clamped his teeth shut to stifle the noise. Stone chuckled in his ear before returning his attention to the screen. Chris tried to concentrate on the action, but the plug had somehow found his prostate and played an unyielding rhythm upon it. He shifted, trying to lessen the sensation. That only made his jeans rub against his cock, emphasizing how hard he was.

He froze, not wanting to come in his pants like an adolescent who'd just hit puberty. Stone's eyes were on the screen, but the curve of the man's lips gave away his enjoyment of Chris's predicament. When the vibration of the plug changed to a pulse of varying strengths, that curve broadened.

Chris closed his eyes and inhaled deeply, trying to calm down, but it was difficult. It became even worse when Professor Stone's hand came to rest on his knee. The action was the least sexual thing the other man could have done, but the heat of his skin soaked through the fabric of Chris's jeans. The sensation shot straight up to Chris's cock. A moan escaped Chris, and he collapsed into his chair in surrender. He barely registered the movie as he watched through heavily drooping eyes, trying not to move beyond the occasional soft moan or rocking hip.

Throughout the film Stone changed the strength of the vibration, sometimes soft, sometimes hard, and sometimes varied, and each change would have Chris startling in his seat, breath coming faster. The film was forgotten as was the popcorn, and when the credits rolled and the lights came up, Chris was a ball of nerves, his cock rock-hard and aching, and sweat dampened his skin.

"Put on your jacket," Stone ordered, rising from his seat.

"But… I…" Chris was afraid to move. If he moved, he'd come. The vibration had stopped, but the effects of the toy had long since made an impact.

In a flash, Stone reached between Chris's legs and squeezed. Chris yelped from the pain, but it made his erection subside enough for him to comply. He slipped on his jacket, and they left the theater through a side door. Chris was grateful for the choice of exit. He didn't want other people seeing him walk funny.

He was still panting as they got in the car. Stone drove them toward the outskirts of the city.

"Drink some water," he instructed, handing Chris a bottle he'd purchased from a vending machine as they left. Chris did as he was told, but what he really wanted was to relieve the ache in his throbbing cock.

"Keep your knees apart," Stone ordered as Chris squirmed to find a position on the seat that was at all comfortable. He spread his knees, hoping something would come of it, but nothing more happened.

He turned his attention out the window. Perhaps the growing density of the surrounding foliage could, in some way, distract him.

When they had left the city behind and were fully driving through the woods, Professor Stone spoke again. "Open your pants and take your cock out."

"What?" Chris asked, surprised by the order.

"The windows are tinted, and there's no one around. I want your cock on display for me."

Chris's dick jumped in eagerness. He popped the button on his jeans and lowered the zipper. He pushed his pants down slightly and lifted his cock and balls out of the fabric. With his cock framed by the edges of his pants, he felt very on display and only ached more.

Stone never took his eyes from the road, but Chris saw the approval on his face.

Chris assumed no more touching would be allowed and returned his hands to his sides and his attention to the scenery out the window. Still, his mind kept returning to his exposed member. Every brush of air against his skin reminded him of how naughty he was. A drop of liquid gathered at the tip from the sensations, and he squirmed in his seat again. He wasn't sure if he'd like being on display for other people, but being so exposed yet safely alone with Professor Stone couldn't have been hotter.

Sadly, the car pulled to a stop in a dirt parking lot. The place was obviously meant for hiking which meant other people could be around and his clothing would have to be put back into order.

As if he knew what Chris was thinking, Stone said, "Don't move," before turning off the car and getting out. He came around to Chris's side of the car, opened the door, and leaned in to unbuckle Chris.

"Come out."

"But—"

"There's no one here. Stop doubting me and get your ass out of the car."

Chris did as he was told and found himself trapped between the car and Professor Stone's solid body. Stone closed and locked the doors. Keeping his body close, he took hold of Chris's erection.

Chris gasped in surprise, and his knees buckled. *Professor Stone is touching my cock. Oh my god, Professor Stone is touching my cock!* The man's grip was firm and purposeful, maneuvering Chris instead of stroking him, but it wasn't until he heard a small snap and felt pressure in his groin that Chris became confused.

"I don't want you coming until I'm ready for you to," Stone explained as he tucked Chris back into his pants and zipped them up.

"What did you put on me?"

"A cock ring." He finished setting Chris's clothing in place and turned away, heading toward a sign marking the beginning of a path.

The pressure from the ring, along with his already throbbing need, was overwhelming, and Chris had no idea how he'd walk, let alone hike.

"I'll turn the vibrator back on if you don't get a move on," Stone warned.

Normally the idea of a vibrating plug would have thrilled Chris, but more stimulation at that moment would have killed him. He hurried as best he could after Stone, half waddling, half groaning from the sensation of his pants sliding over his tortured skin.

Stone pushed Chris ahead of him, obviously wanting to enjoy his submissive's struggle as they hiked. At least it was an easy trail, but in Chris's predicament, he was soon sweating bullets.

"How long are we hiking?" Chris panted.

"We have a couple of hours before sunset, so we can take our time."

Chris wanted to fall to his knees and beg. He'd barely last a few more minutes, let alone a couple hours. Thankfully, Stone wasn't done talking.

"We'll come to our first rest stop just around the corner."

"Oh, thank god," Chris cried in relief.

"God has nothing to do with it. It's me you should be thanking."

Grateful wasn't the emotion Chris wanted to express while his balls felt like melons between his legs.

The rest stop Stone had indicated was a huge boulder on the side of the trail. Chris headed for it without prompting and leaned his body against it, resting his forehead on the sun-warmed surface.

Gentle hands touched his shoulder and hip, guiding him to turn around so he stood with his back against the boulder. He remained limp and pliable as Stone positioned him as he wanted. A soft groan escaped him as Stone unbuttoned Chris's pants once more and lowered the zipper. His cock and balls were carefully lifted and framed by the fabric again.

"You did this perfectly in the car. I was very pleased."

"Thank you, Sir."

"I'm going to reward you for all your patience, Chris. Use the rock for leverage or hold on to me if you need to. I'm taking off the ring now."

Before the words truly registered, the cock ring was unsnapped and the pressure on Chris's balls released. All the pleasure the ring had repressed came rushing to the fore, and he cried out. His cock spurted once before he could stop himself.

"That's it, Chris," Stone coaxed in his ear. "Come for me now. Show me how beautifully you can come for me."

A fingertip trailed down the length of his cock. The sensation was too much after being on edge the whole day. It bordered on painful, but it still wasn't enough.

"Please," he begged, wanting more and yet unable to take it. "Please touch me."

There was a moment of silence before Stone said, "Jerk off for me, Chris. I want to watch you come."

Chris needed no more invitation than that. His hand flew to his cock and pulled with frantic need. The mix of pleasure and pain from overstimulation was ignored for the burning necessity of release. It took longer than he expected to get past that hurdle, but finally, with a cry, Chris fell to his knees as he came. His orgasm ripped through him in a series of waves, and he moaned through it all until he sat, panting and spent, on the forest floor. He couldn't move and hoped Professor Stone gave him time before ordering him to.

Instead, a rough hand landed on his shoulder and held him in place as a gruff voice demanded, "Don't move."

A belt buckle jingled followed by the rasp of a zipper, and Chris gaped in wide-eyed disbelief. Professor Stone pulled his engorged cock from his pants and stroked it rapidly. It was thick and appeared ready to burst.

Chris thrilled at having pushed Stone so far. He couldn't look away from that cock, so close to his face yet off-limits. Tearing his gaze away, he stared up into the man's eyes. They bored a hole right back at him with an intensity that kept him down on his knees more than the grip on his shoulder ever could.

"You want this?" The words were gritted out through clenched teeth.

Oh god, yes. Chris nodded, unable to speak.

"Close your eyes."

He didn't want to. He didn't want to miss a moment, but the urgency in Stone's expression and the growl in the accompanying *"now"* had him shutting his eyes just before hot semen sprayed against his face. He closed his eyes tighter but couldn't resist opening his mouth for a chance taste of the other man. He was rewarded as the next spurt went between his lips. His tongue reached out for more of the salty flavor as another spurt hit his cheek. Professor Stone gushed buckets, and Chris enjoyed every second until the weight on his shoulder increased, and he knew the man was spent. He swallowed and licked his lips clean. His eyes were still closed as Stone straightened.

"I hadn't planned on that, so I didn't bring anything to clean you with. Take off your jacket and shirt."

Chris did as he was told, and the fabric of his T-shirt was rubbed over his face. When Stone deemed it was safe, Chris opened his eyes.

"Put on the jacket before you get cold. You'll have to carry this for the rest of the hike."

"We're still hiking?" Chris asked, surprised.

"Yes. We have an hour left before we need to turn back, and the woods here are pretty. Are you ready to get up yet?"

Chris moved to stand and found one of his legs had fallen asleep on him. Stone helped him up, and they waited until he was able to walk before setting off again on the trail.

"So, you like hiking?"

"I prefer it for exercise rather than a gym."

"Are your hikes always so…intense?" Chris asked.

The other man smiled. "Sometimes."

"I've never been one for hiking, but I can see myself getting into it now."

"Not every hike has an orgasm attached."

"I'll only sign up for the ones that do."

Stone laughed, but his amusement soon faded. "I didn't mean for that to happen."

"It seemed like you meant for me to come. That's what you told me to do."

"That's not what I'm talking about."

"I know, but I don't want you to apologize." Chris sighed. "I never wanted an apology for that kiss last winter, and I don't want you to apologize for coming on my face. Both times, I wanted it. *Really* wanted it. Please, don't ruin it by apologizing."

———

Daniel hadn't realized he might have hurt Chris with his apology, and he didn't want to risk doing it again by apologizing now.

"I'm still your teacher." At Chris's look, he amended, "A teacher at your university then. I don't want to cross lines we shouldn't."

"I think this whole vacation is crossing lines we shouldn't, but as you said, you're not my teacher, and I'm in college, not high school. I'm twenty-six and old enough to be treated like an adult in a situation like this. You said I could be yours for the week, and you said no sex. I've accepted the time limit and the limitation on what we do. I accept you're the one to make the rules, but please, can we, for this week, just be a Dominant and a submissive having a good time? Can we not be a student and a teacher?"

Daniel stopped to look at Chris. The boy was more mature than he'd given him credit for. "Okay. The no-sex rule still stands, but yes, we can be a Dom and a sub for the remainder of the week."

Chris's grin was worth bending the rules for, and Daniel couldn't help smiling back. "But that also means if I plan to go hiking and not give you an orgasm, you're not allowed to object when I take you with me."

Chris's shoulders slumped. "Fine," he whined brattily. "Can I call you Daniel?"

"You'll call me Sir, or Stone if we're not in a kink-friendly place."

"That's not that different from school."

That pout of his could fell the hardest of hearts. Daniel

was finding it difficult to resist. "My best friends call me Stone," he offered as consolation.

Chris's face brightened again. "Does that mean you think of me as a friend?"

"That means you're in good company. Now get moving." Daniel gave him a swipe on the ass for good measure.

"Yes, Sir," Chris said with a salute, and they both laughed as they continued down the trail.

FIVE

The rest of the hike was pleasant, both men relaxing now their roles were clear. Without the strain of hesitancy burdening them, they took the time to enjoy each other's company, talking about their lives and interests. As the sun set, they drove back to the hotel for dinner before their outing to the club that night.

Dinner was an ordinary affair. The intensity of a scene had been set aside for their newly found camaraderie. To Chris, it felt like a date though he wisely kept the thought to himself. He liked spending time with Stone and wished they'd continue after the week was over.

After dinner, Stone escorted Chris up to his room. He pulled a pair of black leather pants from the room's closet and took them into the bathroom to change. Chris would have preferred watching him get dressed, but witnessing his Dominant emerge in nothing but tight leather pants made his mouth water and his cock stand at attention. Catching Chris's stare, Stone winked and pulled something from his suitcase.

"Your turn." He handed Chris a small strip of leather.

Chris examined the fabric in confusion before figuring out it was a leather G-string. He swallowed, his pulse rushing faster with the thought of wearing nothing but the thong for

Stone. He hurried into the bathroom to put it on but hesitated before emerging. The tiny shorts he'd originally worn to the club had been small enough to make him feel vulnerable, but this barely covered his cock! If he became fully hard wearing it, it wouldn't cover anything at all.

"Come out, Chris," Stone ordered.

Slowly, Chris cracked open the bathroom door and stepped through. He resisted the urge to cover himself. Stone would order his hands away anyway. When he finally managed to look the man in the eye, the raw lust he saw there warmed him. His confidence settled into place. His cock grew harder, and he instinctively hid his erection.

Stone didn't say anything. He stepped forward and took hold of Chris's wrists, moving them back to his sides.

"You can't hide anything from me. If necessary, I will cuff your hands behind your back to keep them in line."

Chris swallowed. "I'll be fine, Sir."

Stone nodded and gestured to the bed. "Lean over. I want to re-lube that plug. It's not coming out for a while yet."

Chris moved to the foot of the bed and placed his hands on the duvet, leaning forward slightly.

"Put your face down on the comforter."

Chris leaned farther, turning his head to the side as he put his cheek down on the fabric. The thin line of the G-string made him feel more naked than if he'd had no clothes on at all.

Stone moved the string and twisted the plug. The empty feeling returned once it was removed. He liked the sensation less and less each time. He clenched his buttocks to make it go away faster.

Stone chuckled. "Your ass is doing a pretty dance for me, I see."

Chris froze.

"Oh, don't stop." A fingertip dragged down the cleft of Chris's cheeks. "I like to know I'm wanted."

"Fill me, please, Sir."

The blunt tip of the plug answered Chris's begging, and he sighed as it teased him.

"Please."

The warmth of Stone's body covered him as the man leaned over to whisper in his ear. "I love hearing you beg. I plan to hear much more before the night is out."

Before Chris could reply, the plug slammed into him, making him cry out from the sudden thrust. Stone slapped each of Chris's butt cheeks and told him to stand.

"Now when people see your ass, they'll have a little artwork to admire."

The tingling sensation made Chris want to look in a mirror, but he wasn't given a chance. "Put on your jeans and jacket. We're heading out in a minute after I check my phone."

Chris thought about checking his own phone, but Stone's expression stopped him. "What's wrong?" he asked.

Stone didn't answer.

———

Jesse Harte. Daniel hadn't seen that name on his phone in over six years. He moved to the bed and sat down. What could Jesse want after all this time?

There was only one way to find out. He pushed the button for his voicemail and set the phone to his ear.

"Hey, Stone, it's Harte. Been a long time, huh?" There was a pause before the message continued. "So…I'm getting married. Well, hopefully. I'm asking him this weekend, and I'd like for you to be there when I do. I know we haven't been in touch for a while, but you're still important to me, man. You're one of the suits, you know? That doesn't go away even if high school is over. Anyway, can you believe it? Me? Getting married? I know exactly what you're thinking, so you should obviously come here to meet him so I can prove he does exist. And don't worry about a hotel. You'll stay at my place. There's plenty of room."

There was another pause, longer this time, and when Jesse spoke again, his voice was subdued. "You know, even if you don't want to come, call me. I'd really like to hear your voice again. I think it's high time the three of us talk about what happened and put it behind us. I miss you." There was one last pause. "See ya, Stone." Then the message ended. Daniel listened to the disconnected line for a while before he hung up the phone.

"What is it?"

He was startled to see naked thighs in front of him and looked up into Chris's concerned face.

"I think we'll have to cut this vacation short," he said. "I have to go home."

Chris frowned. "I guess I'll head back too. I don't think I'd feel comfortable wandering around here without you right now."

"That's a good idea." Daniel scratched his head, trying to think. "Look, I know we're cutting our deal short, so if you want to talk about things once I get back, we can do that. I won't leave you hanging."

"I know you won't." Chris's brow furrowed. "What do you mean 'back'?"

"I told you. I need to go back home."

"But... Do you mean where you grew up?"

"Yeah. One of my friends is proposing to his boyfriend, and he wants me to be there."

"That's great," Chris said. "Congratulations."

Daniel nodded.

"You don't seem happy about it."

Daniel sighed. "It's been a long time since I've been there. The last time I was there was not long after...a friend died."

"I'm so sorry. I'm guessing you were close?"

"He was one of my best friends. I killed him."

"You *what*?" Chris exclaimed, the shock making him retreat a step.

Daniel shook his head. "It's my fault he died," he amended. "I called him out when I knew I shouldn't. While we were driving, a drunk driver smashed into the passenger side of the car at high speed. Clover died on impact."

Chris sat beside him and slid an arm over his shoulders. "I'm sorry."

Lost in his thoughts, Daniel didn't respond.

"Do you want me to go with you?"

Daniel turned to Chris in surprise. "You want to spend the rest of your vacation in my hometown with me?"

"Yes."

Chris sounded so sure of himself. It was a sharp contrast to how Daniel felt.

"Besides," Chris continued, "I'm yours for the week. We never stipulated where that week needed to be spent. Are you going to break your word?"

Chris was right. "All right, boy. Go pack your things. I'll make arrangements for us, and we'll leave tomorrow. You don't have a problem with flying, do you?"

"No, but…" Chris hesitated.

"You're mine for the week," Daniel said. "That means you don't get to think about money unless I tell you to. Besides"—his voice softened—"I'd appreciate the company."

"Okay." Chris headed for the door. "Oh—" He paused. "—what about this?" He gestured to the G-string, still the only fabric covering his body.

"I'm afraid the club is out tonight. I don't have the head-space to Dom you properly for a scene."

"I didn't mean that."

Daniel's smile was wicked. "If you slip on a pair of jeans, it'll be fine. Once you're packed, bring everything over here. We'll deal with that then."

Grinning, Chris grabbed his pants, thrust his legs into them, and was out the door.

Once he was gone, Daniel took another deep breath. He was going home. Back to where it all started and—if he was lucky—back to *Harte*. For a moment, he toyed with the idea of introducing Chris to *his* club, but his excitement for the idea quickly faded. Going home meant facing Dillon again, seeing the grave, and admitting his failure. Even after six years, he wasn't sure he was ready.

SIX

Stone was on the phone when Chris returned from fetching his things. He was transferring clothing from the dresser into a mostly filled suitcase on the bed while talking with the person on the other end of the line. He gestured for Chris to put his bags in a corner while he finished packing. He zipped up his suitcase and placed it on the floor before motioning for Chris to lose his pants. Chris was happy to do so. Even if they weren't going to the club as planned, Chris was glad Stone was still interested in playing with him. He folded his jeans and set them atop his suitcase, planning to wear them the next morning.

Finished with his phone call, Stone disconnected and said, "Lie down on your stomach." He informed Chris of their new plans as he approached the bed. "Our flight is at eleven tomorrow morning, which means we need to be ready to go by seven at the latest."

He leaned over and parted Chris's ass cheeks with his palms. The heat of Stone's touch made Chris want to moan, but instead, he replied, "Yes, Sir."

"I'm setting an alarm for six o'clock," the other man continued as he removed the plug from Chris's ass. "If you need more time in the morning, you'll have to set your own alarm. It will be your responsibility to make sure you're ready and checked out by seven. I want to shower in the morning and have a bite to eat before we're on our way. Factor that in when deciding how much time you want to leave for yourself."

Chris was too distracted by the fact he'd be sleeping in the same room as Stone to worry about what time he should get up in the morning. He wouldn't get what he really wanted, but sharing a bed was a step in the right direction. He'd take what he could get.

After washing the plug and putting it away in his suitcase, Stone instructed, "Get into bed. It's getting late, and we have to get up early."

Chris frowned, but it made sense. "Yes, Sir," he said quietly. He sat up and pulled back the sheets. He didn't know what side he should sleep on, so he picked one and curled up under the blankets. He was disappointed not to feel the weight of another body shifting the mattress beside him.

Stone had resumed packing. That was sensible. They had to leave early, so they should have everything ready for when they woke in the morning. Stone would come to bed when he finished.

Chris turned over and closed his eyes. For a while, he listened to the other man move around the room, but he was still alone in the bed by the time he drifted off to sleep.

———

The alarm woke Chris. At first, he didn't remember where he was, but the weight of the cuffs on his wrists reminded him. He felt the other half of the bed. It was empty, and the sheets were cold.

Sitting up, he surveyed the room. A blanket was piled in one of the room's chairs. His eyes narrowed in anger at the sight of it. Stone was taking his vow not to have sex with him too far. Then he noticed some papers on the table and a glass sitting next to a few empty bottles from the minibar. It hadn't been him that had kept his Dominant from sleep.

The bathroom door opened, and he turned in time to see Stone emerge, drying his hair with a towel. Another was wrapped precariously around his hips. Chris's jaw dropped at the sight of so much naked man. Catching sight of his reaction, Stone smirked. "Throw the covers back."

Chris did as he was told before he remembered the skimpy G-string he'd worn to bed the night before. The small patch of fabric was stretched to its limit as an erection proudly held it out from his body.

"We're lucky I was up before the alarm." Stone finished with his hair and dropped the towel on the floor. He pulled a shirt over his head, hiding his delicious skin. The second towel dropped, and a whimper escaped Chris at the sight of Stone's firm ass before it disappeared into a pair of briefs. They were followed by jeans the infuriating man zipped up before turning to face him.

"The sight of you like that makes me want to do all sorts of things to you."

Chris's breath caught in his throat. "Like...like what?"

Stone's gaze raked over Chris's body. "You like it when I look at you."

It hadn't been a question, but Chris nodded anyway.

"You flush nicely when you're embarrassed. I wonder how you'd feel if I looked at you in a pair of lacy women's underwear instead of that G-string."

Chris's face heated at the suggestion.

"You like that idea?"

Chris's face grew hotter. The idea was humiliating, but when he thought of Stone staring at him, alone in a room, just like this... "Yes, Sir."

"You liked it when I came on you as well. You even walked for over an hour with traces of dried spunk on your face."

Chris swallowed. It was true. He'd loved everything

they'd done together so far. He didn't have to admit it either. Even if he didn't say anything, his cock gave him away.

"The question is what to do with you now before we have to catch a plane."

"You can do whatever you want with me, Sir," Chris said, and he meant it.

"Spread your legs for me."

Chris did.

Stone moved closer to the bed but made no move to touch him. All he did was look, and that was enough.

"One day I'm going to wrap your cock in rope, bind it up so you won't be able to come or even pee without begging me first."

Chris had no idea if he'd like that, but when Stone touched a finger to the tip of his cock, he didn't care. He wanted to know what would happen to him *now*.

The alarm went off again, startling them both. Stone blinked, then reached for Chris's wrists. He removed the cuffs, saying, "Go take a shower. We're leaving in a half hour." He turned his attention to other things.

———

Chris emerged from the bathroom much as Stone had, dressed in nothing but a towel and drying his hair. He held up the leather G-string and asked, "What do you want me to do with this?"

"Pack it for now and pull out some simple clothes. We won't get many opportunities to play on the plane." After a short pause, he added, "But don't wear underwear. If I want your cock on display, I don't want anything getting in the way of that."

If that was what Stone wanted, Chris would burn his underwear and never wear any again. He quickly rolled up the thong and thrust it into his suitcase, then pulled out a T-shirt and socks to add to the jeans he'd worn the day before.

Just as he was about to pull on the shirt, he heard, "Stop," and stilled.

"Drop the towel."

Chris dropped both shirt and towel to the floor. He stood naked in the center of the room, still sporting the erection from earlier.

"Come here."

Chris walked closer as ordered.

"Give me your wrists."

Stone put the cuffs back on him. He stepped closer and spoke low in Chris's ear. "You'll have to show these in the airport. The metal buckles will surely set off any detectors. Everyone will see them, but the only thing you'll concern yourself with is *I* am the only one who takes them off you. No one else, not even you. Understand?"

"Yes, Sir."

"Good. Now, I think we'll keep that erection going for the morning. Maybe, if you're good, we'll take care of it after we land. I'm sure there will be a bathroom we can use where I can watch you jerk off." He landed a sharp tap on Chris's ass. "Get dressed. We're leaving in ten."

The rest of the morning went as smoothly as could be expected when dealing with airports. They checked out of the hotel, grabbed some breakfast, and were on time for the recommended three-hour wait for their plane. As Stone had warned, the cuffs had to be removed before Chris could pass security. Stone removed them slowly, eyeing Chris the whole time as if to say, *Everyone can see this. Everyone knows you're mine,* which both embarrassed and thrilled the submissive in him. Once they were checked in and settled, the cuffs had been immediately put back on him. It was a relief when they were returned. Chris didn't feel right without them.

Stone had also warned they would not play at the airport, but that didn't stop him from whispering dirty comments in Chris's ear any time Chris's erection waned. By the time they landed, Chris was ready to beg, but he ended up not needing to. Even before they went for their luggage, Stone pulled Chris into the nearest men's room. He shoved Chris into the accessible stall and locked it with both of them inside.

"Strip," he ordered. "Everything but your shoes."

Since he couldn't take off his pants without removing his shoes, Chris dropped his jeans to his ankles and removed his shirt, which Stone took hold of.

"Face me and jerk off. Don't get anything on our clothes, or you'll have to wear it or lick it off."

Chris was quick to come, spilling on the bathroom floor between them, a mess Stone didn't seem to mind. He probably enjoyed the thought of the next person entering to the sight of Chris's semen on the floor. Chris turned red at the idea but didn't comment on it. He carefully avoided the streaks while he dressed, and they left the restroom.

They promptly collected their luggage and grabbed a taxi. It was only then that Chris wondered where they were going. Would he see Stone's home from when he was younger? Were they staying at another hotel? He wanted to ask, but as they drove, Stone had become quiet, his expression somber.

Chris let the questions pass and settled in his seat, hoping his presence would be of some comfort. He let his legs fall open so one of his knees rested against Stone's. It was an invitation and a reminder he wasn't alone.

The silent car ride ended when they pulled into a circular driveway and parked in front of a large house. The size wasn't overly ostentatious. The home was structured like the others they'd passed on the street, but it stood out for its coloring. Most of the houses were painted neutral tones like taupe, but the building they parked in front of was partially covered with gray stonework and painted in a warm rust color with white trim. It had character. Perhaps the people who lived inside it did too.

Chris admired the residence as Stone paid the driver and got out of the car. The slam of the trunk behind him startled him into movement, and he got out before the taxi could leave with him still frozen in the back seat.

"Where are we?" he asked.

Stone took a deep breath before answering. "Jesse Harte's house. He's…a friend."

Chris wasn't sure why Stone hesitated, but he didn't have a chance to ask. The front door burst open, and a handsome man in a stylish suit bounded down the front stairs, grinning widely. A second man followed at a more sedate pace.

"Stone!" cried the first man. He pulled Stone into a hug, slapping his back enthusiastically. "And here I wondered if I'd have to drag you out of a hotel."

"You offered a room; I'm here," Stone said with a shrug.

"I'm so glad. Dillon will be happy to see you too. I thought we'd all do dinner at the club tonight." He glanced at Chris. "It seems we have plenty of introductions to go around. Hello." He stuck his hand out. "I'm Jesse Harte. And you are?"

"Nobody," Stone interrupted gruffly. "His name is Chris, and that's all you need to know."

A pang shot through Chris, but he forced it away and took the offered hand. Jesse shook it, raising an eyebrow when a cuff peeked from beneath Chris's sleeve. "It's a pleasure to meet you, Chris. I'm sure we'll have much to talk about."

Stone's glare could have cooked bacon. "And what about you?"

Jesse's expression softened as he turned to the man who had followed him from the house. "This is my boyfriend, Adam. I'm working on getting him to move in with me, but I think I'll succeed pretty soon."

Adam's smile was friendly but teasing as he shook hands with them. "He's mostly succeeded. I'm resisting for the fun of it now."

Jesse rolled his eyes at his lover. "Come on in. We can put your suitcases in your room, then get a drink and catch up."

With a glance at Chris, he asked, "Will you need another room, Daniel?"

Stone also looked at him, but Chris couldn't read his face.

"Yeah. I'm sure you have enough space for it," he answered, and Chris had to curb his disappointment.

"Of course. This way."

They entered the house, and Chris was immediately distracted by the spaciousness of it. He made sure to wipe his feet before entering, not wanting to leave smudges on the shiny, clean floor. A winding staircase curved ahead of them in the foyer, and sunlight streamed in through many windows. The place was bright, cheery, and elegant. Still, the character of the exterior continued with the décor inside. There were warm colors and an interesting mix of comfortable and modern furniture. The house was impressive yet welcoming.

"You live here by yourself?" Chris asked.

"Sadly, yes, but hopefully not for long." Jesse looked pointedly at Adam before explaining. "When I bought the house, I wanted to make sure my closest friends could stop by anytime and always have a room available."

They followed Jesse upstairs, and he gave them the ten-cent tour as they went. "I'm over here, and there's a bathroom on your left. Daniel, this is your room—you will be happy to note, I've had the dust cleaned out in anticipation of your arrival—and, Chris, we'll be putting you in here. Unfortunately, I didn't know you'd be joining us, so the bed isn't made yet, but we'll do that after dinner. Unless Daniel has other plans…" Jesse trailed off.

Stone shook his head no. Jesse's curiosity was obviously piqued, but he left the topic alone.

"Get settled. I'm assuming you haven't eaten since you've just landed?" When they confirmed this, he continued, "I'll have lunch ready by the time you come downstairs. See you all in a few." And with that, their host left.

Chris hesitated, not sure what he should do. Stone was quiet and unmoving, an utter lack of help.

"You do remember our deal, right?" Chris asked.

The question pulled Stone from his stupor, and he looked up.

"It's your choice about the rooms, but you remember you're my Dominant, right?" Chris went on. "You're not going to flake out on me now that we're here, are you?"

Stone's lips curved. It was a small smile, but it was there. "I haven't forgotten." He turned to Chris, his eyes focused and intent. Familiar heat pooled low in Chris's belly. "Though it sounds like you've forgotten a few things if you're ordering your Dominant around. I should punish you for that."

A shiver ran through Chris. "Yes, Sir."

Stone stepped closer, an arm sliding around Chris's shoulders. He pulled Chris into a hug. "You're right though. I'm being distracted by my thoughts and not keeping aware of my duty to you. Thank you for the reminder."

Chris melted into the embrace. "Are you sure you don't want to punish me, Sir?"

Stone's chest vibrated with a chuckle. "It's not a punishment if you want it."

"I'll do my best to pretend, Sir."

This statement was greeted with another laugh. "Go get settled in; then meet me downstairs. It's time for you to properly meet my friends."

Chris reluctantly let go when he pulled away.

"Sir?" he called.

Stone stopped and turned back to him.

Am I really nobody to you?

Chris swallowed, unable to ask the question. "Never mind." He waited until the other man had disappeared into his room before he did the same.

SEVEN

It was weird being home again. In some ways, it was as if he'd never left. Jesse was the same animated whirlwind he'd been since high school, and being in his presence didn't give Daniel an opportunity to think about anything other than the conversation at hand. Jesse swept Chris up in his enthusiasm and regaled him with tales of their high school and college escapades. Laughter filled the room, and Daniel smiled along with them, adding his own details and corrections when Jesse's stories drifted too far from the truth.

Chris had relaxed as well. Daniel caught him touching the cuffs occasionally, but the action seemed more of a reminder for himself than a self-conscious tic. Daniel liked seeing the leather on Chris's wrists. He'd be sad to see them go when the week was over.

"So how do you know Daniel here?" Jesse asked Chris.

"I bumped into him at the club I go to," Daniel answered, hoping to avoid unnecessary details. "He's new to the scene, and I offered to teach him a few things over spring break."

"Are you a student?" Jesse asked.

"Yes," Chris said. "I'm studying applied mathematics."

Jesse turned to Daniel, mischief sparkling in his eyes. "You're not very good at lying, you know."

"I haven't lied about anything," Daniel replied.

"Avoidance doesn't work either. It's obvious he goes to the same school where you teach, or you wouldn't be so worked up about it."

Daniel didn't reply.

"Lay it out for me, Stone. I need to know the protocol for later, anyway."

Daniel sighed. "He's my sub for the week. No sex and no sharing, but I might put him on display at the club if he's good. I've wanted to demo him in front of an audience."

"Okay."

"And you?"

"Adam's my boyfriend, like I said. We scene, but outside of the bedroom, the dynamic is generally vanilla."

Daniel nodded slowly, absorbing the details. "What about Dillon? Has he...?" He trailed off, but Jesse picked up the question.

"He's wonderful, actually. He has a full-time sub who you'll meet tonight. The boy has been good for him. I haven't seen Dillon this happy since Clover."

A wave of relief rushed through Daniel even as some of his worries returned. "What's his sub's name?"

"Michael."

"I look forward to meeting him."

———

Later that evening as they were all heading upstairs to get ready to go out, Jesse took Daniel's arm and pulled him into the kitchen.

"I'm glad you came," he said when they were alone.

"I couldn't not come. No matter what, we're still friends." It was true. For years he'd felt as if he'd lost everything when he'd left, but now that he was here, he realized he hadn't lost anything at all. At least not when it came to Jesse. "I'm surprised you let me stay away so long," he added with a smirk.

"Well, it's not like you made it easy," Jesse protested. "You never called or wrote. I had to find out where you were working from your mother."

"You talked to my mother?" Daniel exclaimed.

"No. The news was passed through the parental grapevine. I had to admit to my mom she knew where you were before I did, and I completely blame you for that."

"You could have called."

"So could you," Jesse pointed out. "You're the one who left." He hesitated. "I didn't know if you wanted me to call."

"When has that ever stopped you?" Daniel asked. "It's not like any of us asked to be friends in the first place. It was your decision, and you badgered us until we went along with your whim. You've been an obstinate bulldozer since high school. What in the world made you stop to consider my opinion this time?"

"You'd never been so far away," Jesse said, and Daniel didn't think he meant the physical distance.

"I didn't know if you'd want me to come back," he admitted. "Dillon was so angry. I thought he hated me, and it would be better if I left. One less reminder of Clover's death."

"Dillon was hurt. We all were. Yes, initially, he took out some of that pain on you—you were an easy target—but afterward, once the shock had passed, he could have used a steady friend."

"He had you."

"And who did you have?"

Both men were silent for a while.

"We should get ready," Jesse said.

Daniel nodded and turned to leave the kitchen.

"Hey, Stone."

Daniel looked back at his friend.

"Don't be a stranger when you leave this time, okay? Come home more often."

"You going to hunt me down if I don't?"

Jesse smiled. "I'll drag you right out of the classroom if I have to."

Daniel grinned. "Deal."

———

Whatever hesitation Stone had felt before arriving at Jesse's had been wiped clean by the time he came upstairs to get ready for the club that evening. Chris was happy to see it go.

"This is the club you went to when you lived here?" he asked.

Stone nodded. "Yeah. Jesse owns the place. You're going to be blown away."

"What should I wear?"

Stone's gaze roamed over Chris's body, and a familiar wicked smile spread across his lips. "As this will be your first night at the club, we should do something special." He moved to his suitcase and rummaged through the contents. "How do you feel about public nudity?"

"Uh…I haven't really considered it."

"You'll only be seen at the club, but what I have in mind will put you well on display." As he spoke, he pulled coils of rope from his luggage. "We'll get you put together and see how you feel. If necessary, I can always come up with something else."

With the amount of rope piling up on the bed, Chris's curiosity would have given any suggestion a try.

"Get undressed. I'll be right back." Brimming with an excitement Chris had never seen before, Stone left the bedroom, and Chris heard him gallop downstairs. "Harte! I need to borrow a pair of chaps. They're for the boy."

Chris wasn't sure he liked being referred to as "the boy" but chaps? Weren't they the things cowboys wore? He ran his fingers over the coils of black rope before he remembered he was supposed to be getting undressed. He hastily stripped off his T-shirt and unbuttoned his jeans. The door to the bedroom was still open, and he debated closing it before dropping his pants. Not wanting to upset Stone, he left it open, kicked off his shoes and socks, and dropped his jeans on a chair. He moved to sit on the bed out of the line of sight from the door and with the edge of the comforter close by to scramble beneath if necessary.

He needn't have bothered. It wasn't long before heavy boots bounded upstairs, and Stone returned.

"Where... Oh. Get over here." He dropped what looked like half a pair of black leather pants on the bed and picked up the rope. "Stand in front of me and spread your legs."

Chris did as he was told. Stone uncoiled the rope and found the middle. He wrapped the strands around Chris's waist, pushing the ends through the center loop and pulling them through.

"That okay? Not tight or anything?"

"No."

"Good, because I'll be doing a lot more than this. I want you comfortable and able to breathe. This is meant to be bondage, not torture, so if at any point anything pinches or gets too tight, let me know. If you wait until the end, it will be a bitch to do it all over again."

"Yes, Sir."

Stone knelt in front of him, then hesitated. He seemed to be waiting for something, but Chris had no idea what he could be waiting for. When the man directed his unwavering gaze right at Chris's cock, Chris didn't need to wonder for much longer. The close attention had him rapidly rising to full mast.

Stone smiled broadly. "That's better. If you're going to be on display, might as well make sure you're hard for it."

He maneuvered the ends of the rope behind Chris, then brought them through his legs, over his thighs, and through the waistband again. After that, he began a complicated pattern Chris couldn't follow. He was too fascinated by the resulting design to care how it was done. By the time Stone had finished, he'd used two coils of rope, and the shaft of Chris's erection was covered in black from base to head. Stone had taken his time, laying each turn neatly so not a spot of skin peeked between the coils. Chris's balls were wrapped as well, and the harness that had started around his waist had ended in a braid that went between his ass cheeks and attached at the back.

"Try moving."

Chris groaned at the attempt.

"Too tight?"

Chris shook his head, unable to speak. The rope wasn't too tight, but it was restricting, making him aware of every shift of his crotch. Fascinated, he reached out to touch, but a firm hand kept him from doing so.

"That's mine," Stone said. "You can look, but you can't touch." He stroked a palm over Chris's rope-encased member. "You won't be able to go soft with this. You'll proudly stand at attention until I release you."

Chris bit his lip to keep from groaning again. His cock tried to grow harder, but the ropes prevented him from doing so, just as they prevented him from softening.

"And now for the rest of the outfit."

Stone picked up the chaps and handed them to Chris, saying, "Slip these on." Chris pulled the chaps over his legs, and Stone helped him buckle them closed. The legs were fitted against his skin, nothing like what he'd imagined a cowboy would wear. The waistband rested right above the rope harness and perfectly framed the rest of the work Stone had done. They also left his ass completely on display.

Guiding Chris over to a mirror, Stone asked, "Well? What do you think?"

The young man in the mirror was definitely him. He recognized his face and body, but he had never been so exposed, never worn anything so slutty. Catching sight of Stone in the mirror behind him and seeing the heat in his gaze, Chris didn't feel like a slut. He felt hot. *Really* hot, and he liked the feeling.

"I'll wear this tonight."

"Are you sure?"

Though Stone wouldn't have been angry or upset with him for refusing, he definitely would have been disappointed. Chris scrutinized his reflection. Although the outfit covered more skin than the shorts he'd worn on his first night, the head of his cock was bare. "You can see my pubic hair. Shouldn't I have shaved first?"

Stone ran his fingers idly over the blond curls. "Even if I call you boy, you are a man who submits to me, Chris. I like the reminder of that."

That was true, but by now Chris knew better. "You like it because it's more embarrassing this way, don't you?"

Stone grinned in answer. "No one outside of the club will see you. We can always leave if it becomes too much, or I can bring something else for you to change into just in case. It is completely up to you."

Chris wanted to do this. This was what he had come to the club to do, to let go, try new things, and be brave enough to try them.

"I'll wear this."

Stone nodded. "Let's head downstairs and see what Jesse and Adam think. It'll be your first taste of what it'll be like to wear this for an audience."

Downstairs, they were greeted by a wolf whistle once Jesse was able to pick his jaw up off the floor. "You are going to be the envy of quite a few people at the club tonight," he said. "Damn, do you look good."

Worried Adam might not like his boyfriend being so complimentary, Chris turned to him. "What do you think?"

Jesse smirked. "He thinks you look hot too, but he's too much of a stick-in-the-mud to admit it."

"Are you comfortable?" Adam asked.

"Well, it's a bit restricting, but..." Chris's cheeks felt warm.

"I meant will you be comfortable going out like that in public?" Adam clarified.

"Oh." Chris looked around at them and back at Stone who stood patiently behind him. He remembered the lust in Stone's eyes and the way he had felt in front of the mirror. "Yes. I'm sure I'll be fine."

"You needn't worry, sunshine," Jesse said. "You're a 'Look but Don't Touch' work of art, and we'll make sure everyone knows it. You might belong to Stone here, but we'll protect you too."

"We might need to," Adam said.

"What makes you say that?" Stone asked.

"Wait until he's standing next to Michael. Then you'll know what I mean."

EIGHT

Stone had promised the club, Harte, would blow Chris's mind, and he hadn't been lying. The building was huge with a line wrapped around it for entry into the ground-floor nightclub. He, Stone, Jesse, and Adam went around to the rear entrance and were immediately allowed in. The lobby they entered wasn't as big as a fancy hotel's, but it was similarly designed. A check-in desk and coat check were located where a concierge would be. There was a small lounge off to one side and elevators to take patrons to the club floors. Everything was clean and elegant, and if Chris had had no idea what the club was for, he never would have guessed.

Without the coat, Chris felt self-conscious, but when Stone's hand firmly landed on his shoulder, he felt better.

"I feel like I'm checking into the Marriott," he whispered.

"The Marriott would never let you in looking like that."

The elevator let out into a room much bigger than the lobby. There was a bar against the far wall. Plenty of tables, chairs, and benches for seating filled the space between them and it. On their right was a huge stage, empty except for a Saint Andrew's cross in the center of it.

"They're having a flogging demo in a little while," Jesse

informed him. "We arrived just in time. Have you ever seen one before? Or been flogged?"

Chris shook his head no.

"You're in for something good," Adam said.

Jesse gave Adam a smile that clearly meant something to the two of them, but Chris had no idea what it was.

"There're Dillon and Michael," Jesse said before leading the way through the crowd to a table in the corner. A muscular man clad head-to-toe in black leather sat there. At his feet knelt a slender young man with black hair and creamy white skin. The submissive wore nothing but a thick black collar and a black leather thong.

Stone's hand tensed at the sight of the pair, but their pace didn't slow as they approached the table. The Dominant rose as they came closer, but he didn't smile or do anything welcoming.

Jesse seemed unaffected by the tension. "Chris, meet Dillon Spade and Michael Nole. Dillon, Michael, meet Chris, Daniel's...temporary company for the week."

Stone glared at Jesse.

"Nice to meet you," Chris said, wondering if he should shake hands with anyone. No one offered, so he didn't try.

"Have a seat," Dillon said.

Adam and Jesse moved around the table and sat. Stone took the last chair on the end. Not wanting to be caught without knowing what to do, Chris knelt on the floor beside him, mirroring Michael's position. He remembered not to cross his ankles and clasped his hands behind his back.

"He's well-trained," Dillon commented.

"He learns quickly." Chris thought he heard approval in Stone's voice and smiled to himself. He liked pleasing his Dominant.

The lights around them dimmed, and the ones on the stage brightened, signaling the beginning of the demo. The room fell quiet as a Dominant and submissive took to the stage.

Though the idea of a flogging demo interested Chris greatly, he was too preoccupied to pay attention. The tension he had believed gone from Stone's countenance had returned. Could Dillon be the cause? He was sure it had something to do with Stone's friend's death, but he didn't know the circumstances of the situation. It would be a lot easier to help Stone feel better if he knew the details of the problem.

"Pay attention." Chris jumped at the order. "I may quiz you, remember?"

"Yes, Sir." Chris smiled at the tease and set aside his musing so he could enjoy the demo as instructed.

———

Daniel waited until the demo was over before placing a hand on Chris's shoulder to get his attention. "Go to the bar and get us some water."

Chris rose to his feet. He took a moment to make sure he was steady, then headed off toward the bar. Daniel watched, wary of onlookers' attention. Chris wasn't marked as taken, and Daniel wouldn't chance someone getting the wrong idea.

"Michael, go with him," Dillon said. "Get water for the table."

Michael rose gracefully, obviously more accustomed to the position he'd been in, and followed the blond.

"You were right, Adam," Jesse said. "They make one hell of a pair."

It was true. Chris and Michael were like the opposite sides of the same coin. Both had pale, creamy skin, and they were of a similar height. Their main contrast was their hair, one black and the other gold, like night and day. Their combined beauty was a worrisome temptation for others, but Daniel wasn't the only one keeping an eye out, and Michael was clearly marked as Dillon's.

"How did you meet?" Daniel asked Dillon.

A wry smile curved Dillon's lips. "We met outside of the

club. He was working as a prostitute and asked if I wanted to buy his time."

Daniel's eyebrows rose. "Really?"

Dillon nodded.

"He's not working anymore," Jesse interjected. "Michael's going to school now part-time."

"A university student?"

"I don't have to warn you off him, do I?" Dillon asked, deadpan, but Daniel recognized the humor behind the words. Though he wasn't sure where things stood between him and Dillon, it was somewhat of a relief to be teased like old times.

"I don't date students, thank you very much."

"Could have fooled me."

Daniel sighed. "That's…complicated."

"Oh?" Jesse prompted, his expression eager for details.

"And I don't feel like talking about it," Daniel added.

Jesse frowned, then shrugged. As one, the men's attention turned to the submissives at the bar.

———

"Six waters, please," Michael told the bartender.

"Did they think I would get lost?" Chris asked as they waited for the order to be filled.

"More likely that someone would try to whisk you away. Though if Daniel Stone is anything like my Master, it's probably because he doesn't like leaving you alone, even for a moment."

Chris glanced toward their table, and sure enough, Stone was watching them.

"Your Master is really like that?" he asked.

Michael grinned. "When I need to get homework done, he leaves the house so he won't distract me. I find it amusing."

Chris tried to imagine Stone being that possessive. He wasn't sure he'd like it.

"Jesse said this is temporary?" Michael asked.

"It's only for this week. He's doing it as a favor for me until I find my footing."

"Are you sure about that?" Michael asked, his voice clearly skeptical.

"That's what he says," Chris answered with a shrug.

"Is that what you want?"

Chris rolled his eyes, and Michael laughed. "Of course not. You knew from the moment you met him, didn't you?"

Chris cracked a smile. "You did too?"

"Probably. But I wasn't aware of it at the time."

"How did you two meet?"

"I picked him up outside the club one night. No idea what made me do it, but I called out to him. I guess a part of me knew where I belonged even before the rest of me did. How did you and Stone meet?"

"He's a professor at my university," Chris said. "He's not my teacher, but he doesn't like to cross lines with students."

"You don't call this crossing a line?" Michael asked as they collected the bottles and made their way back toward the table.

"You don't know how hard I had to work for this much, believe me."

Michael sighed. "It takes so much to train a Dominant."

"I don't think you should let your Master hear you say that."

Michael grinned again. "Oh no. That would get me in trouble, big time."

Chris laughed.

As they neared the table, Chris felt pinned beneath Stone's gaze. Dillon was also following Michael with his eyes, but the submissive greeted the glare with a breezy smile and resumed his place beside his Dominant. Dillon's hand automatically went to Michael's hair and began petting, his expression softening easily. Chris felt jealous as he set the bottles he carried on the table and knelt on the floor beside Stone. His hair remained untouched.

"Did you two have fun?" Dillon asked.

"We were getting to know each other better," Michael replied.

"If you'll excuse me." Stone pushed up from his chair and walked off.

"Where is he going?" Chris asked, confused.

"The bathroom is over that way," Jesse said. "I'm sure it's nothing."

"Stay here," Dillon ordered. He got up and followed in the direction Stone had gone.

"Is that a good thing?" Chris asked Jesse.

"It's long overdue," Jesse answered. "Good or not, it's about time they spoke to each other."

Chris was sure it was true, but he couldn't help being worried.

———

"If you stay in this mood, you're only going to make Chris paranoid."

Daniel finished rinsing his hands, then focused on Dillon in the bathroom mirror. Not knowing what to say, he reached for a paper towel and dried his hands. Dillon turned away from the mirror and leaned against the counter, blocking Daniel's way to the exit.

"I shouldn't have blamed you," he said.

The comment caught Daniel off guard. "He wasn't allowed out that night. I made him break your rules."

"You didn't make him do anything. Clover decided to go out on his own. He wasn't going to leave a friend in need. And he didn't break any rules. He left a note for me, so I knew exactly where he was when I got home."

Not exactly where he was, Daniel thought. "But if I hadn't invited him—"

"Neither of you could have known what would happen," Dillon interrupted. "Stone, I only blamed you because I was hurt, and I was angry, and I wanted to lash out at someone. You were the easiest target, but it wasn't your fault. It wasn't anyone's fault except the guy who hit you."

"I know that." Daniel sighed. He leaned against the counter next to his friend. "I know that's the truth, but…it's hard to believe sometimes."

They were silent for a while, not looking at each other but not moving away.

"You know, I think Michael's been good for you," Daniel said. "You seem…softer than you used to. It's nice to see you smiling."

Dillon let out a laugh. "Jesse says the same thing." He sighed, then looked Daniel in the eye. "I forgive you."

Daniel blinked and swallowed. He'd needed to hear those words. "Thanks."

Dillon nodded and pushed away from the bathroom counter. "So, what is it with you and that boy you've got out there?"

"It's a temporary thing. I'm introducing him to the scene, giving him an opportunity to find what he likes while he gets his footing."

"Is that all?"

Daniel's brow furrowed. "What do you mean?"

"Stone, I haven't spoken with you in over six years, but I still know you. You don't spend time with someone unless it's necessary or you actually want to, and you certainly wouldn't fly all the way over here with some kid if you were only helping him to adjust to the scene. You wanted him here. I'm wondering what else it is you want from him."

Daniel didn't answer.

"It's a simple question."

Daniel shook his head. "He's a student at my university. He's young and stepping into a world with a ton of open doors. What I want doesn't matter."

"That's bullshit. If you're too scared to go through with it, at least man up about it. Don't give me half-hearted excuses you don't even believe. Lame excuses are just that—lame."

Daniel glared at Dillon and was about to reply when the door to the bathroom opened and the topic of their conversation walked in. Chris paused when he saw the two Dominants.

"I'm sorry if I'm interrupting. I—"

"I'll leave you two alone," Dillon said. He slid past Chris and left.

In the wake of Dillon's departure, Daniel didn't know what to say. He was still geared up for the fight the other man had started.

He turned to Chris, ready to suggest they return to the others. With the boy standing there, beautiful and half-naked, bound in rope and leather, the words stuck in his throat, and he said instead, "Do you want to go somewhere more private?"

Chris glanced around the empty bathroom. "More private than this?"

"I believe I owe you a tour of the club. You can't be suitably impressed until you've seen everything."

Chris smiled. "I'd like that."

Daniel felt better now that he was taking action. "Come along then." He led the way out of the bathroom and down a hallway away from the main room.

"Shouldn't we tell them where we're going?" Chris asked.

"I'm sure they'll figure it out," Daniel replied.

———

Harte had the same things Chris had seen in the other club he'd visited, but it also offered a *lot* more. Chris spent much of the tour with his jaw hanging open and kept having to remind himself to close his mouth, but a few seconds later, it would just fall open again. Harte was a wonderland for kinky adults with rooms and toys beyond his imagination.

When he could think, he asked questions about the objects he saw. That led to him and Stone sharing ideas of what they could do in each room they came across. It wasn't too surprising when they both fell silent after entering a small schoolroom.

Chris surveyed the desks he hadn't seen since high school, the blackboard, and the teacher's desk. The room was much smaller than a real schoolroom, with only twelve desks for the students, but the size didn't matter. He could easily imagine himself in his senior year of high school, crushing on Stone as he taught at the front of the classroom. He wove his way through the desks and took a seat on one in the middle. The surface of the desktop was cool against his bare ass, and that made him feel even naughtier. He shot a wicked smile at Stone.

"Am I a bad student?" he asked.

Heat filled the other man's gaze as he moved closer.

"No," he said, "but I'm a bad teacher."

Chris's heart raced. When he parted his legs, Stone moved to stand between them. Chris's cock ached with the inability to rise higher. He tilted his head to look at Stone, and the intensity of the man's gaze made him shiver. His lips parted, and he wanted nothing more than to be kissed.

———

Daniel's world narrowed down to Chris's luscious mouth. His whole body thrummed with tension and the desire to give in, grab hold of Chris's head, and thrust his tongue deep between the boy's lips. He could already taste the kiss even though it had been so long since the last one. Chris would taste sweet and sharp, a smooth mix like biting into a fresh apple.

Chris's fingers plucked at the closure of Daniel's pants. Hesitation fluttered through his expression as he silently asked for permission, asked if this was too much. Daniel should have pushed his hands away but couldn't. He gazed into Chris's eyes as the boy unbuttoned his pants and cautiously drew the zipper down. Chris bit his lip, and Daniel waited, wondering how far the submissive would go, how far he would let him go before stopping him.

Doubt morphed into resolution, and in that instant, Daniel grabbed hold of Chris's wrists. He leaned forward, pressing Chris's hands flat against the desktop as he crushed their mouths together. Chris yelped in surprise before surrendering to the assault. His lips parted easily, and Daniel took the advantage, his tongue delving in to explore every crevice it could find. Chris attempted to tug his hands free. He made a frustrated sound when Daniel's grip remained solid and unyielding. Giving up the fight, Chris closed his eyes and melted into the kiss in the most beautiful act of submission Daniel had ever witnessed. His instincts made him deepen the kiss in reward, and his offer was greeted with a moan.

Chris's hips wiggled as the moment continued, a new form of frustration motivating them. Daniel enjoyed the sweet pleas and the struggle and remained just as passionate as the need between them increased. Eventually, it became unbearable even for him, and he broke the kiss with a growl.

"Get on your knees. Hands behind your back," he ordered.

Chris scrambled to the floor, kneeling as he'd been told, back straight and beautiful. He looked up at Daniel, panting and flushed, his lips parted and swollen. Irresistible.

Scrambling, Daniel freed his cock from his trousers. He stepped closer to the boy, bringing his dick as close as possible to that beautiful mouth without touching it. "Don't move," he ordered when Chris strained forward with the desire to please him. Chris froze, his eyes returning to his Dominant.

Their gazes locked, and Daniel began to jerk off. He was so close to coming, but he stretched it out as long as possible, unwilling to waste the perfect image in front of him. When his orgasm ripped through him, he aimed for Chris's chest. White lines marked the younger man as his own.

Spent, Daniel knelt in front of the submissive and rubbed the cream into his skin, covering his chest and belly. Finally, he wrapped his hand around Chris's neck. He squeezed lightly and declared, "You're mine," before letting him go.

He stood and tucked himself into his pants.

"Stand up. We're going home."

Chris stood, his hands still clasped behind his back. Daniel nodded approvingly. He leaned forward and inhaled deeply.

"You smell like sex. When you walk out of here, everyone will know I came on you."

Chris swallowed, and his voice was rough when he said, "Everyone will know I belong to you."

"Yes," said Daniel. "You do."

———

They entered Jesse's house and made their way up to Daniel's room, their footsteps the only sound breaking the silence. Once inside, Daniel shut the door behind them and told Chris to remove his coat, then stand in the middle of the room. He circled the boy once, admiring the look of him before stepping closer to brush his fingers over nearly flawless skin.

"Where did this come from?" he asked of the faint scar on Chris's shoulder.

"When I was ten, I fell out of a tree I'd been climbing. Cut myself on a branch on the way down."

Daniel ran his thumb over the pale line of pink against white. He stepped even closer, letting the heat of his body warm Chris's back. He reached around Chris's waist and unbuckled the chaps. "I want to know every inch of you," he whispered in Chris's ear. "I want to know every mark on your skin and where it came from."

Chris leaned against him. "I broke my arm when I was

seven. I was climbing that time too. I've always liked being high up."

Daniel smiled as he pushed the leather down. "Like an angel."

He had Chris step out of the pants before moving around to kneel in front of him. "Spread your legs for me."

Chris shifted his stance, his arms clasping once more behind his back as Daniel untied the rope. Daniel moved slowly as it unraveled, silent once more.

He's mine, he thought as the coils gathered on the floor. *For now.*

Gradually, Chris's cock was freed from its binding, standing proudly though marked by the rope's caress. He stroked a hand over its length, and Chris whimpered.

I want him to always be mine.

Dillon was right. His reasons for keeping Chris at a distance were wearing thin. He was afraid to mess everything up, but they had already come this far. He'd be making an even bigger mistake to run away. Still, any decisions about their future had to be made with a clear head, and Daniel was in no position to do that right now. He finished removing the rope from Chris's waist, then stood.

"You have a choice to make tonight. You can sleep in the room Harte has provided for you, comfortable in a bed with a mattress, by yourself, or you can sleep in here with me but on the floor. What do you choose?"

"Here," Chris answered immediately.

"Get a pillow and a blanket from the bed in the other room, and bring it here."

Chris ran to do as bid. Daniel hadn't even removed one shoe by the time Chris returned.

"Do you want me to do that?" Chris asked.

"Set the pillow and blanket on the floor next to the bed, but leave me enough space to get out without stepping on you," Daniel answered as he pulled off a boot and set it aside. "I can take off my own shoes."

Chris did as he was told, then returned to the center of the room to await further instruction.

Daniel took his time with the second shoe. He needed to have a talk with Chris if anything was to change between them, and there was something else he needed to do if he truly wanted to move on with his life.

"I'd like you to accompany me tomorrow," he said as he finished removing his footwear. "There's a place I need to visit."

"Where?"

"Clover's grave. I've never seen it, and I think it's time."

Chris was silent for a moment. "Okay."

Daniel nodded once. "Get some rest. We'll go in the morning; then I'd like to take you on another hike."

Chris smiled. "Will this be anything like the last one?"

"Not if you end up being bratty about it, it won't. Go to sleep."

Chris slid beneath his blanket on the floor and closed his eyes. Daniel finished getting undressed and paused before grabbing a pair of pants to sleep in. Chris was obviously feigning sleep, and he seemed a bit too smug for Daniel's liking. With a wicked smile of his own, Daniel made sure to step over the submissive as he got into bed and was satisfied to hear a gasp as he did so. Daniel might not be in the right mindset to change any boundaries between them that night, but that didn't mean he couldn't enjoy working within the ones they already had. He grinned as he slid, naked, beneath the sheets, knowing his submissive was hard and thinking of nothing but his Dominant as he fell asleep that night.

NINE

The next morning, they had breakfast with Jesse and Adam before Stone announced their plans for the day. His only order for Chris before they left was to forgo underwear and dress in comfortable clothing. Then they were off, borrowing Jesse's car and heading to a nearby cemetery.

"Are you sure you want me with you for this?" Chris asked.

"Yes."

Chris would have thought Stone would prefer one of his friends to accompany him. Despite all the time he'd been naked around Stone, this was the first thing they were doing that felt intimate.

Stone parked the car, and they got out. The cemetery was big, and he led the way through the rows of headstones until they came to one that was slightly set apart from the others. The plot was neatly tended and clean. Chris read the inscription on the headstone. Clover had been Chris's age when he'd died. The realization shocked him. Stone had to have been a similar age when Clover died. He couldn't fathom what that had been like.

Chris had been attracted to Stone since the moment they'd met, but there had always been something untouchable about him. Whether it was the professor-student thing or not, there'd always been a distance between them. No matter how much Chris had pushed to close that gap, a part of him had been used to the idea of Stone being a fantasy. For the first time he wasn't seeing the professor or the Dominant. This was Daniel Stone, a man who could be hurt like anyone else, and he had been hurt. Deeply. Chris wanted to comfort him but didn't know what to do or say.

When the silence had stretched, he asked softly, "What happened?"

Daniel remained silent, and Chris wondered if he would answer or if he'd even heard the question. Finally, he spoke. "When my father lost his job, he didn't take it well. The half-hearted attempt he made to find something new was fruitless, and he began drinking when he decided it was hopeless. He was 'too old to learn new tricks,' he would say." Daniel's smile was mocking. "It burdened my mother and frustrated me to no end, and I would often talk to Clover about it. He was a good listener, and being around him usually made me feel better.

"Clover had been living with Dillon for a while already, and they'd put together their arrangement or whatever you want to call it. I knew Dillon liked coming home to Clover, so Clover never left the house in the early evenings, but that night, I went over there anyway and called him to go driving with me. He came, and he listened like he always did." Daniel swallowed once, his voice becoming rougher as he continued. "I had just started to feel better when a car came out of nowhere and smashed into us. It was a drunk driver who'd run a red light. Clover was killed instantly, and I was shaken up pretty badly with a concussion and a broken arm." He stopped talking, and his gaze grew distant as if he were seeing the crash again. "Dillon blamed me when he showed up at the hospital. I didn't argue because I agreed with him. I went to the wake, but I couldn't bear to stay around, so I left before the funeral. I moved away and got a job at the university"—he turned to Chris—"and I've been teaching there ever since."

That was why Daniel had never been to the gravesite before. Chris couldn't imagine what it must have been like for his best friend to die next to him or to feel responsible for it.

"Dillon seems to have forgiven you," he said.

Daniel nodded. "He did."

"But you haven't?"

"It's not that easy."

"It's been six years. More than that even. Do you actually think your friend would be happy to know you're still carrying around your guilt instead of living your life?"

"When did you become the teacher between us?"

"I won't let it go to my head, Sir."

That provoked a smile. "Thank you."

Chris nodded.

"I want to show you something," Daniel said. "Come on."

He led the way to the car, and they got back on the road. They drove for about ten minutes before they pulled into a small parking lot surrounded by woods.

"Hiking again?" Chris teased as they got out of the car.

"This is one of my favorite trails. It runs up the hill to an overlook I thought you might like."

The woods were peaceful, and they remained quiet while walking through them. The air was warm, and sunlight filtered through the leaves above. It was a perfect spring day. At the end of the trail, the woods opened into a small clearing that overlooked the city below.

"It's beautiful," Chris said.

Daniel took a seat on the grass and gestured for Chris to join him. He pulled Chris onto his lap, wrapping his arms around him. Chris was surprised at first, then relaxed into the embrace. He wished they could always stay like that.

"We need to talk."

Chris tensed. "Oh?"

"You and I both know we've gone beyond our originally

agreed-upon terms. Last night alone pushed things further than it should have."

"We haven't had sex. It's not like we broke any of the rules."

"Yes, but we've bent them quite a bit, and that's not something we should do recklessly."

Chris bit the inside of his cheek. There was nothing wrong with what had happened between them. He wouldn't mind if more happened, but he'd known from the beginning he wasn't the one the rules were in place for. "So what should we do?"

Daniel was quiet for a moment. "What do you want to do?"

"I want what I've always wanted," Chris said. "You." He sighed. "I know your concerns, and I understand them. They're legitimate, but rules have no sway over feelings, and mine aren't changing whether we have sex or not."

Daniel was silent again. Chris wanted to see his face, but before he could move, Daniel's arms tightened around him in a hug, and he buried his face in Chris's neck. Chris wasn't sure what sort of an answer that was, but he wasn't going to argue with it.

They sat for a while, enjoying the lazy spring day. Chris's eyes had drifted closed, and he began to doze. He woke when Daniel fumbled with the catch of his jeans. He opened his eyes to watch as his zipper was drawn down, and the fabric shifted to expose his member. People could have walked by, but Chris set the worry aside when Daniel whispered in his ear.

"I'm going to jerk you off, and you're going to come for me."

Daniel worked him leisurely, in no rush to bring Chris to hardness or to hurry the orgasm that eventually came in a pleasant rush. Afterward, his softening cock was left on display as they continued enjoying the morning and the view.

Floating on the remnants of bliss from his climax, Chris

found his tongue loosened, and he spoke thoughts he normally would have kept to himself. His eyes closed once more. "I would spend the rest of my life belonging to you."

There was silence behind him, and he swallowed, instantly regretting the impulse. He wished he could see the other man's face and feared what he would find if he did.

Finally, Daniel spoke. "There's only one proposal scheduled for this weekend."

Chris clenched his jaw as he fought back tears. He'd known the rejection would hurt, but he hadn't counted on how much. Not wanting Daniel to see him cry, he leaned forward to get up. The arms around his waist tightened into iron bars around him.

"Let me go," Chris said, hating how his voice broke.

"No."

"Let me go," he said again, his voice stronger this time and louder.

"Unless you say your safeword, I'm not letting you go anywhere. You're mine for the week, remember?"

"You don't even want me," Chris snapped as he fought harder to get up. He managed to turn sideways, but Daniel pulled him against his chest with a firm tug. His arms were pinned to his sides, and Daniel's legs covered his own, sufficiently binding him without a prop in sight.

"You are *mine*," Daniel growled roughly in his ear. The possessiveness in his voice trapped Chris even more than the physical grip. "You are mine," he repeated. "Not even you can tell me differently."

Chris panted from the struggle. A torrent of emotions rushed through him, but even in the storm, he knew he'd been wrong. However much Daniel was or was not willing to claim him was nothing compared to how much Daniel wanted to. Gradually, he calmed, and the desire to fight abandoned him.

"I'm yours," he whispered and promised himself he

would find a way to prove the statement would always be true.

Daniel relaxed but made no move to release Chris. Realizing they weren't going anywhere anytime soon, he leaned against the warm chest beside him. He inhaled the scent of the woods and man and surrendered to both. His head rested against Daniel's shoulder, and his eyes drifted closed once more. When Daniel's cheek leaned against his head, Chris smiled. There was hope. He was sure of it.

TEN

When Chris and Daniel returned to the house, they found a small party waiting for them. Jesse had invited Dillon and Michael over for lunch.

"Adam's setting the table on the back deck, and the mimosas should already be out there."

"Mimosas? Did we transport to the Bahamas?"

"It's a nice day out. I thought it would be fitting. There's also beer if you want it."

Daniel opted for the latter and took a couple of beers from the cooler, offering one to Dillon. Chris kept himself busy snacking on chips and guacamole as the two men spoke.

"So, how long are you staying?" Dillon asked as he popped his bottle open and took a seat in the shade.

"We're leaving tomorrow actually. Classes resume on Monday, so we can't stay any longer than that."

Dillon nodded, but the words stopped Chris cold. He'd known this adventure would only last a week but hadn't realized how much time had already passed. It was Saturday. He would only belong to Daniel for one more day unless something changed and fast.

"Well, if we only have one more day together"—Jesse said as he emerged from the kitchen, carrying a big bowl of salad and a plate of marinated chicken—"we'll have to do something special tonight."

"I'd planned on taking Chris back to the club."

"Michael and I were planning on going as well," said Dillon.

"Perfect. We'll all meet there tonight. I'm sure we can think of something special to make the evening memorable."

"I was planning on doing some work tonight," Adam said. "I have a deadline coming up I can't afford to miss."

Jesse waved a hand. "Nonsense. One night out won't kill you. Besides, it's Saturday. Deadline or not, no one should work on a Saturday."

Adam sighed. "All right. I'll come too."

Chris was sure Jesse winked at Daniel after Adam agreed. Tonight was obviously the night of the proposal. Chris had been so busy focusing on his own situation he'd forgotten all about it. He smiled. He was looking forward to tonight. He liked Jesse and Adam. He'd only known them for a short while, but he was happy to be a part of this moment with them. He only hoped Daniel would keep him around so he could be a part of more of them in the future.

———

That night as they got ready to go out to the club, Chris decided Daniel had lost his mind. Though it was perfectly acceptable for his Dominant to be hotly decked out in leather pants, he'd never expected to be instructed to wear a pair himself.

"Leather pants? Isn't that...simple for your taste?" Chris asked as he searched for holes or something else revealing among the fabric.

"Last night I wanted to make things special for you, but tonight isn't about us. I don't want you stealing the spotlight."

That made sense, but... "Won't people be confused if I'm

walking around in pants? I'm shocked you let me wear pants to go hiking."

Daniel smirked. "I wouldn't have if I didn't have to worry about public exposure."

"You don't always worry about it. I've had my dick on display more times this week than it has ever been in my life. Are you sure you want me in pants?"

"Are you questioning my decision?"

Chris heard the warning in the query and responded appropriately. "No, Sir. Not at all."

That was a lie, but they both knew Daniel wouldn't be satisfied putting his submissive in a pair of leather pants, no matter how tight the leather. After some consideration, a gleam sparked in Daniel's eye. A better idea was coming.

"Wait here. I'll be right back."

Curious and excited, Chris grinned as he waited. He looked up expectantly when Daniel returned, but the man wasn't carrying anything. Chris's brow furrowed in confusion.

"Close your eyes."

Still confused, Chris did as he was told.

"Lift your left foot." Chris did. "Down. Now your right. Good. You can put it down now and bring your legs closer together."

Something tickled his legs. The edges of fabric slid over his thighs as whatever Daniel was putting on him rose higher. He felt softness against his buttocks before elastic was at his hips, and his hardening cock was tucked into a tight pouch. Hands on Chris's shoulders guided him to move, and he walked as directed.

"Open your eyes."

Slowly, he opened them and found himself in front of the room's full-length mirror. Daniel stood behind him, watching his face in the reflection. Chris lowered his gaze to see what he now wore. His eyes widened, and he gasped at what he saw. A pair of ladies' panties. They were dainty, made of lavender satin with lace on the edges. Chris's face burned. He'd never in his life worn women's clothing and never imagined wearing women's undergarments.

"You're going to wear these tonight," Daniel said. "I'll let you wear the leather pants over them, but you will wear them." He brushed his hand over the fabric, making Chris more aware of the feel of it against his skin. "When we get home, you'll show me how much you've enjoyed wearing them, won't you?"

Chris nodded.

"I can't hear you, Chris."

Chris swallowed. "Yes. Yes, Sir."

"Good. Now, put on your pants. We don't want to be late." He stroked Chris once more over the fabric. "Unless you'd like to wear only these tonight?"

Chris shook his head. That would be too much.

"Get dressed then. I'll meet you downstairs."

Downstairs, Daniel found Jesse pacing in the kitchen. He caught his friend by the shoulders and stopped him.

"You're going to wear a hole in the floor. Relax for a second, will you?"

"What if he says no?" Jesse asked. "What if I embarrass myself for nothing?"

"I personally wouldn't mind that," Daniel admitted. "You're long overdue for a little embarrassment, but you have nothing to worry about. He's not going to say no."

"How can you be sure?"

"I'm taking a page from this pain in the ass I know who automatically assumes everything will work out just as he planned. The annoying thing is it always does."

Jesse rolled his eyes and sighed. "You're right."

"Besides, if you let your nerves get to you, he's going to catch on, and that will blow all your well laid plans."

Jesse nodded. "You're right," he said again. He took another breath. "Okay. Let's do this."

"That's romantic," Daniel teased before leading them out of the kitchen.

When they arrived at the club, Dillon and Michael were already there. Like the last time they'd all been together, Daniel, Jesse, and Adam took the remaining seats at the table, and Chris knelt on the floor. Daniel spotted the matching grins Chris and Michael shared when they looked at each other.

"You don't usually sit in the center of the room," Adam observed as he slid into his seat.

"It was the only one open," Dillon answered with a shrug.

Jesse had just sat down when a hulking man in a black uniform cut through the crowd to whisper in his ear. "Sorry, gentlemen, but I have business to attend to. I'll see you all in a bit." He got up and followed the security guard deeper into the club.

"Perhaps he's planning something special since this is your last day," Adam suggested.

Chris blinked in surprise. "What makes you say that?"

"I wouldn't put it past him," said Daniel.

"Have you enjoyed your spring break, Chris?" Adam asked.

Chris grinned. "You have to ask?"

"What time are you two leaving tomorrow?" Dillon asked.

"One," Daniel answered. "I thought we could do breakfast before leaving."

Dillon nodded. "Good idea."

The lights around the room dimmed. Everyone quieted, turning their attention toward the stage. It was unusually empty and lit only by a lone spotlight. There wasn't a prop or a table to hint at what sort of demo would happen. Murmurs of confusion filled the darkness.

A man stepped forward into the pool of light. It was Jesse. The murmurs continued at the sight of him. He was clad in dark-blue jeans and a black button-down shirt, not at all the sort of attire he wore when performing on the stage. He stood tall and proud but swallowed before speaking.

"Hello, everyone," Jesse said. "May I have your attention please?" The room quieted. "Tonight's demo presentation has been postponed for an hour. I apologize for any inconvenience this schedule change may cause. In the meantime—" He licked his lips nervously. "—I'd like you to have patience with me as I ask my lover to join me onstage. Adam, will you come here for a moment?"

Though he couldn't have seen them, Jesse looked in their direction. Dillon had grabbed this table for a reason. It hadn't been the only one left.

Daniel glanced at Adam. The man was livid. He glared at Jesse with a gaze that could have fried an egg. His arms were crossed over his chest, and he made no move to respond.

"Adam?" Jesse called again.

"Absolutely not," Adam muttered, though only those at their table heard him.

Confusion ran through the audience again as their respectful quiet turned to questions amongst themselves.

"Adam, please," Jesse pleaded.

Jesse Harte never pleaded. Perhaps that was what cracked Adam's resolve. Still glaring, he slowly rose from his chair and made his way through the tables. Jesse's relief was palpable as he offered his hand to help Adam onto the stage. He paid no attention to his lover's expression and didn't let go of his hand.

"From the day we first met, you told me you would never kneel for me in front of a crowd or wear my collar, and I have never asked you to do so. But right now"—Jesse stepped back and lowered himself to one knee—"I am the one kneeling before you, and I ask you in front of all these people if you would wear my ring." He pulled a box out of his pocket, opened it, and held it up before Adam. "Adam Kern, will you marry me?"

The room was silent; not even a creak of leather could be heard in the dark. Adam's jaw dropped. He must have misplaced his voice because he opened and closed his mouth a few times, but nothing came out. Eventually, his face warmed into a smile so full of love it made Daniel's heart ache.

"Yes. Yes, I will absolutely marry you."

Jesse beamed. He pounced on his lover with an enthusiastic hug and kissed him. The room erupted into cheers and applause, reminding the two on the stage they were not alone. Jesse broke the kiss and, still grinning, slid a ring on Adam's finger. There was a second ring in the box that Adam placed on Jesse's finger in return. More cheers thundered through the room, and the lights came up to their usual muted setting. Boys in black shorts and bow ties wove their way through the tables, carrying trays with champagne flutes. When Daniel accepted one, he wasn't surprised to find it was sparkling cider in the glass. All four men at Daniel's table toasted their friends. They would do so again once the happy couple returned to them.

"You know, for a moment I didn't think it would happen," Dillon admitted.

"You thought Adam would walk out?"

"No, I thought Jesse would chicken out. Did you see him sweating up there?"

Daniel laughed. "Yeah. I don't think he's ever been that nervous in his life."

The group settled back to enjoy the celebration. Daniel was surrounded by the people he held most dear in his life, and those friends were happy with people they loved. He remembered the look on Adam's face as he'd agreed to Jesse's proposal, and his gaze fell to Chris. Dillon and Jesse didn't let anything get in the way of their happiness. Once they'd found it, they'd seized it. Daniel wanted to be happy like that. He wanted to be with someone he loved.

Letting the moment of joy buoy his impulse, he set his

flute down and took Chris's hand. "Come on." He pulled them both to their feet.

"Where are we going?"

"Nowhere far. I want to talk to you."

He led the way to a private playroom and closed the door behind them. He turned to face Chris. The boy seemed confused, but in a way that made Daniel think Chris was considering whether or not Daniel had gone crazy.

There were so many ways to say this, so many excuses and problems to sort through and things to consider. He would get to them, but first he'd lay his cards on the table.

"I want more than just this week," he said.

Chris's eyes widened as he caught on.

"This isn't a proposal," Daniel continued. "I'm not promising forever. Hell, I don't even know if this will work. We have a lot to figure out, and there's also the matter of conducting ourselves appropriately on campus, but if you're interested—"

His rambling was cut off as Chris's lips landed on his. After a moment of surprise, he wrapped his arms around the young man's lean body and pulled him closer. Chris opened his mouth to Daniel's probing tongue. He wrapped his arms around Daniel's neck as they became lost in the kiss. When they eventually parted, Daniel asked, "I take it you agree?"

Chris grinned. "Absolutely."

Daniel pulled him close again, enjoying a kiss with no regrets. The first of many if they played their cards right, and Daniel would make sure they did.

"You're mine," he growled against Chris's mouth.

"Yes," Chris agreed. "Sir."

Daniel slid his hands over the curve of Chris's ass and ground their hips together roughly. The drag of leather on leather drew his attention from their embrace.

"Get these off. Now."

Chris quickly complied, and the pants were tossed onto a nearby table in record time. Daniel had forgotten the satin panties he'd made Chris wear, and the sight of them made him even harder. When Chris tried to kiss him again, he pulled away.

"These look good on you." He brushed a hand over the fabric. "Lavender matches your skin nicely." Chris's cheeks colored prettily, and Daniel smiled. "Let me see how much you enjoyed wearing them."

Chris took a step back, showing Daniel how his erection tented the underwear. There was a damp spot on the satin. Daniel caressed it. "I would love to show the world out there how much you love this. I could put you on the stage and have everyone admire you in your dainty panties."

He wanted to see how Chris's blush had deepened from his words, but the look in Chris's eyes was so naked and hopeful that the desire to tease him more vanished. He cupped Chris's cheek in his palm.

"You've been very good this week, Chris," he said. "You've come a long way, and I think that deserves a reward." He dragged a thumb across Chris's lips.

Chris's eyes widened at the offer. Slowly, he lowered himself to his knees, then reached up to undo Daniel's pants. He paused to look up as if double-checking he hadn't misunderstood. Daniel nodded. "Go ahead."

Chris lowered the zipper and licked his lips. Daniel wondered if Chris's heart was racing as fast as his own. He hissed through his teeth when Chris drew him out. He felt the soft touch of lips in a featherlight kiss before that perfect mouth was on him. Warmth and wetness enveloped him, and his eyes rolled back as he groaned in pleasure. It had been too long since someone had had their mouth on him. He put one hand on Chris's head but let the boy do as he pleased. His boy definitely knew what he was doing. It wasn't long before Daniel gruffly called out, "Stop," and had to brace himself until Chris complied.

"Come in my mouth," Chris begged. "Please."

Daniel took a deep breath to keep from doing exactly that. "No." He licked dry lips. "I'm going to come in your ass."

Chris gasped.

"We're going to have to discuss what this means and how things are going to be handled when we get back home, but right now, you're not a student. You're my submissive, and I want to fuck your brains out." It was a big change from the rules they had set initially, but they'd already gone past them, and he was sure Chris wouldn't mind.

Chris obviously didn't. He grinned as he excitedly said, "Yes, Sir!"

Daniel laughed. "Get a condom and lube from the cabinet while I figure out how we're going to do this without a bed."

"I'm sure you've had sex outside of a bed before, haven't you, Sir?"

"If you get cheeky, I won't let you come," Daniel warned.

"I didn't say anything, Sir."

Daniel shook his head, still smiling, and surveyed the room. He spotted a padded bondage table off to one side. The table was shaped like an upside-down Y where a submissive could lie comfortably in the center, and their legs would be spread and fully accessible. On closer inspection, Daniel noticed the sections for legs were hinged and could be lifted to a ninety-degree angle from the center.

"That's convenient," he said.

"What's convenient?" Chris asked as he approached the bench.

"You'll find out another day." Daniel took the lube and condom from him. "Lie down."

Daniel put the condom on as Chris settled onto the bench. On any other day, he would have taken advantage of the restraints the furniture offered, but right then, he wanted nothing more than to be wrapped in Chris's limbs. He lifted Chris's legs and set them on his shoulders.

"This is really happening, isn't it?" Chris asked.

Daniel ran his hands over Chris's thighs soothingly. "Yes,

this is really happening. Are you nervous?" He didn't think this was Chris's first time, but he could be mistaken.

"No, I just… I'm wondering when I'm going to wake up."

With a smirk, Daniel pinched his nipple. Chris yelped in surprise. "If that didn't do it, I think you're safe."

He slid his hands down Chris's body to the waistband of the underwear. "Lift your hips for me," he said softly.

His submissive did as told, and he drew the panties down to Chris's thighs. Even if he wasn't going to tease about them, he liked leaving them on while they fucked. After popping open the lube, he wet his fingers and massaged Chris's hole.

"Oh god, it is real," the boy moaned.

Daniel worked a finger inside him. "I want to be in you, Chris. I've wanted this for a very long time."

"I've dreamt about this," Chris admitted, his face turning red at the confession.

"Ah, no wonder you've been doubting." He circled his finger, working to relax Chris's muscles. "Did your dreams feel like this?"

Chris shook his head. "No. They were nothing like this. Oh!"

Daniel had two fingers inside him now. Chris's body felt hot and tight. He considered skipping the third finger. He wanted to be inside the boy *now*.

He held on as long as he could, but finally he withdrew his fingers and slicked himself with extra lube.

"Please," Chris begged. "Fill me, please."

Impatient, Daniel lined up and pushed inside. He moved slowly but didn't stop until he was in all the way.

"So tight," he groaned as he waited for Chris to adjust. "So good."

Chris's body relaxed around him, and Daniel began to move. Chris rolled his hips in counterpoint, only adding to the pleasure between them. It wasn't long before they moved harder, faster. Daniel held on to Chris's thighs as he slammed into him. Chris moaned with every thrust, his hands clinging tight to Daniel's shoulders and his legs wrapped around the older man's body.

"Kiss me," Chris pleaded.

Daniel leaned forward and sealed their mouths together. Their tongues mingled in a fervent dance that matched the need of their pounding hips. Suddenly, with a yell, Chris came. His body clamped tight around Daniel, making him see stars before he, too, was coming. Spent, they collapsed onto the bench, panting. Sweat made them stick to each other and the padding, but for a few moments, neither cared. Eventually, Daniel pulled out of Chris and threw the condom away.

"Sit up for a minute."

Chris moaned. "Do I have to?"

"Yes."

Once Chris was in motion, Daniel took a seat on the bench, leaning his back against the wall. He pulled Chris into his lap and held him close. They sat in silence for a while, enjoying the afterglow and the comfort of being with each other.

Eventually Daniel spoke. "It can't be like this when we get home. I have to treat you like a student when we're in public."

"What about in private?" Chris asked.

Daniel's smile was wicked. "In private, you'll be lucky if you ever wear pants again."

Chris wiggled around to face him. He was grinning. "I've already decided to throw out all my underwear. It's not like you ever let me wear any."

"You're wearing some now." Daniel gestured to the satin panties still on Chris's thighs.

"That's not the same thing, and you know it."

Daniel did, and he didn't mind Chris's decision at all. "In exchange, you're going to wear those." He nodded toward Chris's wrists and the cuffs there. "Permanently. You can only take them off to shower or if you go swimming. Though if you're going to be in a bathing suit, I might want to know."

"I don't think I'll ever wear a bathing suit again. You can't hide an erection in one."

"I am well aware," Daniel said. He liked that idea, a lot.

"So, does this mean I'm yours? Your submissive from now on?" Chris asked.

"We still have a lot to discuss, and I'm sure the finer details will be a work in progress, but yes. If that is what you want, then that is what it means."

Chris turned to kneel between Daniel's knees. The word "grin" did not even begin to cover the smile on his face. It was so full of happiness Daniel felt his own heart lighten at the sight of it. He took Chris's face in his hands and pulled him closer for a kiss. When their lips parted, Chris curled into him, resting his head against Daniel's shoulder.

"Sex is included this time, right?"

Daniel laughed. "Yes. Though I'm not going to fuck you in your dorm. I don't think I should go in there at all, but I have my own apartment, and I plan to have you over often." He ran a hand down Chris's spine and squeezed his ass. "I plan on taking advantage of this as much as possible."

"You know," Chris said, lifting his head. His eyes sparkled with mischief. "There's no time like the present."

Daniel pushed his face away. "Brat." Then he shifted and turned them over so Chris was beneath him, pinned to the bench. "But you're right. Perhaps you don't have to wait to see what's so convenient about this bench."

ACKNOWLEDGMENTS

I want to thank all the editors that have helped make this series what it is today. As the trilogy has gone through a few iterations, that is a small army, and I am grateful for each of them.

Second, I'd like to thank Kanaxa for the stunning cover art. She took my concept of kinky silhouettes and ran with it. It's even better than I imagined.

Last but definitely not least, thank you to the person who bought this book. My readers mean the world to me.

ALSO BY JACQUELINE GREY

Won't You Be My Master?

Ghost House

Piotr and the Beast

<u>Suit of Harte's Series</u>

Tricks and Bids

Shoot the Moon

Limits and Stakes

Suit of Harte's - The Complete Collection (print only)

ABOUT THE AUTHOR

Jacqueline Grey lives on an island on the east coast of the United States. She spends her time juggling her day job along with her many interests, which include reading, writing, being a cat couch, and drinking tea. Sometimes she does more than one at the same time. She loves M/M romance and looks forward to bringing more stories of love into the world in the future.

You can find Jacqueline on Twitter, in her Facebook group "Tea, Books, and Cats" (bit.ly/TeaBooksCats), or you can email her at JacquelineGreyBooks@gmail.com.

For simple updates on Jacqueline's books and events, check out her Facebook page or visit her website JacquelineGrey.com and sign up for her newsletter.

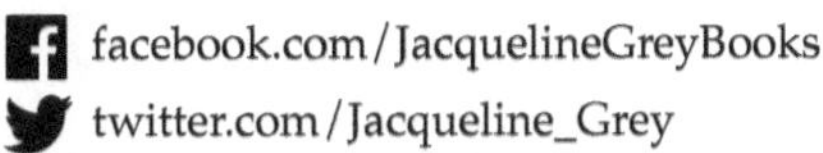

www.ingramcontent.com/pod-product-compliance
Lightning Source LLC
Chambersburg PA
CBHW030807210726
48290CB00002B/467